THE
LIGHT
ABOVE

THE LIGHT ABOVE

a novel of faith and determination

Jean Holbrook Mathews

Covenant Communications, Inc.

Covenant

This volume is dedicated to the thousands of faceless and nameless men, women, and children who worked and died in the pits of Scotland from the year 1600 to the middle of the nineteenth century; they sacrificed their physical strength and mental health, living and dying in conditions that were not of their own making or choosing. The Industrial Revolution of Britain rode upon the strength of their muscle and sinews.

Foreword

During the reign of the monarch who gave the world the King James Version of the Bible, the Scottish Parliament, with that monarch's blessing, turned the Scottish coal miners into slaves. By an Act of Parliament in 1606, mine owners would own their labor force *in fact* for the next two hundred years and in a *de facto* manner for an additional fifty years thereafter.

It was during the reign of James VI of Scotland that the demand for coal and the number of collieries needed to produce it steadily increased. That Scottish coal was required for British industries, including the production of salt, lime, and gunpowder; glass blowing; soap making; sugar refining; and the manufacture of tile. Keeping pace with the demand brought a series of major problems to the industry, such as the invention and supply of the necessary machinery for pumping water from the mines and the transportation of the coal over long distances, but the gravest problem was the ever-increasing need for labor.

The southern uplands of Scotland present a picture of rural beauty and harmony in this day, largely because the many scars of the great coal mines that opened the earth, gouging and scarring the valleys and hills, are now hidden by more recent growth of gorse, bracken, and heather. But a hundred and fifty years ago, and for centuries earlier, these same valleys and hills hid a netherworld of misery, hunger, disease, and death for those thousands who worked the mines.

These men, women, and children were neither highlander nor lowlander; they were just ghosts of the southern uplands—muscle that chopped and blasted out of the rock the fuel that kept the British Isles warm and powered the industries that were spawned by the Industrial Revolution. These wretched individuals were warmed by their own sweat and the heat of the lowest regions of the mines. In the shires of Lanark, Ayre, Fife, Lothian, and others, they lived lives of slavery, seldom seeing the sun, black dust filling their eyes and lungs and covering their skin, making them as dark as the chunks of carbon they dug and hauled from the earth. How did these people find themselves owned by the very mines they worked and by the lairds who owned the mines?

Due to the dissolution of the monasteries under Henry VIII and numerous other causes of poverty, the British countryside was nearly overrun with beggars and vagrants for several decades. Harsh laws were enacted to punish those with no means of support, including the Scots Poor Law of 1579, which altered the usual punishment for vagrants and beggars from public whippings and ear-brandings to servitude for an employer who would keep them at work for a year, while seizing their underage children; daughters were kept in bondage until they were eighteen years old, sons until they were twenty-four. By amendment in 1597, the Scots Parliament made it legal to retain these children in lifelong bondage. The near-starvation conditions of these workers forced them to enslave their children to the same life, generation after generation.

In almost all industries, these laws were never fully enforced because the members of the governing bodies of the cities and towns of Scotland—the Kirk Sessions—did not take kindly to enforcing such harsh legal requirements. The two great exceptions were the coal mines and the salt works, where labor shortages were severe.

To bypass the Kirk Sessions, the Lords of the Articles, who were often owners of mines, passed the Act of Parliament of 1606, which prohibited anyone from hiring colliers, coal bearers, or salters without the written permission of their master. Additionally, if any collier, coal bearer, or salter left the service of his master without such written permission, his master could reclaim him, and the fleeing workman would be deemed a thief, having stolen his labor from his master. Penalties were severe for both the runaway workman and any employer who took a runaway into his service. Lastly, Parliament extended to all masters of coal and salt mines the authority to apprehend all "vagabonds and sturdy beggars to be put to labor."

In November of 1641 a new Act of Parliament expanded the Act of 1606, limiting wages paid to the mine workers and depriving them of their customary holidays, requiring that they work as long as fourteen hours per day a full six days a week throughout the year.

In 1774 the Lord Advocate of Scotland, Sir Alexander Gilmour, presented legislation to Parliament regarding the servitude of the miners and salters in Scotland. Its stated purpose was "to remove the reproach of allowing such a state of servitude to exist in a free country." This statute stated that after July 1, 1775, new entrants into the collieries or salt pans would be free, and those already in the industry would be set free by stages. The law was meant to allow colliers and salters to gradually obtain emancipation. But over the next two decades, it became evident that the law was full of obstacles, making eventual emancipation impossible. To begin the process, the collier had to sue his master in the Sheriff's Court to establish his right of freedom, and as these laborers were generally uneducated, the requirements of this procedure were beyond most, if not all, of them. Even if some of them had been educated sufficiently to proceed through the court requirements, most had fallen into debt slavery, often having followed the old custom of "arling" their children at baptism to the coal master for an amount of money as large as ten to twenty pounds. No collier or salter could ever hope to pay back such a sum. So the colliers and their families remained bound to their old masters.

In 1799 the Lord Advocate brought a bill before Parliament to amend the Act of 1774, and as of June 13, 1799, all colliers bound at that date became legally free, though in practice they were still bound by circumstances. Wages were to be fixed at intervals by local justices of the peace, many of whom owed their positions to the powerful and wealthy coal mine owners. Loans to the miners were prohibited except in the case of illness. Included in the Act of 1799 was a provision prohibiting the miners from forming any organization or combination (trade union) of colliers; the formation of such was punishable by heavy fines.

Wages, which were fixed artificially low, coupled with high prices at the company stores guaranteed continued *de facto* slavery in the mines until the rise of the mining brotherhoods and trade unions in the second half of the nineteenth century.

Had the world known of the conditions under which these men, women, and children labored, perhaps a great upheaval, nearly as traumatic as the American Civil War, would have occurred within the British Isles, for it seems inconceivable that a civilized society could have tolerated in good conscience the conditions thrust upon those who worked the coal mines and salt pans of Scotland.

Knowledgeable LDS historians have estimated that between nine and ten thousand Scots joined The Church of Jesus Christ of Latter-day Saints in Scotland, and between four and five thousand left their homes in response to the clarion call of Brigham Young to gather to the Great Salt Lake Valley and made their way across the ocean and the great American Continent to cast their lot with that of the other Saints previous to 1869. We can only guess how many loved ones they buried before arriving in the Valley.

The author extends thanks to R. Page Arnot for his book, *A History of the Scottish Miners: From the Earliest Times,* published in London by George Allen & Unwin Ltd. in 1955, from which the previous information has been taken.

Though this book is best described as historical fiction, every effort has been made to accurately reflect the conditions of the times and places portrayed in this story. The primary characters, which include members of the Hogge and Smith families, are fictitious, though many of the other characters that form the framework and background of the events of this story will be recognized by readers familiar with LDS Church history in the British Isles. Though I have placed the primary characters of Robert and his sister Helen and their spouses in the first wagon company funded by the Perpetual Emigration Fund, which was led by Abraham O. Smoot (1852), this is not an attempt at a detailed recounting of the experiences of that wagon company. Such an account would entail its own extensive work. The primary characters and their experiences represent the lives of the thousands who lived, labored, and died under the conditions here portrayed.

Any errors, misinterpretations, or inaccuracies contained in the text are solely the responsibility of the author.

—Jean H. Mathews

Glossary

Arle the bairn: To pledge the lifetime services of a child for a sum of money.

Afterdamp: Carbon monoxide and other toxic gases that seeped from the coal seams and gathered in the mine shafts.

Blacklegs: Strike breakers.

Coal face: The wall of the lateral shaft where the coal seam was exposed and could be dug.

Coal master: The manager of the mine, employed by the owner.

Coal pusher: A child between the ages of five and twelve who pulled or pushed a coal carrier from the coal face to the pit bottom.

Coal seam: The exposed layer of coal, which was usually about twelve inches to three feet wide and was encased in hard rock.

Creel: A basket for carrying coal on the back and neck of a fremit bearer. These baskets could weigh as much as 125 pounds when filled.

Croft: Farm.

Crofter: Farmer.

Darg: A work slowdown.

Firedamp: Extremely explosive methane gas that gathered in the mine shafts.

Fremit bearer: A woman or girl twelve years of age or older who carried the coal in a creel from the pit bottom to the pithead. These women and girls usually worked for a husband, brother, father, or son and were unpaid, as their labor increased his output. When working for a non-relative, they were paid between two and three Scots shillings a week.

Gai: Very.

Gin: An area where a horse or mule moved around a center pivot, which operated a winch that lifted buckets filled with the water that accumulated in the bottom of the mine shaft. These areas were sometimes enclosed within a rock wall about three feet high.

Jugs: Leg and wrist irons.

Kirk Sessions: The ruling body of a village or town comprised of the most respected members of the local congregation of the Church of Scotland (which was an extension of the Church of England).

Laird of the mine: *Laird* is Scottish for "lord." The laird owned the mine and its profits. From approximately A.D. 1600 to A.D. 1800 the laird also owned the men, women, and children who worked in the mine. The mines were originally given to noble families by royalty.

Muck: The label given all forms of rock that had to be removed to get at the coal.

Nappies: Diapers.

Pit: The mine.

Pit bottom: The lowest point from which the lower lateral shafts of the mine extended.

Pithead: The area at the surface of the earth around the shaft where the miners entered the mine and where the gin and equipment shacks were located.

Posting of the banns: Formal announcement of an engagement.

Room: The area usually at the end of a lateral shaft where the coal face was exposed and active digging was taking place.

Scots shilling: One-twelfth of an English shilling.

Slype: A coal carrier made of wood. It had a rounded metal bottom, which had to be dragged from the coal face to the pit bottom by a single coal pusher.

Tag man: The employee of the mine who kept track of the amount of coal dug by each miner, for which the miner received a "tag" to represent each 500-pound tub credited to the miner. The miner turned the tags in each week to receive his pay.

Undercutting: When the lateral shaft in a mine was to be lengthened or enlarged, the base of the walls at the end of the shaft were excavated at floor level to a height of two or three feet to increase the wall collapse and better expose the coal seam.

Vicar: A minister for the Church of Scotland.

Wake: The gathering of friends and family before a burial.

CHAPTER 1
Cave-In!

Twilight had come a second time when Jack Kerr was helped out of the shaft by two dust-covered rescuers. The dust from the cave-in still hung in the air, shutting out the view of the sunset and the early stars. With one arm over the shoulder of each man, he was half carried, half dragged out into the cleaner air, where the rescuers sat him down on the ground with his back against the equipment shed. His wife rushed to him. "Where's Rand? Oh, Jack, where's our lad?"

"He's hurt, Maggie. His leg is near crushed."

"But he's alive, Jack, he's alive." She sat down on the ground, leaned against his shoulder, and wept with relief.

* * *

Another hour passed before two men carried sixteen-year-old Rand Kerr out of the shaft entrance, each one holding him by the upper arm and upper leg. His left leg dangled, crushed and bloody below the knee. As the men neared the shed, one called out, "Move the tools so we can put the lad down." The counter where the lanterns were kept was quickly cleared.

Isabel rushed to the two dust-covered miners who followed the young man's rescuers out of the pit entrance, and, hanging on the arm of one of them, she pleaded, "Where's my George and my Jamie? Ye won't leave them in that hole, will ye?"

"Nae, Mrs. Hogge, others are going down to find them." With that he patted her hand and crumpled to the ground in a state of exhaustion.

Five more miners entered the mine and started down the ladders. As the crowd watched them disappear into the mine entrance, one of the children who had been separating coal chunks from rock waste at the top of a steep slope ran to his mother. "Ma," he cried as he pulled at her skirt, "Ma, Billie fell down the hill. Come quick; Billie fell down the hill."

Several men and women in the crowd followed the child and his mother to the edge of the slope where the children had gathered and were looking down the hillside. "Where did he fall, lad? We can't see him."

"There, he fell down there," the child said, pointing. Several men started down the slope. Unable to keep to their feet, some resorted to sliding down the slope in a sitting position. Several others ran back along the path, which wound its way to the miners' cottages and to a place where the ground sloped toward the gully and the stream at the bottom the hill. Several men and women called out, "We can't see him! Where is the lad?"

As a group of men reached the bottom of the hill, Joe Moffatt called, "Laddie, say something. Where be ye?" As they paused to listen, he said, "Shush, I hear something." The muffled cry of a child could be heard. "Spread out, follow the sound." He called again, "Laddie, where be ye?" After each call, they listened for a few seconds for the sound of the boy's whimpering.

One of the men stumbled in the growing darkness and called out, "There's a great hole over here big enough for a coal wagon and a team of horses to drive into. Maybe he fell in it." He started to move large rocks so they could enter the opening. He could hear the child crying.

Feeling his way in the dark he called out, "Come here, laddie. Come, take my hand." The boy did not respond. The miner said louder, "Come to my voice, lad. Take my hand, so we can take ye to your ma." Still the boy did not respond. Then the sound of rocks being pushed out of the way could be heard deeper in the hole.

"Ye found us! Praise God, ye found us!" A filthy figure could just barely be seen in the light cast by the lamp one of the miners held. He was trying to climb over the large boulders and slabs of slate nearly filling a lateral shaft about ten feet behind the child.

"Hogge, is that you?" Moffatt called.

"Aye, me and my lad had just about given up. The blast closed off the tunnel entrance at the pit bottom. We couldn't figure out where the fresh air was coming from, so we started to make our way to the end of the tunnel. It was slow going in the dark. Thank God the blast put a hole in the hillside and we heard your voices."

By this time, a dust-covered George Hogge had reached the crying child. He picked him up and shakily handed him to waiting hands, and the cry went up, "We found them! We found them!" Then the hands reached for George, pulled him out of the hole, and then reached in to help his eldest son, James, out behind his father.

When George and James had half stumbled up the slope of the path to the pithead, they were so black with coal dust they could hardly be recognized. As the crowd surrounding the rescued men moved up the path and reached the pithead, a shout went up from every throat. Isabel ran to her husband and son.

The young mother took Billie from the arms of one of the men. "God be with us, and bless us, every one," she said as she held her five-year-old to her and tears made little trails through the dust on her cheeks. "Praise be; I thought I had lost another one."

The twilight was gone, and the miners and their families stood about in the light of a few lanterns, congratulating each other on their rescue efforts. After looking at George and James in the weak lantern light, William Watson asked, "George, where be your hair? Ye got no eyebrows." Then he and the others laughed the loud, raucous laughter of relief.

George took a fairly clean rag from an offering hand, and as he wiped his face, he said quietly, "The mine was filling with firedamp, and added to the coal dust and the black powder we were ordered to use to open up that lowest shaft, it made for a big blast. I told McBride that we need to be using more wedges to free the coal seams, and less black powder, but he would hear none of it. If we hadn't been so close to the side of the hill, we would nae speak to ye again on this side of life. Thank God the blast put a hole in the side of the hill. Have ye found everyone that was in the pit yet?"

Several men shook their heads, and one said quietly, "There be five or six we can't account for." George dropped his head and said no more.

After a few minutes, some of the men approached the coal master, and Archie Kenny asked, "Who are you going to send to fetch the doctor in the village so he can see to the injured lad?"

McBride stood rubbing his chin, as though he needed to debate the matter with himself. Then he said, "I'll send anyone willing to ride the horse." Three men stepped forward. One of them, a tall and strong young man of about twenty, was chosen. "Ye are to bring the animal back unharmed," the coal master warned.

After the horse was unhitched from the gin, it was led over to the young man, and he was handed the reins. The animal stood so high that it took two tries for him to mount it. Then he pulled its head toward the wagon road to Penston Village. Someone handed him a lantern, and he started down the road, bouncing about on the back of the animal as he struggled to press his legs against its broad sides.

McBride then stated as loudly as he could, "Every one of ye be here by four o'clock in the morning, as we will need to double our efforts to make up for no coal dug for two days."

Joe Moffatt stepped up to the coal master. "What do ye mean, McBride? The lads and lassies have sorted at least six cartweight. Look at that pile. Ye best give credit to every family that had a child sorting through the rubble and the muck, or else."

"What do ye mean, 'or else'?" The men were looking directly at each other, their faces a few inches apart.

"Ye don't have to ask, Mr. Coal Master," Moffatt said with contempt and anger. "How would ye explain a wee darg to the laird? How would ye explain that everybody was suddenly so sick that none could work the mine?"

"Ye're makin' trouble for yourself, Moffatt. I've always known ye to be a troublemaker."

"Troublemaker?" Joe Moffatt did not back down, but instead stepped closer as he talked. "Since when is trying to get miners and their families paid for the work they do being a troublemaker?"

Angrily turning away from Moffatt, the coal master relented and said to those standing close enough to hear, "If your bairn sorted coal today, put your name on the list at the equipment shed."

By this time George was shaking visibly from exhaustion and stress. Isabel found a place for him to sit on a battered stool in a corner of the equipment shed, and his family gathered around him, forming a separate group from the one gathered around the young man on the tool counter. George tried to hide his shaking hands between his knees. It never occurred to anyone to leave while they waited for help for the injured boy.

* * *

The doctor arrived at nearly midnight in his dogcart. "Stand back, stand back," he called out as he pushed his way through the group to examine the crushed leg of Rand Kerr, who lay gritting his teeth to keep from crying out. His mother hovered near him, wiping the coal dust from his white face with the tattered and soiled hem of her dress.

After several minutes, Jack Kerr asked agitatedly, "Well, what can ye do for my lad? How bad is his leg broke?"

"It'll have to come off, above the knee. The bones are crushed."

"Nae, don't take off my leg," Rand cried out.

His mother stifled a sob with her hand over her mouth. The doctor said, "Don't be worried, lad. Your folks will have you fixed up with a timber toe shortly, just like some of the other miners here in the Penston pits."

"You can surely save the leg? Don't take if off," Jack demanded. "It will make the lad a cripple."

"It has to be done," the doctor responded. "Get the biggest bottle of whiskey you can find among the cottages. I know there is plenty to be had. After the lad has had a good drink, he won't feel anything."

Isabel put her arm around the shoulders of the young man's mother and led the nearly frantic woman away. One of the men soon arrived with a bottle of whiskey, and the doctor insisted that young Rand drink until he started coughing and choking. He then took a large drink himself. He responded to the looks of amazement and disgust on the faces of the men standing around by saying, "What's the matter with all of ye? Do ye think this is any easier for me than for the lad?"

But in the end, it was much easier for the doctor than for the boy. The bleeding from the artery in the severed leg could not be stopped, and within the hour, young Rand Kerr was dead. For those who knew the boy, the silence that followed was harder to bear than his cries of pain.

CHAPTER 2
The Death of Rand

The wake was held the next morning, despite the coal master's threats to dock the pay of those attending, as they would be late to work. A small cluster of men stood outside the Kerr cottage speaking in low but angry voices as the women offered their sympathy to the grieving parents. By nine o'clock the group had followed the rough-hewn coffin to the churchyard in the village. After the coffin had been buried, the women gathered around Maggie Kerr like a protective flock of birds and guided her back to the row cottages.

No one had noticed the red and swollen eyes of sixteen-year-old Helen Hogge. Her father and brother had been safely rescued, and for that she was grateful, but her heart ached for the loss of redheaded, laughing Rand Kerr. She would miss him and his constant teasing. They had been friends since childhood, and she had even wondered if someday they might marry. Those hopes were gone now.

His death was not unusual in the Scottish mining community, but that did not make it any easier for Helen or for Rand's parents. Every family she knew, including her own, had buried at least one member, killed by the hardships and dangers in the pits. And Rand Kerr was not the only casualty of this mine collapse. Five men and women were finally located where they had been crushed under the rubble.

Jack Kerr and George Hogge joined the men who were still standing in the graveyard talking together. "It didn't have to happen."

Joe Moffatt's voice was hard with anger. "Hogge here tells me that McBride refused to let him use wedges or take the time to have the room at the end of the shaft undercut. That's why the powder men were told to use near eight pounds of powder in that tunnel. If the undercutting had been done and done right, they could have got away with using maybe no more than two pounds. Might not have been any cave-in at all." As he talked, he grew even angrier, as though his words stoked a fire in his gut. "And he wouldn't even wait until the pit was empty to have the powder lit."

George stepped forward and said weakly, "The blast might have happened anyway, Joe. The shaft was filling with firedamp."

"I say we demand that the laird put in some kind of ventilation system, like they got over in Lanark. I hear that the deepest mines there have an exhaust furnace to vent the bad air." Most of the men stood silently, unsure what to say. Moffatt continued, "And I say we go for a slowdown. If we all get sick, maybe we'll get the attention of the laird."

Someone responded, "And what if we do? What happens then?"

"We'll demand that the laird put in some kind of ventilation to vent the bad air—and we'll demand McBride be fired. Anyone replacing him has got to be better at running the mines."

"Ye never can tell where that will lead," someone said. "Things can always get worse." Slowly and quietly the group began to separate, leaving Joe Moffatt standing frustrated and alone.

When the Hogge family arrived at the cottage, George was shaking again with exhaustion and a deep, racking cough. Isabel fussed over him, something she was not usually prone to do, and insisted that he rest. His family members were surprised to see his quiet acquiescence. His cough had been aggravated by the dust from the cave-in, and his face was white as chalk once he washed off the coal dust. After George had promised that he would rest that day, Isabel, her three sons, and her two daughters made their way to the mine to belatedly begin another day. As they arrived to pick up their equipment, they could hear the voice of the coal master as he berated some of the men as they stood in line at the equipment shed. "Ye had better plan on working a full twelve hours, or your pay will be docked, for sure."

"But we didn't hardly get even one hour of sleep," Archie Kenny stated loudly.

"That's not my problem," McBride yelled back. "The quota is still the same." Then he turned on his heel and walked away.

The day-shift miners and their families worked from midday until midnight, mixing with the night shift, crowding the shafts. But then, one by one, in a state of exhaustion, they climbed to the pithead and turned in their equipment. In the morning, none reported to the mine at the usual time of four o'clock A.M. Two hours later, the coal master was moving from one cottage to another, pounding on the doors. As each miner or a family member sleepily opened the door, he would demand, "Get yourselves to the mine before seven o'clock or ye be fired!" When he arrived at the door of the Kerr cottage, after rousing the family, he demanded to speak with Jack. "The doctor wants his pay on Saturday!" Then he turned away, moving toward the next door. Jack stood still at the open door, stunned by the demand.

CHAPTER 3
Visiting Victoria

On the Sunday night that followed the cave-in, Robert Hogge listened for the regular, wheezy breathing of his father, which signaled that he was asleep. Once it began, he waited for the sound of the steady breathing of the other family members who slept the exhausted sleep of people worn thin by unceasing physical labor. When he was sure they were all asleep, he rose and slipped quietly out of the cottage doorway and into the darkness.

By moonlight, he made his way across the small hillock toward the edge of the village. The small sliver of the quarter moon spilled its light intermittently as the clouds passed before its face, giving such limited light that he stumbled several times as he made his way through the gorse bushes and bracken. Upon reaching a cart path, Robert began to move more quickly.

Eventually he saw the dark, imposing form of a large house rise before him—two stories of hewn stone with seven large casement windows along the front of the second story. The impressive entrance was flanked by three large windows on each side of the enormous door on the ground level. A single-story wing extended on each side, like short, stiff arms. The stone carvings on the eaves above the windows and the front door made Robert wonder if this was what a real castle looked like. The building, the well-kept shrubbery, and the statuary in the garden spoke of great wealth.

He moved stealthily between the darker shadows of the trees and shrubs around the house until he reached the back of the building. Taking a small handful of pebbles from his pocket, he stepped into the yard and tossed one at a lighted window in the center of the upper story. There was no response. He tossed a second and a third pebble. The window sash slowly began to rise. The head and shoulders of Victoria Keith took shape in the splash of light from the room as she leaned out the window. She put her finger to her lips and withdrew.

The window closed, but in a few minutes the back door of the mansion opened, and Robert could see Victoria's face lit by a candle in her right hand. Her long, auburn hair lay across her shoulders where it shone in the light from the open kitchen doorway. Her left arm was wrapped around a water pitcher. She wore a shawl over her ruffled, pink nightdress, her feet kept warm by rabbit-fur slippers.

As Robert moved out of the shadow and into the moonlight, Victoria stepped out of the doorway onto the stoop and emptied the pitcher into a small flower garden near the kitchen door. Then she walked toward Robert with her finger against her lips. She took his hand and pulled him into the dark shadows of the trees at the edge of the yard.

"Can we talk?" he asked.

"At the stream," she whispered.

Without speaking, they ducked under the tree branches and pushed their way through the bracken until they reached the stream, which gurgled over the rocks in its path. When they arrived, they sat on a large rock near the water as it hurried down the hill. "Now you can speak," she said.

Robert spoke quietly, "Will your father find us out?"

"He and mother are sleeping. Father always has a long meeting on Sunday afternoons with the trustees at the Kirk Sessions. He goes to bed early on Sunday nights." She paused and looked at him in the weak moonlight. "This is the fourth Sunday night that we have met this way. Why don't you come to my home on Saturday afternoon for a proper visit?" she asked with a question in her voice.

"Nae, I cannot," was all Robert could respond. "But I think I would die if ye wouldn't see me every Sunday evening."

She smiled modestly with downcast eyes and asked, "Why is that so important to you?"

Robert swallowed hard and then answered, "Ye must know that ever since I saw ye wading in the stream that Sunday afternoon after church services, that I've had to see ye each Sunday or—or die. 'Tis the memory of your laughter and the way ye lifted your skirts above your ankles when you danced in the water that keeps me working until I can come again."

"Robert, if you work at the village store, I am sure I can get Father to let you come for a visit on a weekday evening."

Robert was silent for several seconds. Then he said, "I don't work at the village store. I let you believe that, but 'tisn't so." After a brief silence, as she looked at him with a puzzled expression, he continued, "I can't come to visit on any other day. Ye would never know me."

"I would not know you? What do you mean?" Her eyes grew large as she spoke.

"On every other day I am covered black with coal dust. Victoria, I work in the pit. I am only a miner."

Victoria stepped back in shock, putting her hand over her mouth. "A miner . . . no, not a miner!" She turned to run, but stopped and returned for the pitcher, which was lying by the stream. After quickly dipping it in the stream, she ran with it through the trees back to the kitchen door of her home.

"Victoria, please don't run away," Robert called after her, but she did not turn or look back.

Robert followed her, and as he arrived at the edge of the shadows beneath the trees at the back of the yard, her father stepped out of the back doorway and onto the stoop. "Where have you been, Victoria?" he demanded. His shirttail was partially out of his pants as if he had dressed in a hurry.

Stuttering slightly with nervousness, she answered, "Ah, I . . . I was very thirsty and there was no water in the kitchen. I had to go to the stream." With that, she held up the pitcher as if to show him.

"In the future, please make sure cook leaves a full pitcher of water before we retire to bed, just in case you should feel the need for a drink in the night."

"Yes, Father," she said meekly.

Without looking into the darkness, Laird Isaac Keith entered the kitchen behind his daughter and firmly closed the door.

Robert stood in the shadows for several minutes before he made his way around the house and across the cart path. Then he began the trek back to the Hogge cottage, where he slipped quietly in, wrapped himself in his old quilt, and turned to face the wall. Sleep did not come for a long time.

CHAPTER 4
In the Pit

"Helen! Helen, get up, tired girl." George Hogge's calloused hand on his daughter's shoulder shook her to wakefulness. "Get up and find an oatcake. It will soon be time for the sun to rise, and ye know we must be at the pit before then."

Helen sat up, pushed the well-worn quilt aside, and rubbed sleep and coal dust from her eyes. "Oh, Papa, I dreamed it was still the Sabbath and I could sleep a wee bit longer." There in the one-room, stone cottage, lit only by a single candle, she reached over and shook twelve-year-old David awake before she climbed out of the rope bed and slipped her feet into the blackened, worn clogs she wore each day. She picked up the brush from the little rough-hewn table near her parents' bed and brushed her hair a few strokes. The ragged dress she had slept in would serve as her dress for working in the pit.

Helen followed her father out into the cold, damp darkness of the early fall morning. David followed her through the doorway. She heard her mother step out of the cottage behind him and close the latch.

David said to his mother in a voice filled with exhaustion, "I don't want to go into the pit today, Ma."

"Davy, ye know that we all must work in the pit to earn enough shillings to eat and pay the rent," she responded matter-of-factly. Isabel was not oblivious to the child's feelings; it was just a fact that in coal mining families, sympathy would do nothing to change their lives.

"I don't like the hard work, but mostly I don't like working in the dark," he explained. "I never have."

"Someday ye will get used to it," his mother responded. She could find no better answer.

Only Helen heard him whisper under his breath, "Nae, I never will." Helen shared his feelings. She hated the darkness of the pits, the foul air, and the never-ending creels full of coal that had to be carried to the pithead as many as fifteen times each day.

They made their way single-file along the path toward Penston Pit Number Two in the waning moonlight. In the darkness, no one observed the gentle rolling hills like swells on a sea that rose around them, cloaked in green and heather and lightly touched with the coming colors of fall. The only glaring interruption to the beauty was the great heap of rock piled not far from the pithead on the hillside. The women who entered the pits would be expected to carry several creels full of waste rock, or muck, to the surface each day without receiving pay for the task; this made it possible for the men to more easily reach some of the coal seams. Their creels full of coal would be weighed, and a husband or father would be paid for them. Only the women who carried coal for a nonrelative would be paid—and then, only three or four shillings per week.

George Hogge's cough punctuated the early-morning air. Years earlier, he had been a young man of tall stature with broad shoulders, but the work in the coal pits had stolen his youth and vigor. Now he walked more slowly with stooped shoulders, a bent and twisted back, and a hacking cough, all characteristics common for a forty-year-old Scottish coal miner.

"I'm sorry if I made us late, Pa. I didn't mean to sleep so long." Helen's voice was quiet.

"'Tis understandable, lass. I too slept too long."

"Did Jamie and Robbie leave before we were awake?"

"Aye, and Janet, too. Jamie has hired Eliza Cummins as his coal bearer, and he wants to get a head start on filling her creel. She is a strong girl and will be able to carry a larger load than many of the others. She will make it easier for him to fill his quota, but he will have to pay her for her work."

"Who will Janet be carrying for today?"

"I think she's carrying for Archie Kenny."

By this time, the little group had made their way down the path that led past the front doors of the long row of stone cottages, built one against another, where the miners and their families lived. The cottages climbed the slope like stair steps.

Helen was quiet as she chewed the nearly tasteless oatcake that served as breakfast. While her parents continued down the path toward the pithead, Helen darted to the little stream that gurgled and tumbled past the rear of the row of cottages as it made its way to the holding pond at the bottom of the hill. She scooped up the cold water in her hands and drank as much as she could to suppress the thirst that would plague her much of the day.

Helen was not as tall as her mother, but like her older sister, Janet, she had hair that shone a dark gold when it was not filled with coal dust. Both the daughters had wide, dark brown eyes like their mother's and a dusting of freckles on cheeks and arms. There the similarities ended. At eighteen, Janet was outspoken and forward. Much to the great concern of her mother, she laughed and teased and was teased in return by many of the men and older boys in the pits. Helen, like her twin brother, Robert, was quiet and listened more than she spoke.

With her wide forehead and strong jaw, Isabel would not have been described as beautiful, but she brought a needed physical strength to her work. As a girl, she too had once had golden hair, which had eventually darkened to brown and was now streaked with gray. Without her help, George could never have provided for his family. Her daughters were both fine-boned, and she feared that in future years they would not bear the hard labor of the pits.

As George started down the first of the long, shaky ladders that led to the bottom of the pit, he noticed that the air was unusually dank and dusty from the recent cave-in. David followed him.

David was small for his age and light in complexion with sandy hair, but that was seldom evident through the coal dust. He had eyes as blue as a Scottish morning sky. As they descended, he said, "Oh, Pa, I hate the smell in the pit."

"Ye'll get used to it, laddie. We all do," his father answered absentmindedly, his mind already focused on the work of the day.

They made their way to the end of the tunnel, often dropping to their knees to crawl through the low openings in each of the support walls. There George stood up—as far as the low ceiling would permit—and found his son James already at work.

David stood quietly out of the way in the ankle-deep water to avoid the swinging pickax until his father had a pile of coal large enough to fill the slype.

At the equipment shed, Helen and her mother were each handed a lantern and a large creel to hold the chunks of coal they would carry up the ladders. Isabel had carried coal for George since she was a young bride, and for her father before that. She sometimes helped Helen, who served as Robert's bearer, by carrying an extra load or two on the days that he dug more coal out of the wall than his father.

David gathered the chunks of coal into the slype while his father continued to dig. When it was full, he hitched the leather strap around his forehead and put his arms through two others, adjusting them over his shoulders. Then, while on his knees and using all the strength in his small body, he pulled on the harness until the box began to move. His knees were already calloused and covered with blue scars from cuts that filled with coal dust before they healed. By the time he had dragged the slype the seventy-five feet to the pit bottom, his chest was heaving and his heart pounding in his ears. The foul air was sucked into his lungs with each breath, but gave his body little relief. After a minute or two, he shook his head as if to quiet the pounding in his ears and crawled closer to the creel his mother was filling, where he helped lift the coal from the slype into her basket.

When it was filled, Isabel whistled, and two women working near her stopped what they were doing and with experienced hands jointly lifted the hundred-pound basket onto her shoulders and bent back. She pulled the leather tug around her forehead to steady the load and attached her lantern to it. The lantern swung freely in front of her as she climbed, its weak light dancing on the walls of the shaft as she moved.

When Eliza, James's fremit bearer, had filled her creel and it was lifted to her shoulders, she started impatiently toward the ladder. Eliza was taller and stronger than the girl ahead of her, and she could be heard calling out as she ascended, "Move your feet faster, lass. Ye're slowing all of us who follow."

When each fremit bearer reached the surface, she carried her heavy creel to a large tub that held four and one-half hundred-weight, or about 500 pounds of coal, where it was weighed. Six tubs constituted a day's labor for a miner. At the end of the week, each man would receive the sixteen Scots shillings that made up a week's pay if he had met his quota. More than once David had said, "When I am thirteen I will start to dig, and I will earn sixteen shillings each week. Then we can buy what we need at the company store. Maybe then we will be able to pay down what we owe." George knew that another sixteen shillings would never pay down the debt they owed, but he just smiled and patted his son on the shoulder. It was good of the boy to want to help as much as he could.

As Helen started up the ladders, she could not help but notice that the girl ahead of her was wet from the water dripping from the large bucket that was being hauled to the top by the horse at the gin. She smiled and called out, "Alice, I think ye are getting a bath before the week is done."

To remove the water that gathered in the tunnels and in the pool at the pit bottom, two large buckets were connected to a long rope. As one bucket was lowered and filled, the other was raised and emptied. The horse trotted in a circle, turning a drum that lifted and lowered the rope in one continuous action. The buckets were emptied at the pithead a few feet from the gin, creating a large, muddy area near the mine opening. The buckets rose and dropped between the ascending and descending ladders in a drippy, swinging dance that stopped only when the horse was changed. At midday, the horse that turned the drum at the gin was replaced, but not so the humans in the pit.

CHAPTER 5
"Will We Ever Leave the Pit?"

Helen was serving as Robert's coal pusher as well as his bearer. Her twin was a quiet young man with a shock of black hair, dark, intense eyes, and the high cheeks and straight nose of his father. His previous coal pusher, seven-year-old Alexander Kenny, affectionately called "Sandy," had been standing near the bottom of the lowest ladder in the main shaft several days earlier when a large chunk of coal fell out of the darkness from a creel being carried to the surface. No one would ever know which basket it fell from. It had bounced off the wall of the pit before it hit him in the head, leaving him bleeding and unconscious.

Archie Kenny had sought a small loan from the mine owner to pay the village doctor at Penston Grange to come and tend to his boy, but the doctor had refused. "Ye all know that I don't treat the filthy miners or their children unless McBride sends for me," he had yelled at Archie before he slammed his door.

Archie was working near Robert, and as Helen stooped to lift the coal chunks into the carrier, she paused and asked, "Mr. Kenny, how's your lad this morning? Is he still so sick?"

Archie paused and leaned on the handle of his pickax and said briefly, "Aye, he burns with fever and talks some out of his mind. We fear that he will not be with us much longer." Then he swung his pick as if to vent his anger against the coal seam embedded in the rock wall. As he did so, he said under his breath, "Curse the doctor who won't give us the help that might save him." Then he swung the pick again, harder, his lips pressed into a thin line.

When the slype was full, Helen put the leather harness around her head and shoulders and started to drag the carrier toward the opening in the support wall. As she labored to get the slype moving, Archie put down his pick and stepped over to give the slype a push with his foot to help her. She smiled her thanks at him, then she dragged the slype through the opening in the mine wall and about eighty feet to the bottom of the pit. There she loaded her creel. She was working nearly alone, so she whistled when the basket was almost full. Robert appeared and lifted it onto her hunched shoulders and back before he returned to the coal face.

When Helen reached the pithead with her last basket that evening, she saw her parents talking with Archie Kenny in the darkness, which was lit only by the lantern hanging on the side of the equipment shed.

She heard her father say, "We keep Sandy in our prayers, Archie."

Archie responded sadly, "Do ye think the God who permits us to be kept in these holes in the earth cares about a little lad of the pits?"

Isabel Hogge responded by putting her hand on his arm. "We know He hears our prayers, but we nae can know His will."

"I dearly hope it is His will to heal my lad." With sagging shoulders and slow step, Archie turned and started up the path toward the row cottages.

As Helen followed her parents up the sloping path, she heard David ask, "Pa, why does God make us work in the pits?"

George Hogge was quiet for a moment, and then responded in a tired voice, "'Tis not God that keeps us in the pits, laddie; 'tis the lairds who serve in the Parliament who own the pits that keep us there."

"Why do they keep us there?" he asked. Helen could see her little brother's face in the moonlight as he looked up at his father. His eyes were wide with perplexity.

"To keep themselves warm and rich."

David continued, "How did they put us there?"

"We were put there by a hungry great-grandfather and the cruel laws of a king."

"A hungry great-grandfather?"

"About one hundred and fifty years ago, my grandfather's father lived in Inverness in the Highlands. 'Twas beautiful country with many lochs and mountain peaks. He had a small croft and raised a few sheep, but the time came when the great laird who owned the land determined that the tenant farmers had to pay him more for the use of the land or leave it. Maybe he could have paid more rent for the farm, but the sheep took sick that year and he couldn't sell them. He couldn't find any work in the Highlands, so he traveled to Edinburgh to find work, but before he found a trade, he was arrested for having none. He was taken before the Kirk Sessions and committed to work in the pits. Sir William Douglas claimed him, and we have all been here in the pits since."

David was quiet for a few minutes as they walked, but then asked, "Who was the cruel king, and what did he do?"

"Ah, that was King James of the Royal Stuart family. He was a Scotsman but never showed any kind feelings for poor Scots. That king lived almost a hundred years before my great-grandfather was born, and he allowed the Parliament to pass the laws that put every poor man and beggar into the pits as punishment for having no work."

"Why did he do such a thing?"

"Because no one would willingly work in the pits, but the coal is needed to warm the houses in the great cities and to fuel the great furnaces in the factories where they make the glass and iron."

"Did your grandpa work here in Penston, Pa?"

"My grandfather worked in the pits at Nitshill Colliery where he was killed by the firedamp. That pit is gai deep, maybe the deepest in Scotland, and many a miner has died because of the bad air or explosions in that pit."

David was quiet for a few minutes. As they neared the row cottages he asked, "Where does the firedamp come from?"

"Firedamp seeps out of the rock and fills some of the deepest pit shafts where it mixes with the coal dust. If someone strikes a rock with his pick and it makes a spark, it sometimes sets off a blast that will bring down the ceiling of the pit on top of the folks digging in its belly. And then there is the afterdamp, which is almost as bad as the firedamp. It fills the shafts and kills the light in the lanterns, and if ye don't get yourself up out of the pit fast, it will kill you."

"Does it make a blast like firedamp?"

"No, Davy, it just sneaks up on a man and smothers the life out of him."

David was quiet until the cottage was in sight. Then he asked a question he had asked before: "Pa, will we ever leave the pits?"

"I don't know, laddie, I just don't know." Then he added as an afterthought, "Maybe, God willing," as if to avoid killing any hope his youngest son held.

By this time they had reached the stone cottage with the sod roof and found the door unlatched and the pot of porridge still warm where it hung above the turf fire in the fireplace. George could see the tousled black hair of James under one corner of the old quilt he had rolled himself into to sleep on the floor near the fireplace.

Robert was sitting near the fireplace where the glowing embers reflected on his coal-blackened face and fell on the battered, cover-less book he was reading in the limited light. He looked up as his parents entered and then returned to the book.

Janet looked up from her nearly empty bowl of porridge and said quietly, "Ma, the coal master, Mr. McBride, wants me to marry him." She was quiet as her parents stood still, stunned and wondering if they had heard her correctly. Then she added, "I think maybe I'm inclined to tell him aye." With that, she stood up from the battered table and crawled into the rope bed in one corner, where she wrapped herself in her old, worn quilt. Then she closed her eyes as if to say she did not want to talk about it and pretended to go to sleep.

Isabel and George looked at each other in alarm. "Janet, ye must talk to us about this," her mother said, but Janet continued the pretense, even when Helen and David climbed into the bed and wrapped themselves in their quilts. It was evident that she would not talk about the matter until she was ready.

CHAPTER 6
Sabbath in the Cottage

On the Sabbath, after eating the porridge that served as Sunday breakfast, the members of the Hogge family gathered around the old table in the middle of the small cottage and shared an hour of reading from the well-worn family Bible. The Hogge children were among the few that lived in the miners' cottages at Penston who could read. Isabel had been permitted to attend school for a few years as a child, and she had taught her children. When the Bible was closed, the two oldest boys went down to the stream and, shivering, washed the coal dust off their bodies as best they could.

Rain or shine, Isabel sent Helen and David to the little stream with two buckets and a small washtub to carry water back to the cottage. George shaved with an old straight-edge razor and cold water each Sunday morning. With her daughters' help, Isabel set about washing the family's clothing.

"Ma, I like the Sabbath," David said to his mother.

She asked, "And why do ye like the Sabbath, Davy, my lad?"

"Because I can see the sunlight all the day. Even when I lay down to rest when ye wash my clothes, I can open my eyes and see the light anytime I want to."

This Sunday, while Isabel washed and ironed the family's clothing, she determined that she would not be put off, and she asked her oldest daughter, "Janet, ye are a bonnie lass, and I can see why the coal master would want to marry ye, but why do ye want to marry him?"

After a minute or two she answered, "If I become the wife of the coal master, I can have a nice dress and go to Sabbath meetings, and maybe even have a cook to fix meals. I would never have to work in the pits again." She added longingly, "Life would be so much nicer."

Isabel spoke firmly as she expressed her concern. "Mr. McBride is known as a man of much temper and drink. He is much older than ye are, and he just buried his second wife not three months ago. He has had no time for proper mourning. His next wife might be . . ." Isabel let the sentence trail off. Her forehead was wrinkled with worry.

"Ma, I will not think he would turn his temper on a wife." Then Janet added wistfully, "And he lives in such a big cottage."

"A small and simple cottage is a happier place with those ye love, than a palace shared with those ye cannot love," her mother admonished her.

Strong-willed Janet started to cry and refused to talk about the matter any further.

As soon as his clothing was dry and mended, David would disappear from the cottage, except on the coldest or wettest of Sundays, and return a few minutes after his father had stood at the door of the cottage and called for him to come for the evening meal. Finally, his father asked him where he went each Sunday.

"I go to watch the rich folks on their way home from Sabbath meeting," he answered simply.

"Why do ye do that?" his father inquired with a raised eyebrow.

"I like to see them in their fancy clothes."

"Where did ye get the notion of going to watch the rich folk on the Sabbath?"

"Robbie goes to watch them. I followed him one day."

George and Isabel both turned to look at their second son. George asked, "How long have ye been doing such a thing, Robbie?"

Robert's head dropped, and he said nothing, but James answered, "He's been going to watch Victoria, Sir Isaac's daughter.

When she's all dressed up in her finery, she's a sight to see—ribbons in her hair and a pink hat with feathers."

Robert continued to look at the floor, but he turned red all the way to his hairline.

Isabel, her face white with alarm, looked at Robert and said, "If the laird should see ye watching his daughter, he would make ye go the round—or worse."

David's voice piped up. "What's 'going the round'?"

Silence hung in the air for a few moments before George answered. "'Tis a punishment that ye don't want someone ye love to go through."

Robert moved to his seat near the window, where he began to silently study the old book again. His hunger for learning was almost a curse, since there was no school for the children of the miners in Penston. He was always like a hungry man searching an empty cupboard for something to eat. He spent every night reading the tattered book until the last embers grew dark in the fireplace.

His mother spoke. "Robbie, what is the book ye are reading?"

"I cannot say, as it has nae cover and some of the pages are missing."

"Where did ye find it? How came ye by it?" Then answering her own question she stated angrily, "Ye have been to the rubbish heap! Ye know that ye will find nothing but trouble there. That rubbish heap is on the laird's property. Ye have been trespassing."

"Aye, I trespassed, but how can anyone mind if I go through the rubbish heap? When the laird is at Sabbath meeting, many of the lads go there to see what he and his family have cast off. That's where I found the book."

"Oh, Robbie, ye worry me so," his mother said quietly, shaking her head. Then she added, "But I am glad ye are reading. What's the book about?"

"'Tis like the Bible, but not like it, too. Perhaps I can say more after I have read awhile."

At the close of the day, Isabel made the oatcakes they would use for breakfast the next day as the fire in the fireplace burned down to embers.

CHAPTER 7
The Wake

One of the women had brought the news of Sandy Kenny's death as the Hogge family was preparing to enter the pit. "Did ye know that Sandy Kenny passed last night? His folk are hard-pressed with grief."

"Nae, we hadn't heard," Isabel had answered.

When she sought out her husband where he stood in the line of men waiting to descend the ladders into the pit, he responded, "We'll go over for the wake when we finish at the pit. That's all we can do."

That evening when the Hogge family, exhausted and covered with coal dust, made the trek up the hill to the cottage, they found the Kenny family and a few other friends from the pit gathered around the small, white-faced form of Sandy, which lay on the kitchen table. He bore a great purple and red swelling on his forehead. As Isabel put her arm around Carrie Kenny's waist, Carrie laid her head on Isabel's shoulder and whispered, "He looks like he's sleeping."

"The lad *is* sleeping. He's sleeping in the Lord," Isabel responded, offering the only comfort she knew how to give. "And he's free from the pits."

"But I don't have my laddie anymore, and I think my heart will break. My Archie can't deal with it. He will not talk to anyone." Then new tears started down her face, and her shoulders shook with renewed grief.

Isabel put both arms around her and held her as she wept. Then Carrie lifted her head and spoke again. "Archie was given the wood for the coffin by the coal master, but we don't have the money to buy a small plot in the churchyard. Where will we bury our lad?" Then the convulsive sobs shook her shoulders again.

George said quietly to Carrie, "How many shillings will it take to buy a spot in the churchyard?"

"About ten shillings, and we don't have more than two."

"Some of us will help." Then George walked across the room and spoke quietly to the men gathered there. After speaking with each one, he stepped out of the cottage, and as each family arrived to share the grief of the Kenny family, George spoke quietly to the husband. In the morning, before it was time to leave for the pit, George went to several cottage doors, and after about thirty minutes he climbed up the slope to the Kenny cottage and knocked.

When Archie opened the door, George simply handed him coins totaling eight shillings collected from those he had spoken to the previous evening. Then he said quietly, "Go and buy the place where ye can lay your lad."

Archie stood quietly in the open doorway, looking down at the coins in his hand, a lump growing in this throat, unable to speak.

That evening in the dark, lit only with one small kerosene lamp, a few of the miners and their families gathered in the church graveyard—the unkempt corner reserved for the miners and their families—and as Sandy's coffin was lowered into the ground, the small crowd stood with heads bowed. The vicar was not present. No one had expected that he would be. George offered a short and simple prayer. "God, take home to yourself this wee laddie, and give his parents comfort, we pray, in the knowledge that he is with Thee and not in the pits."

After the soil was shoveled onto the small coffin, George quietly urged Isabel to go home and take Carrie and the children with her. Then he sat down on a corner of a headstone and said, "'Tis time to talk, Archie."

Instead of talking, Archie took a deep, shuddering breath and said nothing. George sat quietly and waited. After a few minutes, Archie spoke in a near whisper. "There is nae comfort in the death of a bairn, George, but I thank ye for what ye did for us." He would speak no further.

On his way out of the churchyard, George removed his cap and paused with bowed head for a moment at an unmarked spot beneath a tree. Under his breath, he said, "Agnes, my lassie, we still miss ye."

When he arrived at the cottage, his porridge was nearly cold, and he ate in silence. Then he said thoughtfully, "In my father's day they would have had to arle the next bairn to buy the grave. I'm glad that time is passed."

David looked up from his nearly empty bowl at supper and asked, "Pa, what does it mean—to arle the bairn?" The boy's curiosity had been roused, and the questions began.

Isabel sat down and tried to answer him. "There was a time when each bairn was born that the parents would take it to the church and there, when it was baptized, they would sign a paper saying that the bairn would work in the pit all its life, starting when it turned six. Your pa and I were arled by our parents. Then the laird of the pit would give the parents enough money, maybe as much as ten pounds, to buy what they needed."

"Oh," was all David had to say for a few minutes. Then he added thoughtfully, "That was like selling the bairn to pay for the grave."

"Aye, Davy, my lad, that's about right," his mother responded quietly.

"Did God like it when the bairns were sold to the laird?"

"Nae, laddie, He did not like it, but such old customs died slowly," his father stated softly. "About fifty years ago the Parliament said it would nae be legal to arle the bairns anymore, but many of the lairds and the coal masters still did it when a family was hard-pressed and couldn't find the money for something as important as a grave."

David did not speak anymore that evening, and he was a long time falling asleep, thinking of hardships past and hardships present.

CHAPTER 8
Janet's Wedding

"Will ye tell me about the book ye are reading, Robbie?" Helen asked at the end of the day as they made their way up the path to the row cottages.

"'Tis about a rich family that leaves their home and their gold and silver to take a long journey to an unknown land."

"Why?"

"Because God told their pa that they should."

Helen was quiet for a few seconds and then asked, "Do ye think God will ever tell our pa that we should leave our home and go to a new land?"

Robert responded angrily, "I hope He does." Then he fell silent.

David was so tired that he could hardly put one foot in front of the other as they made their way toward the cottages, but he still had more questions to ask his father. "Pa, can we ever leave the pit?" Though he had asked the question before, he seemed to think that if he asked it enough times, the answer might change.

"Nae, son. There's no way. Once there was hope. A few years before I was born, the Parliament passed a law that the miners could leave after seven years if they could get all the right papers sent to the Sheriff's Court, but most miners don't know how to do that, and we must pay all our debts at the company store—but we won't ever be able to do that. If we get sick, we must get a loan to buy our oatmeal and pay the rent. The debt just keeps rising till the day we die."

"Why can't we run away?"

"There's always been a fearsome punishment for those who try to run away. They're thieves. When they are caught, they are made to go the round. In my grandfather's day, the runaways were whipped or branded in the ear."

"If a runaway is a thief, what did he steal?"

"He tried to steal his labor from the laird of the mine that owned him."

David was quiet for several minutes and then asked, "What else did the laird do to the runaways?"

"Sometimes the laird had the blacksmith make an iron ring that the man had to wear around his neck. On it was printed the man's name; it also said that he was the property of the laird of the mine, so he could be returned if he ran away again."

"How long did he have to wear it?"

"Until he was sold—or dead."

"Can the laird do that now?" David' eyes were big with alarm.

"Nae, as we are no longer considered to be the property of the laird of the mine by law, but as long as we owe the company store, we might as well be." George's voice was bitter.

"If the laird doesn't own us anymore, how can someone who runs away be a thief?"

"Because he stole from the laird when he left without paying his debt at the company store."

"Did anyone ever get away?'

"Once we heard of a lad who made his way to Leith, where he got a post on a warship and signed on with the English navy, or at least that's what folks say. We never heard more about him. Maybe he's drowned in the sea by now."

David was quiet the rest of the way home.

On the following Sunday, McBride visited the Hogge cottage and formally asked for Janet's hand in marriage. He was a short, stocky man with a gray shock of hair under a flat, woolen cap, and he had gray lamb-chop sideburns above heavy, florid jowls. His manner was brusque as he entered the cottage. He did not remove his cap. His manner suggested that the decision was predetermined.

Janet looked at her father and said, pleadingly, "Oh, Pa, say it will be all right. Please say aye." There was no changing Janet's mind, so he gave his permission.

The wedding followed a week after the banns had been posted at the village church. Janet wore the previous Mrs. McBride's wedding dress. The Hogge family was not invited to the wedding, and Isabel wept the entire day. "I know this is a foolish thing she has done," she said quietly.

"Why can't we go to the wedding? She's our sister," David asked his mother.

"Because we own nae suitable clothes," she answered. But other family members knew it was because Janet had married above her station.

The Hogge family walked home from the pit on a Saturday evening in late October, a week after the wedding, with slow and tired steps. James and Robert walked ahead of Helen, who was just a few steps behind her brothers. She heard James say to Robert, "Ye can't go again. Ye must have more in your head than straw. If ye get caught, ye will have more troubles than ye can guess."

Robert responded quietly, trying to keep his voice low enough so Helen would not hear his answer, but she caught part of it. "I must try one more time. I must make her understand . . ." but the rest of the words were too low to be heard.

The Sabbath was quiet in the Hogge household. Janet's absence weighed heavily on everyone. Even David was quiet until the evening meal was finished. Then he asked of no one in particular the same question that was on the minds of every other family member. "If Pa gets so sick he can't go to the pits, and Janet won't be carrying coal anymore, will we have enough shillings to buy our oatmeal?"

His mother said with more confidence than she felt, "Of course, Davy; we are lucky to have two strong lads to dig the coal. Many families in Penston have only one who can dig." That seemed to satisfy him.

Each of the family members prepared for sleep except Robert, who sat at his usual place near the fireplace, reading the coverless book by the light of the dying fire.

After the firelight was gone, Robert sat in the darkness for several minutes without moving, waiting to hear his father's even breathing. Then he quietly moved across the room and slipped out the doorway, catching the latch as he silently closed it behind him. James and Helen lay with eyes open in the darkness. Helen whispered, "Jamie, where is Robbie going?"

"To find trouble," was his only answer.

In the morning, when Helen awoke, she rushed to James and shook his shoulder to wake him. "Where's Robbie?"

James sat up and looked around. "Maybe he went to the pit early. Don't worry, I'll go after him." Then James grabbed an oatcake from the table and hurriedly left the cottage. When the rest of the family was ready to leave for the pit, James had not returned, so Isabel's worry about Robert eased but was replaced by her concern for George. He was too weak and feverish to go to work that day.

CHAPTER 9
"Going the Round"

"Stop right there, you filthy hole digger! How dare you approach my daughter! I should shoot you here and now. No one would blame me!"

Robert turned to look at Laird Keith and raised his hands. The man's face was scarlet with rage. Stuttering and cold with fear, Robert spoke, "I, ah, I meant no harm, Sir Isaac. I only wanted to be Victoria's friend. She's been kind to me."

"Kind!" he raged. "Kind! I will show you kindness. I won't kill you, but for sure you will go the round." Sticking the gun into his nightshirt pocket, he picked up a rope, which lay near the stoop where he stood, and threw it around Robert, tying it so it kept his arms pinned to his sides. Then he took the gun from his pocket and fired it into the air. Lights began to come on behind the windows of the house, and the door of the carriage house opened. The laird's carriage driver stepped out with bare feet and disheveled hair, wearing only his nightshirt.

Laird Keith yelled at him, "Get the dogcart ready to go." Taking the gun from his pocket, he pointed it at Robert and added, "We're going to the pit."

Robert stood still, feeling much colder than the night air. He shivered and desperately hoped the sick feeling in the bottom of his stomach would not worsen. The cold perspiration of fear covered his face.

A servant brought the laird his greatcoat and shoes, and the carriage driver quickly appeared, his nightshirt only partially tucked into his waistband, and his feet in shoes without stockings. When he drove the dogcart around to the front of the big house, Laird Keith tied the end of the rope to the back of the cart and got in. The driver sat on the small front seat and slapped the reins to make the sleepy horse move.

A few minutes earlier when Robert had arrived at the big house, he had made his way to the back as he had done several times previously. His heart was pounding so loudly in his ears he felt that everyone in the house would hear it. The frost on the ground was thick and crunched under his feet. Ice crystals hung like delicate lace from the branches of the rowan trees in the yard. Tossing a pebble at Victoria's bedroom window, he had been surprised to see it open immediately. Victoria put her head out of the window and, shaking it vigorously, had whispered forcefully, "Go away. I cannot see you again." She closed the window forcefully, and the candlelight behind the lace curtains went out.

Robert waited for a few seconds and then threw another small pebble at the window. It remained closed. He waited a minute or two and then he threw a third pebble, but nothing happened. After waiting for about five minutes, stomping his feet to ease the chill, he had dejectedly started across the backyard, toward the side of the house. This visit had required all the courage he could muster, and now she would not see him. As he had turned away, the kitchen door had opened, and that was when Sir Isaac Keith had stepped out with a long-barreled revolver in his hand.

The cart road was longer than the shortcut Robert had always taken to visit Victoria, and he was stumbling with exhaustion by the time they reached the pit; he had been forced to follow the trap at a near run. There, the laird climbed out and pulled Robert to the pit entrance. Inside were several sets of rusty and seldom-used wrist and ankle irons attached to the rock wall. Laird Keith and his cart driver pulled Robert to the first set, where he could be seen by everyone reporting to work in the pit. After they put his wrists and ankles into the irons, they climbed into the cart and departed to return to their houses.

When James arrived at the equipment shed, several men were standing nearby and were talking in quiet whispers. James asked one of the men if he had seen his brother. One of them grabbed his arm. Pulling him aside he said, "Robbie's in the jugs. What did he do to make the laird so angry?"

Alarmed, James ran to the pit entrance where it was dug laterally into the hillside. There he could see his brother with his wrists in irons above his head. "Robbie, I told you to give it up. Why did ye go again?" he asked, exasperation filling his voice. Robert just hung his head. James continued with a tone of frustrated anger. "What does it take to teach ye some common sense?" Robert looked at the ground. He had no answer.

Within a few minutes the laird arrived, and, in the presence of the coal master, who carried a whip, Robert was released from the jugs and tied in front of the great draft horse that stood at the gin. With his wrists tied together in front of his face, he was connected by a short length of rope to the bridle of the animal. Then the coal master hit the hindquarters of the horse to start it moving around the gin, forcing Robbie backward into the mud. The horse reared and almost struck him with its front hooves.

When Isabel, David, and Helen arrived at the pit, Helen cried out, "Ma, the laird has put Robbie in the gin. He's making him go the round."

Upon seeing her son in the gin, trying to run backward in front of the horse, Isabel cried out, "Robbie, what did ye do to earn such a punishment?" She started to run toward the gin, but the coal master caught her by the arm and stopped her.

"Teach your boy his place, and in the future he won't have to go the round. Now get to your work or ye'll all have your pay docked. And don't come near the gin until your shift is over." He let go of her arm and turned away.

Carrie Kenny laid her hand on Isabel's arm and said, "We are so sorry for ye, Bell, but he is a strong lad. He will come through it." James put his arm around his mother's shoulders and guided her toward the line where the women were collecting their creels and lanterns.

James spoke to her quietly and said, "We must do double work today, Ma, or we will have our pay docked. We can't help Robbie." Helen stood watching her twin brother, unable to take her eyes from the sight, until the coal master yelled at her to get to work.

Isabel's shoulders drooped. Looking up into her son's face, she said, "Jamie, who will I carry for with Robbie in the gin and your father sick?"

"Mr. Moffatt needs another fremit bearer. Find him and ask if he will pay you to help him." She took her basket and started toward the pit shaft. Looking over her shoulder in the direction of the gin, she stifled a sob. Descending into the pit, Isabel asked everyone she met if they knew where Joe Moffatt was working. Finally, she found him. He was glad to have her help.

For the next fourteen hours, Robert stumbled and half ran backward in front of the horse, trying to match his stride and speed to that of the animal. By evening, as the miners began to come up out of the pits, Robert was staggering around the gin in front of the horse, sometimes falling to his knees and struggling to avoid the animal's hooves.

After Isabel reached the pithead she rushed to the gin, where James was helping Robert to his feet. The big animal was glad to have the rope and the cumbersome young man attached to it removed from its bridle, and it stamped its feet and tossed its head impatiently.

James said, "Robbie, put your arms around my neck and I will lift ye up." Robert could hardly stand. His exhaustion was so total that Joe Moffatt pushed a company wheelbarrow over to the gin. James helped Robert lay down in it and started to push it toward the cottages. The coal master objected as James pushed the barrow past him. "Make him walk; he earned his time in the gin," the coal master called out.

Joe Moffatt stepped up and said to him quietly through clenched teeth, "Ye'll keep your mouth shut, or risk a work slowdown the likes of which ye have yet to see."

Isabel hurried after the heavily loaded wheelbarrow. When they reached the cottage, they helped Robert into the room, warmed by the fire in the fireplace. George had started the porridge cooking. As his wife and sons stumbled into the room, he rose from the chair by the fireplace with a look of confusion on his face. "What happened? Robbie's hurt?"

"Aye, husband. The coal master made Robbie go the round."

George looked from James to Robert and back to James for an explanation. As James lowered Robert onto a quilt near the fireplace, he said grimly, "Seems that Robbie went visiting Victoria Keith last night and got caught. The laird is more than a tad upset about it, so he made Robbie go the round today."

As Isabel knelt to pull Robert's tattered shoes off his feet, Helen threw the door open as she entered, breathlessly asking, "Will Robbie be all right?"

Her mother answered, "Helen, go to the stream and get me a pail of water so I can wash the blisters on his feet." When she returned with the water, Isabel carefully washed one foot while Helen washed the other. He bit his lower lip but said nothing. As Isabel wrapped Robert's feet in a few clean rags, George asked, "What did Jamie mean, ye were visiting Victoria Keith? Ye must remember how your mother warned ye that ye mustn't be watching or speaking to the laird's daughter."

Finally Robert spoke. "I know, Pa, but I just had to talk to her." He stressed the word *had*.

"What did she say to you?"

"After I told her that I was a miner, she didn't have any more to say to me."

"Ye were seeing her before that and she didn't know who ye were?"

"She thought I was a clerk at the village store. I didn't tell her otherwise until Sunday a fortnight ago. When I told her, she ran away like she had been burned." He dropped his head before he continued. "I just thought she, well, she seemed to like me the way I liked her."

Helen's voice was full of amazement that her brother would do something so foolish. She spoke as though she were speaking to a child who had thoughtlessly touched an obviously hot kettle hanging in the fireplace. "Ye only thought she could like you. If she had known who and what ye are, she would never have looked your way."

When Robert did not answer, George added quietly, "Some lessons are learned hard but for a profit, if learned well."

The next day Robert had to wrap rags around his torn shoes to keep them on his feet. His walk to the pit was slow, and Helen hung back to walk with him. "Robbie, tell me how ye met Victoria. What made ye do such a thing?" Robert just shook his head. He would not talk about the matter, even with Helen, with whom he shared most of his thoughts.

That evening after a long day of work, he stopped at the company store, where he purchased another pair of shoes on credit. The amount of coal Robert dug for the next several days was diminished by his exhaustion and sore feet. He was even quieter than his normal self the next few weeks, and in the evenings he spent more time reading the coverless book.

One winter day after Robert had come at her whistle, Helen said, "Tell me more about the book, Robbie. Are ye learning something as ye read?"

Robert scooped the gritty water from a pool on the tunnel floor into his tin cup, and after taking a drink, he answered, "Aye. I'm learning about a family who left all they owned to go across the great waters to a new country, a 'promised land.'"

"Was the promised land far away?"

"Aye, it took them many years to get there. 'Twas a long, hard journey."

"Do ye think we will ever get to a promised land, Robbie?" Helen's words were strung on a frail thread of hope.

"Only if God be willing," he answered. With that, he heaved the heavy creel onto her shoulders and arched back, and Helen started for the bottom of the ladder.

CHAPTER 10
"More Than I'm Willing to Give"

About a week later, as Helen was bringing her last creel load out of the pit, she could see McBride talking with Eliza Cummins on the opposite side of the gin in the shadows, almost behind the equipment shed. With his left hand he had Eliza by the right arm, and she was leaning against the shed wall. His body was blocking her way as he leaned on his right arm, which was at the height of her head. Eliza was looking around with frightened eyes. As she caught sight of Helen, she called out in a voice that quavered with fear, "Oh, Helen, there ye are. I've been waiting so we could walk home together." As McBride turned to look at Helen, Eliza pulled away from his grip, ducked under his arm, and darted past him. Helen was too surprised to speak.

Eliza put her arm in Helen's and started to pull her toward the path. As she did so she chatted nervously. "Ye are nearly the last one out of the pit tonight. Ye must be tired, for sure." As they walked together, Eliza pulled Helen along, almost faster than she could walk.

Helen looked back over her shoulder and could just barely see McBride in the darkness, standing with his fists on his hips, looking angrily their way.

"Eliza, what did Mr. McBride want of ye?"

"More than I am willing to give him, that's for sure," she said with fervor.

Both girls were quiet the rest of the way up the path as Helen wondered about Eliza's words. Why would Mr. McBride be so interested in Robert's fremit bearer? Without another word, Eliza separated from Helen and walked toward the door of the Cumminses' cottage.

When Helen entered the room, she stepped to her mother's side and asked in a perplexed manner, "Do ye know why Mr. McBride would try to keep Eliza from going home when she finished her work?"

Her father heard her, as did all three of her brothers in that small room. "What do ye mean, lass?" James asked.

Helen explained what she had seen, and asked her mother what Eliza meant.

It was Helen's father who responded while everyone in the room watched and listened. "Ye are young, daughter, but ye must be able to see that Eliza is almost a woman. She's the same age as you and Robbie, and when the coal dust is washed off, she is a bonnie lass. McBride has been looking at her in the wrong way."

"But Mr. McBride is married to Janet!" Her voice rose in anger.

"Aye, but that has not stopped him from looking at and sometimes touching some of the lassies that work in the pits."

James broke in. "Helen, if ye ever see him touch Eliza again, ye will tell me and I will see that he never does it again, if it means a week in the jugs." His voice was hot with anger.

* * *

David crept away from the cottage on the following Sunday, after his clothes were washed, and sought out the large, two-story, stone house of the coal master, which was set apart from the miners' row cottages. He knocked on the door and waited, but nothing happened. Thinking that his knock had not been heard, he looked around and found a rock the size of his hand. He used it to knock on the door again. A stout woman came to the door. She wore a soiled apron over her dress and a dust cap on her gray hair. "What d'ye want?" she asked gruffly.

"I want to see my sister," he said simply, looking up into her face.

"And who be your sister?"

"My sister married the coal master, Mr. McBride."

"Oh, ye mean Mrs. McBride. She and the master are gone to services. Come back some other time." With that, she firmly closed the door.

David slowly walked home. For some reason he did not believe the housekeeper. He returned each Sunday for the next four weeks and was always told the same thing. He grew more determined to see and talk to Janet.

* * *

In mid-December, Carrie Kenny gave birth to a baby boy, which she and Archie named Alexander, after his brother. Many of the miners and their families gathered at the public house to celebrate the birth. When some of the men began imbibing too freely of the cheap ale that was passed around, George and Isabel told their children that it was time to go home.

As they walked back to their cottage, David asked, "Why did some of the men talk and laugh so loud? Why do we need to go home?"

George tried to explain. "Sometimes, Davy, my laddie, men will drink a bit too much ale, and they get loud and say and do things that disgrace themselves."

"Why do they drink the ale if it makes them do such things?"

"I don't know, laddie, but too often too many of them drink too much of the stuff, to the great regret of their families."

* * *

On the second Sunday of March, a day with a leaden sky that poured rain, the banns were posted announcing the pending marriage of Victoria Keith and David Gray, the son of Sir Ian Gray, the laird of the pits at Dalkeith. As Helen walked back to the cottage with her brother a few days later she asked, "Robbie, did ye hear about the posting of the banns for Victoria?" He nodded his head once in a brisk, short action but said nothing. For the next several days, he was even quieter than usual, and on the following Monday morning he was not in his old quilt when it was time to rise.

CHAPTER 11
"Runaway!"

David's voice woke James and Helen. "Robbie's not here, Pa. Maybe he's run away."

George tried to quiet Isabel's fears by telling her, "He's just gone to the pit early. Don't worry yourself." But intuitively, Helen knew they would not find him at the pit. And besides that, several oatcakes were missing.

When Isabel and her children got to the pit and asked if anyone had seen Robert, the answer was always just a silent head shake. By this time, Isabel was distraught. "Oh, Helen, what if he's gone to see Victoria Keith again? The laird will see that he gets ten lashes."

At the end of the day Isabel said, "I know ye are tired, Jamie, but I need ye to go look for Robert." She was insistent. James visited every miner's cottage and asked about his brother. He stopped everyone he saw on the way to the village store. He continued to make his way in the dark for three miles on the road to Musselburgh, stopping at every crofter's cottage that had a light in the window. He returned home exhausted. "I can't find any trace of him anywhere, Ma. I'm sorry." Then he dropped onto his quilt. The last thought he had before drifting into an exhausted sleep was of the burden his brother's leaving would thrust on him.

As the dawn lightened the eastern sky, George struggled out of bed and, against Isabel's wishes, insisted on returning to the pit. "We must have another man digging, or it will be hard times without Robbie," was all he said.

With Robert gone, Helen began to carry coal for Joe Moffatt—replacing her mother, who returned to carrying for her father. She missed her brother. When everyone else had been too tired to talk, they had always been able to share their thoughts with one another. When the family ate their porridge that evening, David asked, "Did Robbie run away to join the navy?" No one had an answer for him.

Before lying down to sleep, Isabel asked each to kneel with her while she offered a simple, short prayer. "Dear Lord, please watch over our Robbie. Wherever he is, he is in Thy hands." In silence they each lay down to sleep.

The next evening, Helen rushed back to the cottage through the cold rain that fell from a low, gray sky, hoping and half expecting to find Robert there, but it was empty and silent. "Oh, Robbie, where are ye?" she whispered as she sat down on a stool and fought off her tears. "I miss ye so." Before the others arrived at the cottage, she started the fire in the fireplace to cook the oatmeal. Soon the heavy, blue smoke rose up the chimney and filled the cottage with the sharp, acrid smell of a turf fire.

After supper, she picked up the coverless book and sat near the fireplace so she could read the book that had interested Robert so much. She read as long as possible before the fire began to die out.

* * *

Robert had waited until his wages were paid at the end of the week before he acted on his plan. Ever since the banns had been posted for Victoria, he had felt an angry rush of blood to his face every time he thought of her. His humiliation left him confused. Why had he ever thought a young woman of such quality could look at him, a miner?

On that Sunday evening he waited until everyone had fallen asleep. When the moon was high, piercing the thin clouds with a weak light that filtered though the small window, and he could hear the regular breathing of several family members, he rose from the quilt he had used for sleeping for so many years. Taking his Saturday pay of sixteen shillings out of his pocket, he looked at the coins in the spill of moonlight, and after a moment he carefully placed four on the table.

Looking at the sleeping form of Helen as she lay on the rope bed wrapped in her quilt, he knew she would be hurt that he had not shared his plans with her, but he had decided that it was better that she did not know where he was going. What she did not know, she could not tell. He took a comb from the bed table near his parents' bed and some of the oatcakes his mother had made for the family's breakfast the next day and wrapped them in his old sweater, tying the sleeves together around his waist. He picked up the coverless book but then laid it back on the table, knowing he had no pocket big enough to carry it in. He quietly let himself out of the cottage door.

He paused for a moment and once again weighed the choice he had made. Then, as if a renewed determination had filled him, he made his way along the cart path with long, firm strides. He passed several crofters' cottages, avoiding any where light still shone in the windows. At about one o'clock in the morning he finally found his way to the rutted road that would take him west to the village of Musselburgh and from there to Edinburgh.

By this time, a thick fog had settled around the east Lothian landscape, swirled by a light, chill east wind. Bone-deep exhaustion settled on him, brought on as much by nervousness as by the long walk and cold night air. Stumbling with nearly every step, he located a haystack behind a dark crofter's cottage where he rested for a few hours, buried in the hay so as to be hidden should the crofter rise early. How he missed his old quilt.

He did not have to worry about the farmer finding him. Before the sun had begun to dispel the fog, he was wakened by a large sheep trying to eat the leather shoes on his feet. He stood and brushed the hay off his clothing, and, putting the comb through his hair, he continued his walk toward Musselburgh.

As he ate one of the oatcakes he had taken from home, he began to think more deeply about the effect his leaving would have on his family. They would greatly miss his wages, and with his father still so weak, the burden of digging enough coal to feed them all would fall heavily on James. At this thought he paused and considered turning back, but then remembered the humiliation he had felt as he had been pulled behind the cart from the great house of the laird to the mine and forced to go the round. "Somehow—someday," he whispered fiercely as he doubled up his fists, "I will go back—and I will pay down their debt and free them from the pits."

CHAPTER 12
Mrs. McEwen's Boardinghouse

Robert walked and whistled through Musselburgh trying to appear as if he had every right to be there. When he reached the other side of the village, he was perspiring with nervousness, which added to the discomfort caused by the cold air. By early evening, he reached the outskirts of Edinburgh, out of oatcakes and very tired.

He was shocked by the crowded, narrow streets where children in ragged clothing were trying to make themselves comfortable for the night in the alleys and a few of the doorways of the shops. Tradesmen were closing up their shops and stalls, and the lamp lighter was well into his task for the evening, leaving the streets behind him lit with pools of light.

After walking through the often muddy, sometimes filthy streets, he turned south onto a side street where he stopped at an inviting house that had a sign in the window reading *Boarders Accepted*. It was made of whitewashed stone with a window on each side of a door in the middle of the front wall. Its thatch roof rose to a second level in the rear. He nervously knocked, and the top half of the divided door was opened by a short and somewhat stout woman with an apron over her dress, her white curls spilling out from under her dust cap. Her round face was marked by the smile lines of many years.

Robert nodded and asked respectfully, "What is the cost of boarding with ye?"

She smiled and answered, "Ten pence a day for the night and two meals—if I accept ye as a boarder."

He swallowed hard and asked, "Would ye be willing to accept me?"

She took a long minute to look him up and down, and then answered, "Aye, I will accept ye. How long will ye be staying?"

"I don't know. Will that be a problem?"

She shook her head and opened the lower half of the door. Robert entered the little house, and she pointed to a chair near a large fireplace in the main room, which served as both kitchen and sitting room. He sat. She asked, "Have ye had any supper?"

"Nae, ma'am."

"Ye be hungry?"

"Aye."

"Then be patient a few minutes while I warm some porridge." Robert noticed that the coal fire had left a black smoke smudge up the wall above the fireplace but that the kitchen lacked the acrid, stinging blue smoke of a turf fire.

Robert's face grew perplexed when she set a pitcher of cream and a bowl of hot oatmeal porridge before him. Robert had never tasted cream and was not sure what to do with it.

As he put his spoon into the porridge, she asked, "Are ye averse to using the cream on your porridge? Ye will find it a trifle hot if ye don't put the cream on it."

Without speaking, he poured a little cream on the porridge. He looked at her while he still had the pitcher of cream suspended above his bowl. She nodded and said, "Ye will need more than that." He poured the rest of the cream onto the porridge. She shook her head and turned away so he would not see her smile.

He had never tasted anything so wonderful in his entire life. He emptied the bowl and looked at it with longing when it was empty. She laughed and filled it again. Then she filled the cream pitcher half full and set it before him. As he emptied it over the porridge, she said, "Ye eat, young laddie, like a starving man. Ye do look too thin. If ye will board with me for awhile, I will put some meat on your bones."

Robert's stomach had never before been so full that it hurt. It was a very new feeling. As his landlady led him up the stairs near the rear of the tiny house to a small bedroom with a narrow bed and a small table near it, he asked, "How shall I call ye, ma'am? I mean, what would be your name?"

"My name is Elizabeth McEwen. And your name?"

"My name is Robert Ho . . . Hoggan, ma'am, Robert Hoggan. But I'm Robbie to most folks."

"Well, Robbie, here be your room. Ye will be welcome to board with me as long as I find ye to be respectful."

Robert looked at the bed and its patchwork quilt coverlet for a moment, and then crossed the room to sit on it. He pulled off the worn shoes that had not been off his feet for two days, and stretched out on the bed. "This is wonderful, Mrs. McEwen. I thank ye . . ." Before the last word was out of his mouth, his eyes closed and he was asleep.

Mrs. McEwen closed the door as she stepped out of the room. With a smile on her face, she shook her head and said in a whisper to someone only she could see, "He can't fool me, William. I know those blue scars on his hands. I can tell a runaway miner when I see one. But he'll get no trouble from me. He's had enough of that in his short lifetime."

CHAPTER 13
The New Dress

"Two drowned and three nearly so!" The coal master had been pacing in the equipment shed. He stopped and angrily smashed his fist against the counter where the stains from the blood of Rand Kerr were still evident. The tools there jumped as he struck it a second time. "How am I to meet the weekly quota?"

The spring brought more rain than was usual, and in the deepest of the tunnels that day the water had risen so rapidly that two miners had drowned and three others had gotten out of the flooded tunnel just in time. The coal master approached the laird to suggest that a waterwheel powered by a steam engine be installed, but the laird had little concern for the safety of the miners and made that clear.

"I can buy the debt of thirty miners for the price of a water wheel," he answered with contempt. That ended the conversation.

* * *

On the last Sabbath morning in April, a day of sunshine that filtered between light clouds, dappling the green hillsides and lifting the heads of the wildflowers, Helen's mother put her arm around her shoulders and said, "This is the day of your birth, Helen. Ye are seventeen years today. Ye are a young woman. I have saved enough shillings to buy a length of muslin print to make ye a new dress."

"Oh, Ma, don't spend your shillings on a new dress for me. We need to pay down what we owe at the company store. How else will we ever be free of the pit?" For weeks Helen had thought almost continually about the prospect of someday leaving the mines and finding a "promised land." How she wished she had been able to go with her brother. The thought of having a new dress did not please her as it would have pleased most of the other coal bearers. She regretted the spending of the shillings it would require.

"Don't worry your head about such things, lass." George said the words quietly but firmly. "Ye are of a height to need a longer dress to cover ye more than that old, ragged one can."

"But Pa," she started to respond.

James answered, "What Pa means, Helen, is that nae matter how many shillings we pay to the company store, we can't buy ourselves free of the pit. Ye might as well have a new dress."

"Is that true, Pa?"

"Aye, daughter. You see, the debt we owe the company store is a much heavier load than ye can guess."

"Oh, Pa, we will never get free of this place." Tears trickled down Helen's cheeks, and she abruptly sat down cross-legged on the floor like a puppet whose strings had been cut. She put her face in her hands.

"We may have few pleasures, daughter, but today we will take pleasure in making a new dress for ye." Her mother's forced cheerfulness was mandatory.

Helen smiled for her mother. Then, rising, she said, "Give me the pails so David and I can get water from the stream. When we are washed, I will go with ye to the village store."

The dress was simple, of dark blue muslin, but Helen was pleased with it. "Oh, Ma, it is a bonnie dress." It had short sleeves, and the skirt fell below her knees. Her father smiled at her as she turned around slowly for everyone to see her mother's work.

"Aye, and ye do look like a bonnie lass in it, daughter," George said with pride.

The next morning, as Helen started the walk to the pit, Eliza Cummins joined her. "Ye have a new dress, lass. Be careful or some of the lads may look at ye," she said with a smile.

"Look at me?"

"Ye are old enough to make the lads think about posting the banns." Eliza laughed heartily at the look of embarrassment on Helen's face.

After the two girls had walked along the path in silence for a few minutes, Eliza looked at Helen again, this time with a serious face. "Ye keep out of the way of the coal master. He likes bonnie lasses. Don't give him reason to like you. Ye would regret it."

Helen said nothing but thought about Eliza's words for much of the day.

* * *

The weeks passed, and George's cough became worse. Between that and his twisted back, it was difficult for him to sleep. Even Isabel's determination to pretend that her husband would start to feel better soon gave way to the realization that he was sick with what the miners called the black spit. She knew that before long he would not be able to work, and the day would come when he would not be able to do anything except sit by the fireplace and cough into a blackened, blood-spattered rag.

One morning Isabel deliberately left for the pit after everyone else so none of the family would see her weep. Helen waited for her a short way up the path and watched as her mother wiped her tears with a corner of a ragged sleeve. "Ma, why are ye crying?"

"Oh, Helen, your father is growing weaker every day, and how will I ever live without him? He has been my friend, my companion since we were children. Twenty-two years we've been married." She wiped her eyes with the back of her hand, then continued in a more resolute tone. "But ye must not be concerned, daughter. Jamie and Davy will provide for us when he is gone."

Helen was silent as they walked for a few minutes, but then said quietly, "I suppose I have known he was sick with the black spit, but I never let myself think about him dying." All day she thought about what life would be like without her father. She felt empty inside.

At age twenty, James worked as hard as any man in the pits to provide for his parents and younger brother and sister. He knew his father was dying, but like his mother, he never spoke of it. He put his pick to the coal seams with determination, but if he had been asked, he would have admitted that he missed his younger brother. He worried about providing for his family when his father could no longer work in the pit.

* * *

Determined to see his sister Janet the next Sunday, David waited until late in the afternoon. It was an hour before supper when he walked to the coal master's house and knocked. The same woman opened the door, but before she could tell him his sister was at services with the master, he darted past her into the hallway and called out as he ran past the stairs that rose to the second level, "Janet, 'tis me, Davy. I come to see ye. Are ye here?" He stopped in the sitting room and looked around.

As the housekeeper tried to grab him, he darted past her and into the kitchen, calling out the same thing. At that point, the coal master stepped out of the room adjacent to the kitchen and said, "What in damnation is going on here?"

"I couldn't stop the lad; he just bounded in here," the flustered housekeeper replied.

"Well, get him out of here," he yelled. Then he turned and reentered the room he had just left, slamming the door behind him.

As the woman reached for David again, he ducked and darted back to the hallway. There he heard a familiar voice. "Davy, Davy, I'm here." He looked at the top of the stairs and saw his sister on the upper landing. He stopped still and stared. She was dressed in a lavender dress with lace at the neck and on sleeves that ended at the elbows.

"Janet, what be the matter with your face?" he said. She bore a large purple bruise on her jaw, and he could see bruises on her wrists.

"Oh, Davy, 'tis nothing," she said as she saw him stare at the bruises. "I . . . I just fell on the stairs. Please don't worry."

At that point, the housekeeper grabbed him by the ear and pulled him to the doorway. She pushed him over the threshold and slammed the door behind him.

David burst into the Hogge cottage, breathless from running. "Ma, Pa, I saw Janet! I saw her, and she's hurt on her arms and face."

His mother sat down at the table and put her face in her hands. "This is what I feared."

"We must do something, Pa. We must go and take Janet away from that place. There are more of us than him," David demanded angrily.

"There is more power in the bonds of marriage than in any of us," his father said quietly, looking at his hands as if he knew they were helpless to aid his daughter.

CHAPTER 14
"Sold!"

McBride stood in the back of a wagon so he could be heard. He made the announcement as the miners were lining up to go down the ladder into the pit. "Some of ye have been sold to the laird at Dalkeith. Laird Keith has made an arrangement with the coal master at the Cowden Coal Pit to take some of ye and your families. Your debt to the company store has been bought by him, and ye will take up your belongings and be ready to climb into the wagons that will take ye there on Saturday evening at sundown. These families will be going—Moffatt, Kerr, Kenny, and Hogge." With that, he jumped down from the wagon and walked into the tool-shed.

George looked at Archie Kenny and said quietly, "Perhaps this will be a blessing."

Archie responded, "Or maybe a curse."

As they ate their porridge that evening, Isabel was very quiet. Finally, George said, "Something is troubling ye, Bell."

"How will we know of Janet's condition when we are so far away? I fear for her."

"Ye are right, but I don't know what we can do about it," George said quietly.

Late on Saturday evening as the twilight was turning to dark, the Hogge family gathered with the other three families and waited for the wagons that would take them to the row cottages at

Dalkeith. Each was resigned to the move. Joe Moffatt said as they waited, "One pit's about the same as another."

The four families climbed into the two wagons pulled by a team of draft horses. They were crowded, but that helped keep them warm in the cool night air. None of them had much to take. Each had his or her few belongings wrapped in a well-worn quilt or straw mattress. The battered furniture they had used in the miners' cottages, like the cottages themselves, belonged to the laird.

They rode in silence. Many of the passengers in the crowded wagons were tired enough to sleep, despite the rough ride. Helen looked at the stars as they swept in a great mass across the night sky. Though there was no moon to light the way, the stars lent sufficient light for the teamsters to see the road standing out white against the dark of the gorse and bracken on the hillside.

"I know there is a God in heaven who made those beautiful stars," she whispered to her mother, who sat next to her. "But if He is a just God, why does He leave us in the pits to work in the dark all our days?"

Her mother made no response. She had drifted off to sleep.

Not noticing that her mother slept, Helen continued quietly. "I hope Robbie is far away from here, where he will be free from the pits for all his days. I hope he finds a promised land, like his book said. If I could know he had, I would work in the mines the rest of my life a bit easier."

* * *

Archie Kenny's words were proven right. Dalkeith was worse than Penston. Arriving in the dark, the wagons suddenly stopped, and the driver of the first wagon turned in his seat and said loudly, "Here's where ye get off. Take any one of the first six cottages. They're empty."

The four families climbed out of the wagon, and taking their few belongings, they walked in a group to the first cottage. When the door was opened and a few of them stepped inside, they could see the night sky through the roof. Someone said, "This won't do. Hope the others are better."

But none of them were much better. Isabel asked stoically, "Oh, George, if it looks this bad in the dark, what will it look like in the daylight?" She did not expect an answer. Each family finally made a decision and hoped they had not made a bad choice. In the cottage the Hogges had selected, the ropes on the bed were rotted through, so George and Isabel lay down on the floor to sleep, along with their children. The cottages were made of brick but other than that, they differed little from the stone cottages of Penston. In the morning some of the families who lived in the row cottages came to offer what help they could to make the new families welcome. Several of the women brought homemade brooms and sent their children to carry water back from the nearest well.

Isabel and Helen scrubbed the floor and walls of the cottage with the rags they had brought with them to rid it of dust and vermin. When they were done, Isabel said, "Davy and Helen, the well is not far. Fill the pails again and bring them back so we can have enough water to wash what we are wearing and the quilts."

Around midday, the coal master at the Cowden pit, Mick Fergusson, appeared in a wagon, and as soon as he was recognized, someone knocked on the door of each cottage where the new families were housed. "Come out and meet your new coal master," one said loudly.

Mick stood in the wagon and, speaking in a strong voice, said, "Ye are new to Cowden Colliery here at Dalkeith, but ye will be expected to dig your quota this coming week, just like everyone else. The laird has bought your debt from the Penston Company Store, so whatever was owed there is now owed here. All of ye here will work the day shift. Consider yourselves lucky. Ye will be expected to be at the pit by four o'clock tomorrow morning. Any questions?"

James called out, "We got a leaky roof and the ropes on the bed are gone. When will they be fixed?"

"Whenever ye get 'round to fixing them," the coal master responded. "The company store will be glad to sell ye some rope and thatch—on credit, of course." He gave a great bark of a laugh and turned his wagon around and started down the road.

James said to his father, "I'll find the company store and get us some rope and thatch. If we help Archie, then maybe he will help us. What else do ye want me to get?"

"Ask your Ma; she will know better than I do."

James and Archie Kenney walked to the company store with Richard Smith, one of the Dalkeith miners willing to show them the way. Smith was a tall, broad-shouldered man with a head of dark brown hair, thick eyebrows, and a square chin. He was a man of few words who still had much of the strength of his earlier years. When they arrived at the store, James and Archie took a few minutes to look at each item for sale, all of which were substantially more costly than similar items had been at the Penston Company Store. Both men just shook their heads in disbelief. On the way back to the cottages, Archie said to Richard Smith, "Now that we know that everything is costing us more at the company store here, what weekly pay do we get, and what is our quota?"

"Same as at Penston," was the brief answer.

"How do ye survive?" James said.

"A man can drown in a creek just as easily as in an ocean. When the debt is over your head, does it matter how much over your head it is?" he answered.

Upon returning to the cottages, each man put out his hand to shake the hand of each of the other men. When James shook Richard Smith's hand, he asked, "What do your friends call ye? Richard or Dick?"

"Smith will do," was the response. Then he nodded, turned on his heel, and walked away.

As James rewove the rope onto the frame of the bed with some help from his father, George asked, "What kind of man is Richard Smith?"

"A man of few words, but he will nae hide his meaning, I think."

"If a man's words are true, then oft a few will do."

The afternoon was spent constructing a second rope bed for Helen and David and filling the holes in the thatched roof of the cottage. James had slept on the floor, wrapped in a quilt, for years. It never occurred to him that he might sleep in a bed.

Helen, wearing her old dress, spent much of the day collecting sticks to burn in the fireplace, walking as far as a mile or two from the cottages to find enough to make an armload. Richard Smith's eighteen-year-old son, John, showed her and David where to look. John's little brothers and sisters, all five of them, tried to help.

Helen asked, "What do family and friends call ye?"

"Most folks call me Johnny."

"Johnny, how do folks find enough wood or turf here to cook their meals?"

"Most of them buy coal at the company store, especially in the winter when it's cold."

"But if they buy coal at the company store, they will owe so much more to the laird."

"What difference does it make?" Johnny answered in a quiet manner. "Owe a little, owe a lot, makes no difference. We still can't ever get away from the pits."

Helen lowered her voice. "My brother did."

"How? Did he run away?" Johnny's interest suddenly grew. "Tell me about it."

Helen immediately wondered if she should have said anything about Robert. She wondered if her words could hurt him. She hesitated for a moment and then said, "Davy, I see a stick way over there. Go get it for me." After her brother had run a few yards, she spoke quietly, "He ran away a few weeks ago. He said nothing to any of us. On a Sunday night we all laid down to sleep, but in the morning he was gone. We don't know where he went." She paused. "I miss him," she added quietly. Then she added with fervor, "But if he has got away, maybe more of us can do it."

Johnny's brown eyes were somber and thoughtful as he studied Helen's face, but he said nothing.

CHAPTER 15
Apprenticeship

"'Tis time for your breakfast, Robbie. Or are ye not hungry?" Mrs. McEwen's voice was cheerful as she knocked on the bedroom door.

He sat up, forgetting where he was. After a moment or two, he remembered and answered, "Oh, Mrs. McEwen, I'm more than hungry enough. Did I sleep the day away?"

"Not yet, but if I did not knock, I thought ye might. Put a comb through your hair, laddie, and come and sit at the table."

The meal was simple by many standards: oatmeal with cream, scrambled eggs, haggis, and muffins. But Robert exclaimed, "Mrs. McEwen, never have I seen so much food before! 'Tis a feast." Robert hardly knew how to eat the muffins. To him, they were like cake.

"Put some butter on it, my lad. That always makes a muffin better."

Not knowing how to split the muffin, he smeared the butter on the top and took a great bite. Mrs. McEwen simply smiled and said in her mind to that unseen individual, *Oh, William, he is so like the boy we buried. He makes my heart warm.*

After the meal, she invited Robert to sit by the fireplace and tried to draw him out about his background. "Do ye have a family, Robbie?"

Her questions made him uneasy, so his answers were short. "Aye."

"Where are they?"

"Far away, in the Lothians." He had decided that he would not be any more specific when asked where he came from.

"What plans do ye have while ye are here in Edinburgh?" She pronounced it with four syllables—"Ed-in-bur-ah"—as did all Scots.

"To learn a trade—or maybe to go to Leith to join the navy."

"What kind of trade?"

"Whatever trade will feed and clothe me."

"Can ye read or write?"

"Some. I read better than I write."

"Can ye cipher?"

"Enough to know if I get the right change when I buy at the com . . . er, market."

"Well, laddie, I know a printer and book binder who might need an apprentice. He is my dead husband's brother. He might take ye on to learn the trade. He is but two streets over."

"But I know nothing of such a trade."

"That is the purpose of becoming an apprentice. That is how ye will learn." She laughed and added, "Now that ye are finished eating, we will go to see him."

Robert was not sure that he wanted this trade that had dropped on him so quickly but determined that it was far better than none. The landlady led him through the streets crowded with people hurrying to their many places of work or business, some selling fish from baskets on their heads, others bumping into one another as they watched where they were stepping, trying to avoid the filth in the narrow streets, which were darkened by the two- and three-story buildings on either side.

Robert had to walk quickly to keep up with Mrs. McEwen's short but rapid steps. They arrived at the book bindery and print shop, which had a sign over the door that read *Ballantyne and Hughes, Printers and Book Binders*. She pushed her way in and called, "Walter, where are ye? It's Elizabeth with someone for ye to meet."

A big man with a short gray beard, a shining dome peeking through thinning gray hair, and a leather apron around a large belly appeared from the shadows in the back of the shop. "Ah,

Betty, how is my best sister-in-law?" He gave her a hug with one arm and stooped to put a peck on her cheek.

"Your only sister-in-law," she firmly responded. She pushed him away with a laugh, and, turning toward Robert, she said, "I have brought ye a good apprentice. I hope ye can use him. He's willing to learn the trade."

"Well, business is a bit better that it has been. I just received a good order to print and bind two thousand copies of a hymnal and several thousand copies each of some religious pamphlets. If our work is good enough, there will be more orders to follow. That will give me need for an apprentice. Are ye ready to go to work, lad?"

Taken aback, Robert could only stammer, "A-Aye, sir."

"I will pay ye seven shillings per week until ye learn the trade. That will take ye about a year."

As Robert reached out to shake the printer's offered hand, he thought to himself that a year seemed a long time to learn a trade; but at the present, there were no other opportunities on his horizon.

"Now take good care of him. I will expect him by eight o'clock this evening," she said over her shoulder as she moved toward the doorway. With a swish of her skirts, she was out the door, and Robert stood facing his new employer.

"Well, put on an apron over there by the door, and I will put ye to work. What's your name, lad?"

"Robert Ho . . . Hoggan, sir."

"Robert Hohoggan?" Walter raised one eyebrow and grinned at the expense of his new apprentice.

"No, sir, just Robert Hoggan." He fidgeted a little. "And most folks call me Robbie."

"My name is Walter McEwen, and most folks call me Mr. McEwen."

Robert's curiosity temporarily overcame his manners, and he impulsively asked, "Then who is Mr. Ballantyne—or Mr. Hughes?"

"They've both been dead some twenty years," Walter McEwen responded. "I bought this establishment when Mr. Ballantyne died. I don't know who bought the Liverpool establishment."

With that, Robert's new life started at a run. The first day, he was taught to set type and, more importantly, how to pick it up off the floor and sort it when he dropped a large tray. Mr. McEwen stood with his fists on his hips and laughed heartily as the type scattered across the floor. "That happens to most every apprentice once." He paused and added with a more serious emphasis, "but only once."

By evening Robert was tired and discouraged. After bidding his new employer goodnight, he quickly became lost in his own thoughts and almost became lost on the way back to Mrs. McEwen's little house. As he rubbed his eyes, he said under his breath, "Aye, I'm tired, but not so tired as I would be in the pit." For the rest of his walk, he let his thoughts stray to home, where he guessed his family would be sitting down to eat their evening porridge. He wanted very much to tell them where he was, what he was doing, and how he hoped he would become proficient at his new trade.

* * *

A few weeks after arriving in Edinburgh, Robert entered the kitchen in the early evening and saw a stranger with his hat in his hand. Mrs. McEwen said, "Robbie, we have another boarder, at least for awhile. This gentleman is Mr. Pratt, Mr. Orson Pratt from America. He will be staying with us for a few days." Mr. Pratt was a tall man with finely chiseled features and longish, light brown hair, that curled around and above his ears. There was not a woman in Edinburgh who would not have called him handsome. "Come, Elder Pratt, and I will show ye up to the same room ye used so long ago. I can hardly believe it has been near eight years since ye first came to my boardinghouse. The Saints are so happy that ye have returned to the British Isles for another mission. When ye have had time to wash your face and hands, then we will have supper." Her voice trailed off as she led him up the stairs.

CHAPTER 16
"Ceiling Fall!"

The first day of work at the Cowden coal pit in Dalkeith was difficult. At midday, Helen sought out her mother and said, "Ma, my head hurts. I think there might be afterdamp in the tunnel."

"Find Davy and get yourself to the pithead," Isabel responded as she stopped filling her creel. She immediately went to look for George. The Hogges were not the only miners whose families climbed the ladders to the surface to get away from the foul air. They sought the shade of a rowan tree about a quarter of a mile from the pithead. Each had a throbbing headache.

As they sat down, Helen quietly said what had been on their minds. "This pit is worse than Penston—it may kill some of us. I am so glad Robbie has made it far away, so they can't find him and force him back into the pits."

"Ye are right, Helen," Isabel responded in the same near whisper used by Helen. "I pray every night that Robbie is forever free of the pits."

After a few minutes David asked, "What happens to the money we owe at the company store in Robbie's name?"

His father responded, "'Tis divided and falls upon the rest of us."

"So we must pay Robbie's debt?" David asked with a question in his voice.

"Aye, lad."

They rested for about ten minutes until their headaches had eased in the fresh air. They had started to get up to return to the pit when the coal master approached the little group. Looking down on them, he cursed and said, "Get yourselves back into that pit before I dock your pay for lazin' about."

James stood up and, as he was three inches taller than the coal master, looked down at him and said, "Ye can't keep us in the bad air all the day or we won't live out the week."

"Just get yourselves back to work or the laird will hear about it," Fergusson said harshly as he turned on his heel and walked away.

After a long day in the pit, George walked slowly back to the cottage, and Isabel slowed her walk to be with him. Each day saw his strength fading. During the late summer evenings, while George rested, Helen and her mother spent their time sitting outside, each on a large rock, stitching the scraps left over from the making of Helen's blue muslin dress into curtains for the little window in the cottage.

"Do ye think that with the dark curtain at the window Pa will be able to sleep in a bit longer on the Sabbath?" Helen asked as they stitched. Her mother nodded. Helen had found a broken teacup and planted a small fern in it. She put it in the window, between the blue curtains. The rest of the cottage was stark and barren.

During the third month of working in the Cowden coal pit, while George and James were in the lowest tunnel, they heard a boom and a thud, almost as if a great tree had been felled above them, followed by a loud cracking sound. James yelled, "Ceiling fall, ceiling fall! Get out of the tunnel!"

With that, he dropped his tools and grabbed his father's arm. The two men started to run for the pit bottom as quickly as they could in a stooped posture. The other men and boys in the tunnel hesitated just a moment, and before they could follow, a large portion of the tunnel ceiling collapsed. Coal dust churned in the air, and the tallow lamps on the miners' bonnets went out.

Without looking back, James continued to pull his father toward the pit bottom. He called to anyone within hearing, "Get up the ladders. There's been a ceiling fall. Beware of afterdamp!" Upon arriving at the pit bottom, he tried to push his father up the bottom ladder. "Hurry, Pa. Pull yourself up the ladder!"

With his son's encouragement, George struggled to mount the ladders, one after another, with many of the miners and coal bearers calling to them, "Hurry, our lamps are going out. The afterdamp will get us."

The men, women, and children working in the pit made their way up both the ascending and descending ladders, pushing past James and his father whenever they paused on the ladder platforms for George to catch his breath. They streamed out of the shaft opening where most sat down on the ground and tried to pull fresh air into their lungs.

When James had finally reached the second ladder from the top, his father collapsed on the platform. In desperation James lifted him over his shoulder, and, driven by the urgent need to get out of the pit, he struggled up the ladder and finally reached the pithead. When he laid his father on the ground, he looked over his shoulder in time to see his mother, sister, and brother along with twenty or thirty others pouring out of the shaft entrance. Behind them, the dust from the ceiling fall was rising like smoke from the embers of a dying fire.

The coal master approached some of the men where they were sitting on the ground and asked angrily, "What brought ye up to the pithead this early in the day?"

"A ceiling fall and afterdamp forced us up the ladders," one man said between racking coughs.

One of the women ran to James and asked, "Is Angus still down there? Did he get out with you and your pa?"

The coal master answered brusquely, before James could respond, "If they're not here at the pithead, then they're still down there."

The woman turned to the coal master and asked with fear in her face, "When will ye send somebody down to find them?"

CHAPTER 17
Elder Pratt

When the three of them were seated at the little table to eat the supper Mrs. McEwen had prepared, Mr. Pratt bowed his head and offered a short prayer. Robert had never seen anyone but his mother offer grace over a meal, and that was the Sabbath meal, so he was surprised. After the short prayer was finished, the little landlady asked, "Elder Pratt, please tell us how the work is going and how many ye have baptized."

With that, Robert's head came up, his spoon halted in midair. "Ye are a priest or a minister, Mr. Pratt?" he asked.

"I am neither priest nor minister, Robbie. At least, not as you are thinking. I come to preach a gospel message but attended no seminary or college of divinity."

"Ye have a congregation and a church?" Robert asked.

"We are a growing congregation, but we often meet in the homes of our members. On the Sabbath we rent a hall. This evening, some of us will meet here in Mrs. McEwen's kitchen. We would like you to join us and listen to our message, if you will."

Robert said nothing, but nodded and returned to his supper. Of course he would be present for the meeting. He had never met someone from America before. Anything Mr. Pratt had to say would be of great interest.

As the small group of nine souls found places to sit in the crowded room, Mrs. McEwen fluttered about, making each as comfortable as her limited space would allow. Robert sat on the floor. Two women sat on the small wicker settee, and a third sat on the backless hassock. Four men were seated on the chairs around the kitchen table, and Mrs. McEwen stood near the fireplace, her eyes moving around the room so she could anticipate the needs of her guests.

After a short and simple prayer during which he asked the blessing of Deity upon the meeting, Elder Pratt, as the guests addressed him, began to discuss the book he took from the large pocket in his overcoat. He discussed how a young man had been led to a place on a hillside in New York State where an ancient record had been buried centuries before, and how the young man had translated that record with heavenly help. Then he began to read. "I, Nephi, having been born of goodly parents, therefore, I was taught somewhat in all the learning of my father . . ."

After a few minutes of listening, Robert began to sense a familiarity in the words—the rhythm, the names, and places. He could no longer restrain himself. "I know this book. I have read this book myself."

Elder Pratt stopped reading and asked with a look of pleasant surprise on his face, "How did you find a copy of this book?"

"I didn't know what book it was. I found it in a rubbish heap. It had nae cover."

"What did you think of it?"

Robert was quiet for a few seconds as he gathered his thoughts. Then he answered forcefully, "It gave me hope. If God could lead one family out of danger to a promised land, I thought maybe he would do the same for me and mine. But what's its name?"

"This is the Book of Mormon, Robbie."

With a smile, Elder Pratt returned to his reading, and after a few more pages, he put the book down, and the small group talked well into the night before each guest took leave of the hostess and Elder Pratt. Robert excused himself to go to his room. There he lay down on the bed, and his thoughts eventually became dreams— dreams of his family on a great ship sailing on a great ocean toward a promised land.

In the morning, Mrs. McEwen knocked twice at the door to Robert's room. Finally, getting no response, she opened the door and saw him lying fully clothed on the bed, still asleep. She went to him and shook his shoulder gently. "Robbie, 'tis time to come to breakfast so ye will not be late to the print shop."

Startled and embarrassed that he had to be awakened, Robert stood up quickly and said, "I will be there, Mrs. McEwen, as quick as I wash my face and put a comb to my hair."

As he sat down at the table, it was apparent that Elder Pratt had eaten and left a few minutes earlier. The empty bowl was still sitting on the table. "I'm sorry, ma'am. I didn't mean to sleep so late."

"'Tis no matter, Robbie. It was a late evening, and Elder Pratt will explain that to Walter. Now eat your porridge before it gets cold."

"Elder Pratt is going to the print shop?" he asked between spoonfuls of hot oatmeal swimming in cream.

"Aye, he placed the order for the books and pamphlets that made Walter take you on as an apprentice."

As Robert rose from the table and thanked his landlady, she took a cap from a peg by the kitchen door and put it on his head. "This belonged to my late husband. Now 'tis yours. No self-respecting boy or man should be seen on the streets of Edinburgh without a cap."

"Aye, ma'am, thank ye, ma'am." Robert smiled and darted out the doorway. When he arrived at the print shop and bindery, Walter looked up at him and said, "Well, it seems ye meant to sleep the day away."

"Nae, sir, it will nae happen again," Robert apologized. As he put on his leather apron, he asked, "Is Elder Pratt here?"

"He gave your excuses and looked over the plans for one of the pamphlets and the hymnals he has ordered and then was on his way."

"On his way?"

"On to whatever business a man of religion from America has to do in a big city, I suppose. Mr. Pratt said something about taking the boat on the canal to Glasgow—to entice more fools into baptism into his church, I would guess."

"Fools?"

"Ye don't believe that religious stuff he's preaching, do ye?"

"I don't know—I think I want to learn more before I decide. Mrs. McEwen believes. Do ye think her a fool? "

"My brother's wife has a good heart, but she is a bit daft."

* * *

When Robert arrived at the boardinghouse that evening, he could hardly stay awake through the evening meal. When he left the table, he thanked his landlady and went to his room, where he found an unusual garment lying on the bed. It appeared to be a long shirt. Mrs. McEwen stepped up behind him and said, "'Tis a nightshirt, Robbie. Most folks don't sleep in their clothes. They take them off and put on the nightshirt and sleep under the blankets on the bed."

Robert picked up the nightshirt and held it up to his shoulders. It came nearly to his feet. "They sleep in this?" he asked curiously.

"Aye, laddie, the men sleep in such a shirt. That belonged to my William."

Robert went to the bed and lifted the first blanket. Then he picked up another blanket, and beneath it he found a sheet of muslin. He looked up at her and asked, "Ye say a person is to sleep on the sheet and under the blankets?"

With a smile, she said, "Aye, my boy. Ye put your tired body on the muslin sheet and under the blankets."

"I will try it tonight, Mrs. McEwen."

She hid another smile as she pulled the door shut behind her. Then she said, under her breath, "William, 'tis a joy to have such a lad in the house."

CHAPTER 18
The "American Religion" and a Wee Darg

When Elder Pratt entered the small kitchen, Mrs. McEwen looked up from the pot of soup she was stirring over the fire. Robert was sitting at the table reading the *Edinburgh Examiner,* which he quickly put down.

"Where have ye been these past three days? I expected ye back yesterday," the landlady kindly chided.

"Mrs. McEwen, I took a trip to Hunterfield, where there is a growing branch of the Church. Seventy of the ninety individuals in that village were baptized there some time ago. The Church is growing, and the Saints are increasing in numbers. Upon my return here, I climbed Arthur's Seat again."

She stopped stirring and looked at him with wide eyes. "And why would ye do such a thing?"

Robert looked from one to the other and asked, "What's 'Arthur's Seat'?"

The landlady responded, "Ach, lad, 'tis a great cliff to the west that looks over the city from above the great castle. Now some of the Saints here call it Pratt's Hill."

"Why do they call it that?"

She smiled and told him, "When Elder Pratt came to Edinburgh on his first mission, he climbed that hill and asked the Lord for two hundred converts. I told him then that I believed he was counting his eggs before they were put in the pudding, but the

Lord granted his request, and the work of preaching the gospel has gone forward ever since that time."

"This gospel ye are spreading—this is the American religion I heard ye preach some nights ago?" Robert asked.

Elder Pratt answered as he sat down at the table. "Yes, Robbie. It is the gospel of The Church of Jesus Christ of Latter-day Saints."

As Mrs. McEwen ladled the cabbage and chicken soup into their bowls, Elder Pratt asked Robert, "How is the typesetting for my pamphlet *Voice of Warning* coming along?"

"Not as fast as I know ye would like, Elder Pratt. I am so new to the work that it goes slowly. It will be finished in a week, I think."

"That would be good, as I need to be getting back to Liverpool soon. I love Scotland, and it is hard to take myself away, but I have much to do to assist the Saints in their gathering to Zion." He paused and continued to eat for a minute. Then he asked, "Would you be interested in going to America some day, Robbie?"

The spoon paused between his bowl and his mouth as he answered with fervent feeling, "Aye, Elder Pratt. Indeed, I would be glad to go to America."

* * *

At the end of a day in the Cowden coal pit, which saw the death of two small coal pushers and many other children made sick by afterdamp, the miners turned in their equipment and stood around talking in low but angry voices. Fergusson had demanded that the mining families return to the pits the next day despite the bad air and the children's deaths. Jack Kerr said angrily, "What makes that man think that we are going to go back into the pit before those two bairns are cold in the ground? Fergusson tells us that we have to enter the pits before the afterdamp has cleared. If we do, we'll see more bairns dead. I won't do it!" Jack Kerr's face was flushed with anger.

Seeing his opportunity, Joe Moffat asked of the men standing around, "Now do ye think that maybe a slowdown—a wee darg— is in order? Maybe that way we can make the laird give some attention to the conditions here. Are ye with me?" Joe Moffatt's voice was low and intense.

Several of the men nodded their heads and, looking around to make sure the coal master was nowhere near, most answered in the affirmative. Archie Kenney stepped forward. "Joe," he said, "what will we use to buy at the company store if they dock our pay? I understand your anger. I lost a boy not so long ago too, but we might find ourselves in a worse situation than we are in right now."

Moffatt answered, "We'll just have to run up our debt at the company store."

"But what if Fergusson cuts off our credit?"

"Then we'll burn it down!" Joe said, the muscles hardening in his jaw.

James had stood at the edge of the group, listening, but had said nothing to that point. Then, stepping forward, he spoke. "What would ye expect of us if we agree to use the darg?"

With that, Joe put his hand on James's shoulder and said to everyone within hearing, "Let's get ourselves back to the cottages where we can talk without being overheard." Looking over their shoulders, each man started down the path to the cottages at his own pace.

As James and Joe Moffatt walked side by side, Joe explained, "A darg is a slowdown and is just what it says, Jamie. We just don't work so hard. If we get asked why the coal production is not as high as Fergusson demands, we tell him we all got the fever or the ague. If we all stick together, he can't fire us all. The laird would nae tolerate it. He's got no one to replace us with."

James asked, "Have any of the other mines ever had a darg—a slowdown?"

"Aye, over at Lanarkshire, there's been a score or more that have done it. That's how they got the ventilation system put into the deeper pits there. We've got to do the same as they did in the Lanark pits. And we've got to have an oath."

"Oath? What do ye mean?"

"We will each take an oath to stand by each other, and we'll have a watchword, so we know who is with us and who is nae with us."

When the men had gathered in a small, tightly knit group near the Moffatt cottage, Joe put forth his idea. "This is what they do in the West Country. I say we do the same thing. That way we have a brotherhood. What do ye all say?"

Many in the group nodded. James interjected, "What happens to a miner who refuses to take the oath?"

"We fine him. If he refuses to pay the fine, we force him to leave the pit," Joe answered. "If we stay together, then we can defend ourselves. And I know what the watchword will be. If ye are all in agreement, the watchword is 'Rand,' so those of us who knew the lad will never forget that he gave us the courage to stand up for ourselves."

Most of the others appeared to be in agreement, though George had said nothing. "I guess it seems the only way of getting the laird's attention," was all James said. But his mind was full of foreboding.

When George and James entered the cottage, George said quietly, "This is just what they did in Ayreshire—two, maybe three years ago. It didn't turn out so well."

"What happened?"

"Many a miner lost his place in the pits, and a miner has nae skills for any other way of making a living."

At the end of the next day, as the miners and their family members trudged wearily up the path to the cottages, Joe Moffatt, walking faster than the rest of them, passed each one. As he passed he said quietly, "The password is 'Rand,' and we meet near the stream tonight when the moon rises." Each miner nodded his head but said nothing.

When it appeared that the majority of the miners had gathered at the appointed time, Moffatt stood on a rock to get above the group.

"Tomorrow, we start the darg. We report on time but dig only half as much as usual. If Fergusson comes to fuss at us, we pretend that we can't hear him. Just do your work but not too fast. Does everyone agree? Instructions will come only with the password."

James stood where he could hear but said nothing. George did not attend the gathering. The night air made him shake and cough uncontrollably. When James returned to the cottage, he told his father what he had heard. George said with irony in his voice, "Dig about half our normal weight of coal? That's about all I can do anyway."

The miners continued the darg for a week and knew they were making their point when they saw Laird Gray arrive in his great carriage pulled by four matched, black horses. The sun glinted on the polished brass fittings and the family crest on the doors. He and the coal master met for a few minutes in the equipment shed, and when Laird Gray left, Fergusson exited the building with his face nearly apoplectic with rage. As the men turned in their equipment that evening, he shouted at every one, "Ye will be here tomorrow, on time, and dig your quota, or I will have every one of ye in the jugs." The men walked past him as if he were not there. The darg continued for another week.

At that time, Fergusson went from cottage to cottage, pounding on each door and yelling, "If ye continue this slowdown, I will see that ye have no job."

Some of the men gathered in the Moffatt cottage, a few spilling out into the night air on Saturday evening, expressing their fears that they might be fired. Moffatt responded, "He can't replace us all. There are too many of us. When he has had enough, he will come to us and ask how to settle our concerns. Now go to your homes and stick together. Right now, we have the stronger hand."

But in the morning there were rumors that the coal master had taken one of the horses and left for Edinburgh early that morning.

CHAPTER 19
The Print Shop

"How is the printing coming, Mr. McEwen?" Elder Pratt entered the shop and shook Mr. McEwen's ink-stained hand. Taking a rag from his back pocket, the printer wiped his hands and pointed Elder Pratt to a large table where the printed pages were carefully stacked. "It looks like you will soon have the pamphlet finished," Elder Pratt said aloud as he carefully lifted a few pages by a corner to examine them.

"Ye're right in that, Mr. Pratt."

As he started to turn away, Pratt stopped and said to both Robbie and Mr. McEwen, "We are having another meeting at your sister-in-law's house tonight, Mr. McEwen. I do hope we will see you there, along with your apprentice, Robbie."

"I wouldn't count on seeing me, Mr. Pratt, but I am sure Robbie will be there." With that, he turned back to his work.

Robert smiled and nodded. "I will be there." He was looking forward to the opportunity to hear Elder Pratt preach again.

That evening another group of people, made up almost entirely of faces that Robbie had not seen before, sat around the small kitchen-sitting room. Elder Pratt began to read from the book again, and several of the listeners asked when they could have a copy of their own.

The conversation turned to the willingness of those present to be baptized into the new religion that Elder Pratt preached. Some had questions about the need for baptism, as they had been baptized as infants. He explained that the baptism of infants could not be valid, because a person had to understand the difference between right and wrong before they could make a promise to God to do what was right, and an infant could not understand such a thing. He added that it was necessary to be baptized by those who had the proper authority. That led to a discussion of what constituted proper authority to act in God's name. Elder Pratt quoted from the Bible where it said that "No man taketh this authority unto himself, but he who has been called of God."

One of the men present asked, "And what are your credentials, Elder Pratt?"

"I bring a heart and mind willing to serve mankind, and many years of prayerful study of the scriptures. I seek no pay, and most importantly, I was ordained to this work under the hand of a modern prophet."

"A modern prophet!" the man exclaimed. "Every real Christian knows the heavens were closed after the Bible ended. Why," here he paused for a moment, "it would be easier to find an honest man in Parliament than a modern prophet! There is no need for prophets in this day and age! God has said everything He needed to say." He took his wife's hand and said, "Come, my dear, it is time for us to leave this group to their confused groping for enlightenment." With that, he pulled her up from the settee and almost dragged her through the doorway and out into the night.

"Some will listen with an open mind and heart, and others cannot be educated," was all that Elder Pratt said. At the close of the evening, three people had agreed to be baptized into the new church. When Elder Pratt looked at Robert, he dropped his head and said nothing. He wanted to be part of this new religion, but he also knew it was wrong to lie to Elder Pratt and God about his identity.

On a Friday morning a man entered the print shop and asked Mr. McEwen to print a handbill. When he shook Mr. McEwen's hand, he introduced himself as Mick Fergusson, coal master of the Cowden coal pit at Dalkeith.

Mr. McEwen read the proposed handbill aloud.

Notice to labourers: Whereas the coal-heughers of the pits at Dalkeith have caused much suffering and inconvenience to Sir Isaac Gray, and the public at large, and allow no person unconnected with their brotherhood to go into the pits to work the coal and also threaten them, notice is hereby given that the laird and coal master are now determined to put a complete stop to this illegal action and in order to effect this, from 50 to 60 weavers or labourers are immediately wanted to whom Mr. Fergusson will pay ten shillings a week till they learn to work the coal and can earn more. Those wishing for work should apply as early as possible to Mick Fergusson, Coal Master, Cowden Colliery, Dalkeith.

"Print me five hundred copies. I will pick them up tomorrow." With that, Fergusson turned and left the print shop.

On Saturday of that week, Elder Pratt borrowed a wagon with a team of old horses and hired a driver, so he could take a small group to Leith, where they would be baptized in the Firth of Forth. As Robbie put on his cap and started for the print shop, he stopped for a moment and watched them as they rode away from the boardinghouse. They had gathered early that morning, happily looking forward to formally joining their new "American" faith. He deeply regretted that he was not going with them.

CHAPTER 20
Strike!

Within five days of the return of the coal master, several men in worn and ragged clothing appeared, seeking work in the pits. The thinnest and weakest of them were turned away, but five of them were hired to work in Shaft Number Two. After the first day, Moffatt and several of the other miners surrounded them as they started their walk back to the cottages. "What was your trade?" Joe called to them.

William Watson added, "And where did ye come from?"

They were weavers from Paisley, displaced by the great mills. Moffatt stepped in front of the cluster of men, stopping them there on the path as they neared the cottages. "Ye were brought in to break those of us who want better working conditions," he said in a quietly threatening manner. "If ye want to get along here, ye better become part of our darg."

One weaver responded, "We ain't looking for trouble, just a way to feed our families."

Another added, "We been out of work for near six months. Our families been near to starving."

"How much you being paid?" Joe asked.

"We been promised ten shillings a week if we learn the trade quick."

Moffatt gave a loud, harsh laugh. "Ye're being robbed. Since they only want to pay you a part of what you will soon be worth, then it is only right that ye only give them a part of what they want."

"Then tell us what a darg is," one called out.

"A darg is just a bit of a slowdown, not so much as to make it easy to tell that there is a slowdown, but enough to bring up only half as much coal as the coal master wants."

"New as they are to the pits, all they dig will be just about right to be part of the wee darg," William Watson stated with a smile.

Moffatt slapped the first of the weavers on the back and asked, "Are ye with us or against us?"

The man nodded, and as the miners watched, each of the weavers nodded, some hesitantly, but each giving his assent to becoming part of the miners' brotherhood.

"Then ye are ready to know the password. The password is 'Rand,' and whenever ye hear it, ye do as ye are told. Do ye all understand?" Moffatt waited for each one to nod his head. Then each miner shook hands with each of the weavers, now fully accepted, and all started up the path again.

Helen and her mother were standing in the doorway watching for James and George. James was slowed by George's labored walk, and they had arrived at the small group of miners and weavers just as the conversation between the two groups had ended.

"It looks like Joe has made some converts to the darg," George commented.

The work slowdown continued, and each day one or two more weavers came to apply to work in the pits. Each received the same welcome from Joe Moffatt, and each new arrival quietly assented to the pressure and became part of the brotherhood.

Two weeks after Mick Fergusson's return, a few thin and nearly starving Irishmen from County Cork came to apply for work. None of them would join the brotherhood when approached by Moffatt, and threats were made. When they still insisted on entering the pits without agreeing to the darg, Joe started a fight with one of them at the pithead.

The coal master broke up the fight with an ax handle and yelled, "Joe Moffatt, ye're fired. Get out of the pit and get your family out of your cottage by tomorrow." As he stomped away, he yelled over his shoulder, "But ye still owe the company store. Ye and yours have got thirty days to pay your debt or I call the sheriff."

Moffatt stood still, his face gray with rage and his hands in fists. Then he moved closer to the nearest man and said, "The password is 'Rand,' and ye will meet at my cottage this night when ye leave the pit. Spread the word." Then he turned and walked up the path toward the cottages with long, determined strides.

Throughout the day, the word was passed to every miner to meet at Moffatts' cottage that evening. The darg continued for the day.

When most of the miners had gathered at the cottage, they stood in a large group around the doorway where Joe stood and spoke loud enough for them to hear. "Now we are going to show that we won't back down. Are ye with me?"

"What do ye mean, 'we won't back down'?" one called out.

"I mean that we strike. There's no way that Fergusson can run the pits with a handful of weavers and blacklegs from Ireland."

Another spoke loudly, above the noise. "Some of us can't afford to do without our pay."

Moffatt continued. "I'll be moving my family out of the cottage and over to my sister's croft in Lasswade tomorrow. After that, I pledge to go to every pit here in the Lothians and get the miners to donate to a fund to help support us through the strike. I say again, are ye with me?"

The miners talked among themselves, some shaking their heads, others nodding. After a minute or two, Archie Kenny stepped up the single step to the threshold of the cottage doorway, and, standing beside Joe, he put his hands out to quiet the group. Then he spoke. "We've got to stand together. If Fergusson can fire Joe and get away with it, he will do that to every one of us as soon as some Irishman is hired to replace us. Do ye understand?"

The crowd stood unresponsively for about three seconds and then Jack Kerr shouted, "We're with ye, Joe!" Then others took up the cry. "All ye that are with us, hold up your hand," Joe called out over the noise of the group. A large majority held their hands high above their heads. "Then tomorrow we strike!"

Some of the men yelled in excitement and slapped each other on the back, but others turned and quietly walked to their cottages, filled with apprehension. James was one of the latter.

When he entered the cottage, Isabel asked her son what was going on. "It seems that the brotherhood has decided to strike. The only good thing about that is that Pa will be able to rest," he replied.

David looked up and asked, "Is a strike different from a darg, Jamie?"

"Aye, we don't go to work tomorrow or for awhile after that."

"I think I like a strike. I'm going to go to the Smiths' and tell Andrew."

After David ran out of the doorway, Isabel looked at George and James with a worried expression and said, "We only have maybe four shillings in the jar. That won't go far to feed the five of us for very long. What do we do if the strike goes on for a long time?"

"Joe Moffatt has promised to go to every pit in the Lothians, if need be, to ask the miners to donate to a fund to help us through the strike. All we can do is hope he is as good as his word," James answered.

So the strike began. The miners' families refused to leave the cottages. Within a week, Joe returned on a late July evening and gave five shillings to each family, money that had been raised for them from the miners in Haddington.

Ten days later, Joe came after dark and was able to give each family nine shillings raised from the miners in the Mauricewood pit in Penicuik. By this time, several of the other miners had joined his efforts. So the summer passed into fall, and the women worried, the children played, and too many of the men sat around and drank the cheap ale they could get from the company store. With increased rest, George looked a little better as the weeks passed.

Helen spent time each day with Johnny Smith when the weather allowed. They often sat near the stream and talked about the book Robert had left behind. Helen spent time teaching Johnny to read from it. Their friendship grew. As he haltingly read the words, she watched his forehead as it wrinkled with concentration. She studied his strong hands and long fingers and thought with sadness that, like her father's hands, they were likely doomed to work in the dark of the pits all his life.

He brought her a little bouquet of snowdrops and heather, and with a quiet stammer, he said, "I, ah, I thought ye might like these." Then a smile brightened his eyes, which was reflected in Helen's. When his hands brushed hers, her heart beat faster.

By fall, the coal master had hired more than sixty Irishmen to work in the pits, but their output of coal remained less than he wanted. The laird came weekly to the pit in his fancy carriage and demanded better production from Mick Fergusson, but little changed.

By late October, the Irishmen began to complain that the water in the pits was about to drown some of them, and the bad air was threatening to kill others, making it impossible to work. They sent a spokesman to Jack Kerr to ask if they could join the strike. When no one appeared for work the following Monday, Mick Fergusson sat in his office in the equipment shed, clenching and unclenching his fists, knowing his job was over.

CHAPTER 21
An Admission and Open Conflict

By February Elder Pratt had returned to Edinburgh and ordered the printing of several thousand copies of another pamphlet he had written entitled *Reply to a Pamphlet Printed at Glasgow.* Robert commented, "It seems a strange name for a booklet."

"Recently a minister by the name of Joseph Paton published a pamphlet attacking the missionaries and the gospel message we are preaching. It was full of lies and half-truths, and I felt that I must respond to it. When this one is completed, I will take many copies of it with me to the Church conference that will be in Manchester, England, in the spring. There I can share it with the elders who must answer the questions raised by the Reverend Paton's booklet. Would you like to travel to Manchester with me, Robbie? There I will preach a message of gathering to America."

"Ye know how I want to go, Elder Pratt, but I don't know if Mr. McEwen can do without me."

* * *

By the third week of February, the booklet was ready to be assembled. After each group of pages was stitched together, they were gathered on a large table where Mr. McEwen trimmed the pages with a great blade that fell with a thud. "Watch your hand, Robbie, or ye'll be known as Three Fingers Rob." The printer laughed as he demonstrated the process. Robert's skill as a printer and bookbinder was growing.

When Elder Pratt came to collect the pamphlets, he said to Robert, "I want to find some good men to go to the pits to teach the miners about the Book of Mormon. Will you go with them, Robbie?"

Robert stood silent for a few moments, and then, looking into Elder Pratt's face, he took a deep breath and said, "Elder Pratt, I cannot go to the mines—at least, not yet." His face began to grow red. "I'm a runaway from the pits. If I go back before I can pay my debt at the company store, I will be punished and put back into the pit as a thief, and Mr. McEwen will be fined for hiring me. Please don't make me face that." He was quiet for another moment. "My name is Hogge, not Hoggan, and I have promised myself that I will try to free my family from the pits."

"When did you leave the pit, Robbie?"

"It will be one year next month."

"You must continue to save your shillings and have faith that the day to help them will come." With that, Elder Pratt put his hand on Robert's shoulder and added, "Be patient and stalwart."

When Mrs. McEwen heard of Elder Pratt's plans to leave Edinburgh, she laughed and shed a tear at the same time. "Well, Elder Pratt, I will miss ye greatly." With that she gave him a motherly hug and stood on tiptoe to plant a kiss on his cheek. "Ye must be careful in that great city of Glasgow and more careful in Manchester or wherever the work of the Lord takes ye," she instructed him. "There is danger there, sure as there's carts to horses."

So Elder Pratt returned to Liverpool, where he was charged with leading the Church in the British Isles and the continuing oversight of the publication of the *Millennial Star,* the official arm of the Church in Europe.

* * *

The pounding at the door woke the entire family. They recognized the voice of Jack Kerr as he yelled, "Get up and defend yourselves. The laird has called the sheriff to drive us out of the cottages." By the time James had gotten to the door, Jack was on to the next cottage. Many of the miners were standing outside their cottage doors with ruffled hair and sleepy faces.

"What means all the noise?" Many voices filled the air, men's voices mixed with the cries of women and children. Some called, "Get yourself a stick or a rock. We can't let them push us from our homes. We must fight! Hurry!" Additional men's voices were raised in shouts.

As those only just awakened stared about and tried to understand the situation, a group of about twenty-five men with lanterns and clubs neared the cottages in the early-morning light. The sheriff led the group and carried a rifle.

The sheriff raised his hand, and the group stopped. "We didn't come to harm anyone here. The laird has grown tired of your unwilling attitude and has sent us to claim his property—that being the cottages and all that is in them. Ye will leave them by morning, or ye will report to the pits to work. That's your choice."

Joe Moffatt, who had recently brought a few shillings for each family, had been staying with Jack Kerr and his family. He stepped out of the cottage, and several other miners gathered behind him. James stepped closer to hear more clearly.

Joe moved forward and raised his voice. "Ye come to remove them from the cottages? All here are willing to return to work if the laird will just ask us our needs. But he has not once come to listen to the troubles we face in the pits. We bury our sons, our daughters, our fathers, and our mothers, with no more notice from him than if he had run over a dog in the path with his fancy coach." Joe moved closer to the sheriff until he was nearly in his face.

"Ben Crary, your pa was one of us. Now the laird has made ye sheriff. Do ye think ye are better than the rest of us? Ye know the hardships we live with. How can ye stand there with these men and their clubs, telling us to go back to those holes in the ground filled with firedamp and coal dust without giving us a chance to tell our needs?"

Ben Crary looked uncomfortable but continued to face Joe Moffatt. "What good is it for ye to tell me your troubles? I can't do anything to solve your problems. I didn't want to tell ye to get out, but I got no choice. Ye have got to return to the pits or get out of the cottages."

Joe looked Ben in the face and said, "Then ye will have to put us out." He turned and looked at the miners standing clustered around him and said, "Are ye all in agreement? We'll make them put us out."

Most of the miners nodded, and many shouted, "Aye, try to put us out. See if ye are men enough."

"If that is your thinking, then that's what we will do." With that, Ben Crary raised his hand and brought it down in a forward arc. "Empty the cottages," he called to the men behind him.

"If any of ye touch our homes, ye will be in for a fight," Joe called.

"Then stand your ground, because we will stand ours," Ben responded.

The twenty-five men behind the sheriff spread out and began to swing their clubs. As the miners fought, sometimes two or three hanging on to each one of the sheriff's men, many of the women came out of the cottages, some of them bringing stools and planks from the tables as weapons. As the weapons on both sides were swung, the crack of wood on skulls could be heard.

For an hour the fighting continued. Isabel stood at the door, wringing her hands with fear and concern. Helen stood behind her, and between the two of them they kept George from going out into the fray. He could hardly have withstood a blow from another man, but he wanted to help James, who had been drawn into it.

Isabel couldn't see James for some time, but when she did he had a great gash on the back of his head. His clothing was torn and bloody. He had grabbed William Watson, who had fallen to the ground and was bleeding from a cut over his eye, and was struggling to carry him back to his cottage.

By this time, the men who had accompanied the sheriff were either lying on the ground moaning or were stumbling down the path away from the cottages. Many of the miners sat or lay on the ground, with their wives or mothers bent over them, struggling to help them to their feet. Sheriff Crary lay facedown on the path.

Joe leaned over him and turned him over. As Ben groaned, Joe stood up and wiped the blood out of his eyes with a dirty sleeve. "Ben, ye're a durn fool to think that ye could walk in here and tell us to get out without a fight."

Ben sat up and carefully stretched his arms and hands as if to see if anything had been broken. "Joe, we've known each other for many a year, and ye know I hold no hard feelings toward ye, but I had my orders. Now, tell me, what's it going to take to get the men and their families back into the pits?"

As the two men talked, several of the other miners slowly gathered around them, some limping as they did so. As if to answer Ben's question, one said, "Give us better prices at the company store. We can hardly feed our families, and our debt keeps growing."

Another said, "Get us some ventilation in the deepest shafts so we don't lose any more bairns to the afterdamp."

Another called out, "Don't make us work the bairns so many hours each day. Get us a schoolteacher to teach them their letters."

Putting his hands up over his head to silence them, he said, "All I can promise to do is tell the coal master to get the laird to listen to your complaints. That he may or may not be willing to do, but I'll try."

Joe Moffatt smiled through a swollen lip and an eye fast swelling shut, and put his hand out. Ben shook his hand and turned and started down the path. He paused to look around for his rifle, but saw it lying in two pieces on the ground. He shook his head and limped into the darkness.

Two days later, a group of three men no one recognized came to the miners' cottages. One wore a black coat with two rows of brass buttons. It was fitted at the waist, and the skirt reached his knees. He wore a beaver-skin hat. The other two were large, stoic men, coarsely dressed. The shorter, better-dressed man stood by while one of his sturdy companions knocked hard on the door of the Kerr cottage. They announced themselves as representatives of the laird of the Cowden Colliery. When the long and some-times loud meeting was over, several of the other miners hurried to ask what had happened. They crowded inside the cottage.

"Jack, what did they say? What will we be doing?" Many questions filled the air.

Joe Moffatt, who had continued to stay with the Kerr family, put up his hand and said, "We didn't win everything, but we won something. We start back to work tomorrow morning, and the laird has promised to put in a ventilation furnace in each of the deepest pits. 'Tis going to take some time, but in a few months we will have cleaner air, so we will nae loose any more of our wives or bairns to the afterdamp."

More questions flew at him. Joe put his hand up again and said, "They promised to set up a school in the evening, at the church in the village, for the miners' bairns. There was one there years ago, and now there will be one again. That's all we got, but that's better than we had before."

Archie Kenny and several other miners crowded around Joe and Jack and shook their hands and patted them on the back. "Ye done good by us, Joe," Archie said, voicing the feelings of most of the men present.

William Watson muttered, "We should have got more," as he left the cottage.

James conveyed the information to his family. David chanted, "I get to go to school! I get to go to school!" George and Isabel looked at each other, knowing that David would find school a heavy burden after pushing coal in the pits each day. But for the time, they said nothing to diminish his happy anticipation.

CHAPTER 22
Sabbath Services in Edinburgh

When the dark clouds had lifted for a few hours on a Sabbath morning in early March, Mrs. McEwen and Robert made their way through the muddy streets of Edinburgh to attend a meeting in the rented meeting hall near Holyrood Palace. Mrs. McEwen kept her hand on Robert's arm as they walked, giving him occasional directions. At eleven-thirty they heard the bells of St. Giles, which were rung in anticipation of the twelve o'clock mass.

When they came upon the Royal Mile and Robert could see the great Edinburgh Castle more completely than he had ever seen it, he stopped and stared in amazement.

"There it is, Robbie, the great castle. Have ye ever seen the like? The great castle was built for a defense and has oft been used as a prison. But the Scottish kings and queens, the Stuarts, lived in Holyrood Palace, as does Queen Victoria when she comes to visit Scotland once a year. Ye will soon be able to see Holyrood Palace at the other end of the Royal Mile."

"Aye, how can there be two great palaces in one city, Mrs. McEwen?"

"Those of royal blood do take good care of themselves, Robbie." She chuckled and continued, "After James the Sixth of Scotland became James the First of England, royalty turned their backs on us in the North. 'Twas called the Union of the Crowns but 'twas actually just the hand of England laid heavy upon Scotland. 'Twas a union the way a hungry man is united with a potato. 'Tis no union;

'tis only a small meal." The two of them made their way along the street. Robert was fascinated by the public houses filled with boisterous men and gaudy women, and by the merchant shops where, if one had enough money, almost anything could be purchased. Occasionally they passed a great two-story wood and stone house owned by a rich merchant. Mrs. McEwen had to quickly pull Robert out of the way when an upper window in one of them opened, and the cry "Gardyloo!" was heard as a servant emptied a chamber pot onto the street.

"Ye must be quick on your feet in this place, Robbie," was all Mrs. McEwen said to him.

As they came in view of a large public house called the Ram's Head, she said, "Now keep an eye open for the meeting room, which should be behind it. I hear the room is for rent for large meetings. Walter aided Elias Brown in obtaining it."

"Mr. McEwen helped us find a room to use for our Sabbath meeting?" Robert asked in amazement.

"Walter's head may be hard at times, but his heart is soft as mush," she responded. Robert didn't completely agree but said nothing.

They pushed between two men who had obviously been drinking too much, and Mrs. McEwen determinedly pulled Robert behind her, like a small ship under full sail pulling a skiff against the current. They made their way about twenty feet into an alley, and there they found a building where Elder MacDougal opened the door to their knock. When they entered the room, they could see that it had not seen a charwoman's hand for many months. Cigar butts and chewing tobacco littered the floor around the overflowing spittoons. Mrs. McEwen put a handkerchief to her nose. "Walter will hear about this," she said.

Over the next hour, men and women entered the building, and by the time the one o'clock gun sounded over the city, there were about one hundred and fifty-five people present. Robert recognized several as having sat in Mrs. McEwen's kitchen, where they had been taught by Elder Pratt.

The sermon on faith and repentance had gone on for almost two hours, and a few heads were nodding when a great pounding on the door disrupted the meeting. The door burst open, and a tall man in a tattered hat and dark coat entered the room and demanded that the meeting stop. Behind him were three men, one of them dressed as a vicar of the Church of Scotland. Elder Brown paused and asked the man in the lead who he was and by what authority he disrupted the meeting.

"My name is Charles MacGregor, and I own this building, and there shall be no Mormons meeting here."

"But our benefactor, Walter McEwen, has paid the rent for the day so that we might meet here," David Brown responded.

"He can have his rent back. I'll have no Mormons meeting here. Now all of ye, get out."

The men and women present looked around in surprise but rose and started to exit the room, talking in low voices. As they pushed past the men standing with Mr. MacGregor near the door, Robert heard the man in the minister's collar say to him, "Now, let's not hear about any more Mormons using your rented buildings, MacGregor, or ye'll loose your place on the parish board."

On the way home, Robert asked Mrs. McEwen, "Why do ye suppose those men were so angry that they insisted we stop our meeting? I thought Mr. McEwen had paid to rent the room from a friend."

"Well, when I get home I will straighten him out about this 'friend,'" she said with vigor. "None of us need 'friends' like Mr. MacGregor."

"But I still don't understand why he would treat folks that way just because they're Mormons."

"Robbie, it seems that 'tis the nature of most men, that when they hear a new thought or philosophy, they feel they must oppose it. As small a group as we Mormons are, it seems that many ministers of the cloth in this city berate and condemn us in nearly every sermon. They spread rumors and outright lies. Elder Pratt told me that many of our elders have found themselves driven out of neighborhoods by those who throw rotten fruit and vegetables at them, and in others, they are driven out by men who threaten and sometimes beat them bloody."

Robert was quiet for a few minutes and then asked, "If ye could go to America, would ye do so? I hear that some of those baptized have done that."

"Ach, why dwell on that, Robbie? I shall never have the funds to make such a journey, and even if I could, I wonder if I could bring myself to leave behind the graves of my dear William and my boy, Willie."

As they neared the boardinghouse, Robert said what he was thinking. "I would give everything I have to go to America. Do ye think that day will ever come?"

The landlady had no answer.

CHAPTER 23
Robbie's Return

The Benbow School for the Poor was begun two weeks after the miners returned to work. It was held in the lower room of the little stone church in the village. In addition to the miners' children, several children of local crofters as well as some from the poor house were permitted to attend. David could hardly contain his enthusiasm as he darted about on the path to the church.

The assistant vicar met the children coldly and assigned them to the rough, backless benches by age groups. It was apparent to even the youngest that he was not pleased to be called on to teach them.

Even though Helen and David were always exhausted after a day of working in the pit, she would not let him stop attending the school, even on days when he could hardly stay awake while they walked to the church. "Davy, it is important for ye to learn to read and cipher. Every man needs to know these things." Helen was afraid to let David attend without her, lest he feel the assistant vicar's rod. She sat behind him and watched him carefully. When he seemed to be falling asleep, she would kick the bench where he sat to keep him awake.

As they made their way home in the late twilight on a warm Friday evening in April, Helen noticed two men walking the path from the village to the miners' cottages ahead of them. She could not help but notice something familiar about one of them. They both wore poorly fitting dark suits. Helen started to walk faster, pulling David along with her, until he complained, "Don't go so fast, Helen."

She dropped his hand and started to run toward the men. Hesitantly, she called out, "Robbie, Robbie, is that ye? Have ye really come back?"

He turned, and Helen flew into his arms. "Robbie, oh, how I have missed ye."

"Helen, how is everyone at home?"

"We are all fine except Pa, and he is growing weaker. Oh, Robbie, have ye come back to stay?"

"Nae, Helen. I have come to teach the family about the book I was reading before I left. And I have brought enough money to pay my debt at the company store so no one can make me go back into the pits. I am going to be free from the pits."

By this time the other children had reached the little group of three. "Helen, this is Elder Brown from Edinburgh. I am his missionary companion. I have come to teach you about a new religion from America."

"Missionary companion? What kind of missionary?"

"We are Mormon missionaries."

Elder Brown interjected, "We are missionaries from The Church of Jesus Christ of Latter-day Saints in America. Some folks call us 'Mormons.'"

Taking his hand, Helen pulled Robert toward the miners' cottages. Many of the other children followed. When they reached the Hogge cottage, Helen burst through the doorway pulling Robert in behind her. David followed, leaving the door open. As Elder Brown entered the cottage, the other children gathered around the doorway watching everything going on inside.

"Pa, look, Robbie's come home! See, Ma, he's come back! He's come back to teach us about the book he left behind and a new religion. He's a missionary." Helen's voice was filled with pride. "And this is his companion, Elder Brown."

"Oh, Robbie, ye should never have come back. They will try to put ye back into the pit." Isabel put her arms around her son and laid her head on his shoulder. Raising her head, she stepped back and looked at him. In a surprised tone she added, "Ye have grown. Ye are nearly a man."

"On my most immediate birthday I turned eighteen, Ma, like Helen, and I have a good job in a print shop in Edinburgh."

By this time George had struggled to his feet. He put his arm around his second son and said, "It is good to see ye, Robbie. I didn't think I would ever see ye again. But your ma is right. Perhaps ye should not have come back. There are some that will try to force ye back into the pit."

James stepped forward and offered a stool to Elder Brown, then he stepped to the open door and shooed the children away before closing it. He put his hand on his brother's shoulder and said with a solemn voice, "Robbie, your leaving put a heavy burden on Pa and me." There was no resentment in his voice; it was just a statement of fact.

"I know, and I'm sorry, Jamie. But I've come back to pay part of our debt at the company store, and more important, we have a message to teach ye about a new American religion."

Isabel cooked a pot of oatmeal for Robert and Elder Brown. While they ate, the other family members sat on the rope beds. Robbie told his family about his experiences since he left the Penston pits. After the bowls were empty, Robert got out his new copy of the Book of Mormon.

Before he began to read from the book, he said to his mother, "Ma, when we couldn't find you at Penston, I asked Mrs. Boyd where ye had gone. She told me your debt was sold to the laird here in Dalkeith, and she also told me that Janet married the Penston coal master, Mr. McBride. I went to his big cottage to see her, but the lady at the door said Mrs. McBride was not home. Ma, did she really marry Mr. McBride?" His mother only nodded her head.

David broke in, "I saw her, and she had bruises on her face and her arms. I think Mr. McBride's mean to her."

"Ma, is that the way it is with her?" Robert asked.

"Aye, Davy is the only one of us to see her since she married. We fear for her, but we don't know what to do."

With a look of concern still on his face, Robert turned to the book and led a discussion of the new religion from America, which lasted long into the night.

"It must be nearly midnight. We must go to the pit in the morning," Isabel said, insisting that the discussion end so they could rest. George was exhausted and coughing.

In the morning, the tired family rose and left for the pit, but George stayed at home, too weak to work that day. Robert and Elder Brown walked to the company store, where Robbie paid one-quarter of the debt owed by the Hogge family, freeing himself from any claim that he had stolen from the laird. It took nearly every shilling he had.

The next evening, which was Saturday, Robert and Elder Brown knocked on the door of every miner's cottage and invited each family to a meeting on Sunday at the Hogge cottage, where they could learn about the new religion. The group of miners and their families that were interested in hearing what Robert and Elder Brown had to say was much too large to fit into the cottage the next day, so the group gathered at the stream, and Elder Brown stood on a big rock so he could be heard and seen as he preached.

The miners reacted in various ways as Elder Brown spoke. Some were quick to ridicule, others tried to shout him down, but he continued until he grew hoarse. He promised that if there were any who wanted to learn more, he would gladly teach them in their own cottages.

After he had stopped speaking, Archie Kenny approached Robert and said, "Ye would have received rougher treatment, except that some of us have known your family for many years. Ye would be wise to cease this preaching. Some of us have heard many things about the Mormons that we don't like."

Robert answered, "Then ye can't have heard the truth. Come to our cottage and listen to the truth."

Archie just shook his head and walked away. Only the Smith family permitted Elder Brown and Robert to enter their cottage to preach. Richard Smith said little, but his wife, Euphamia, whom everyone called Effie, had many questions. Like his father, Johnny said little. When Robert offered them a copy of the Book of Mormon, Effie looked at her husband for permission to take it. Richard made no response, so she smiled and accepted the book.

Robert and Elder Brown stayed with the Hogge family for another five days, teaching them and the Smiths each evening. On Friday, Robert asked his family if any of them would accept this new religion and be baptized.

"Robbie," Helen asked, "have ye been baptized?"

"Aye, Elder Brown baptized me some weeks ago and then ordained me an elder. I have known for many months that the book is true and that this new religion teaches the things that are in the Bible."

"Then I will be baptized." Helen then looked at her father and added, "If it is all right with Pa." George thoughtfully and slowly nodded.

Isabel added, "I would like to be baptized, George, if it's acceptable to ye."

He smiled weakly and said, "Aye, ye have my permission. I would like to be baptized, too, if I didn't think the cold water would kill me."

On Sunday, the little group stopped at the Smith cottage, and when the Smith family had joined them they made their way to the little stream where the men spent more than an hour building a small dam so a pond would form, deep enough for them to be baptized. By the time they were ready for the baptism, several miners and members of their families had gathered to watch.

Helen nervously looked at those who had gathered and then said to Robert, "Robbie, will ye baptize me?"

"Aye, I will be glad to baptize both you and Ma."

Then Elder Brown baptized Effie Smith, and as the women and Helen stood wet and dripping, William Watson called out, "Hey, Smith, can't ye control your woman? Don't ye know that ye be damned for being baptized into another religion?"

Without answering the taunts, the little group made their way back to the cottages. The next day, when Elder Brown and Robert took leave of the Hogge family, George and Isabel each briefly held their son in a firm embrace, and Isabel said, "How we wish ye could stay here with us, but we can only be happy that ye are free of the pits. That makes it easier for us to see ye leave."

"I must leave so I can return to the print shop where I will save my money until I can pay your debt at the company store; then someday ye will be able to come with me." Looking at James he added, "Jamie, ye will take care of them 'til then?"

James answered, "Ye know I will."

The family watched while Robert and Elder Brown walked about a half mile down the road from the miners' cottages toward Dalkeith. Then they turned, and, taking off their hats, they called out as they waved them three times in the air, "Huzzah, huzzah, huzzah for Zion!" Then they disappeared from sight down the winding cart path.

CHAPTER 24
Intolerance

One evening, when he arrived at the boardinghouse, Robert found that Mrs. McEwen had made a small pound cake to celebrate his success as a printer and book binder's apprentice. "Now 'tis time to ask Walter to raise your salary. He promised to pay seven shillings a week for the first year, and now ye are worth much more than an apprentice. Ye must ask him for ten shillings for each week."

Robert answered, "I fear that Mr. McEwen may not be able to pay me more, as he has nae so much work as he had a year ago. I hope he will keep me on, as I want to continue to work in the print shop, but I think I will ask him, instead, if it will be acceptable to him for me to take some days to preach the gospel when the work is slow in the shop. Then he wouldn't need to increase my pay; he would pay me only for each day I work."

"Well, laddie, that sounds like a workable plan. Now eat your cake."

Walter McEwen was agreeable to Robert's proposal. The first task the young man had to do was to locate another hall to rent for Sabbath meetings. He found the Carpenter's Hall available, but it was unsightly and smelly. Elizabeth McEwen came with him on Saturday evening, and with her scullery skills and his young muscles, they soon had the place clean and acceptable for Sabbath meeting the next day.

The meeting drew nearly two hundred people, many of whom were strangers to Robert. Elder Franklin Richards, who had returned to Britain to aid Orson Pratt in overseeing the Church there, spoke that afternoon. He addressed the subject of several New Testament scriptures and compared their simple language with the beliefs and practices as they now existed in churches claiming to be followers of Christ. His remarks so angered and exasperated some who were present that one man, the Reverend Jonathan Pendleburg, who claimed to be a Methodist minister, stood and began to speak so loudly that Elder Richards paused and requested that the interruption cease. But Mr. Pendleburg called out more loudly, "This is a new doctrine you preach, and we demand proof. We ask for a miracle before we can be expected to believe this new doctrine." His voice was almost drowned out by those who insisted that he sit down and listen, but he would not be silenced. "Give us a sign, and we will believe. Give us a sign."

Then another man stood near him and demanded, "Tell us where you obtain your authority to preach this new religion. What is this Mormon Bible from which you preach?"

Elder Richards stood at the table he was using as a pulpit and raised his hands, asking for quiet, but the confusion increased. Elder Richards started to sing, and most of those present joined with him as he sang the familiar words to "Rock of Ages."

As the congregation sang, Robert made his way between the benches until he could reach the Reverend Pendleburg. Putting his hand upon Pendleburg's collar, he pulled the man to the aisle, where the minister struggled free of his grip and, turning on him, landed a hard fist on Robert's jaw. Robert staggered back, and the minister was on him immediately, pummeling him with his fists. Three men pulled the man off Robert and forced him outside. Two other men placed their hands on the minister's loud companion and ushered him outside as well. As the congregation completed the hymn, Robert and three of the men returned to their seats. The other two stood at the door to block any further unwanted attempts to enter. The meeting continued.

By the time Robert escorted Mrs. McEwen home, his left eye had begun to swell shut. Clicking her tongue, she said, "Ach, 'tis a terrible thing when a person claiming to be a Christian minister behaves like a hooligan from the streets." She laid a cold, wet cloth on his eye.

When Robert arrived at the print shop the next day, Walter McEwen looked at him and laughed. "Did ye have some difficulty getting one of your converts into the waters of baptism?" Then he laughed again at his own joke.

"We were at Sabbath meeting, and a particular minister differed with the doctrine we were teaching, so I tried to help him out of the meeting. Seems he did not want to go."

Robert spent some weeks preaching—sometimes with Elder Brown and sometimes with John Leishman, a Scotsman who, like Robert, had dreams of going to America. They preached in Edinburgh, and for several weeks they traveled from Aberdeen to Inverness. When hunger became so prominent that it had to be dealt with, Robert would knock on a crofter's door and ask, "Can ye spare some supper to the both of us in exchange for a religious message?" Some farmers were willing; others were not. Often they had to work at odd jobs to earn their bread, and many times they slept in haystacks, something with which Robert was well acquainted. Occasionally, their supper consisted of the vegetables that had been thrown at them by angry villagers at noontime.

CHAPTER 25
Marriage and Death

By May, George had given up working in the pit. He could hardly sit up at the table long enough to eat a bowl of oatmeal. Isabel had begun to serve as a bearer for James. Helen became the fremit bearer for Johnny Smith, who at nearly twenty was as tall as his father, though with a more youthful slenderness.

As they sat together near the stream on a mild evening, Johnny said quietly, "I know that a future in the pits is not what ye want, Helen. If I could see any other future for us, I would promise it, but I have thought a long time, and I think we should marry." Helen was not surprised at his statement. She only felt relief that he had finally gotten around to asking her. He was a good man, and she could not hope to do better among the young men in the Cowden pits. In June, with the blessings of their parents, the banns were posted.

After the vicar had performed the ceremony, they rented one of the vacant cottages, and Helen was able to put some curtains at the window. They hired Johnny's ten-year-old brother, Andrew, as Johnny's coal pusher, and he came to live with them.

As the Hogge family sat at the table eating the usual supper of porridge a few weeks after Helen's wedding, Isabel said to James, "Jamie, you're a man now. 'Tis well past time to take a wife. We have not spoken of it, but I need to know if ye intend to marry."

After a few moments, James answered her, "Aye, I've been thinking on it."

"Tell me what ye've been thinking."

George was lying on the bed, almost asleep, so James dropped his voice so his father would not be disturbed. "I know that Pa will soon be so sick that ye will not want to leave him alone to go to the pit to carry coal. If I marry, I would have a coal bearer, and ye could stay here with Pa."

Isabel waited, saying nothing. Then James continued. "I've been thinking that I would like to go back to Penston and see if Eliza Cummins would be willing to be my wife. Maybe she is already married to someone else, but if not, she would be a good wife. She is a strong, hardworking girl, and when she is all washed, she is a bonnie lass with her long, reddish hair and green eyes. I don't think I could do any better."

"Then go and ask her."

The next Sunday James set out on the long walk to Penston.

The family waited to eat supper, hoping he would be back by that time. Finally Isabel said, "I think we had best eat and go to bed," but she lay awake with worry. A knock came on the door about midnight, and as the door opened, Isabel sat up and called out, "Jamie, ye are back. We've been so worried."

"Aye, Ma, we're sorry we've been so long in getting back."

Isabel slid out of bed. "Davy, light the candle."

Davy rose from his bed and located a match on the small shelf near the fireplace. As he lit the candle, he was startled to see Eliza with a baby in her arms. As the candle brightened the small room, Isabel pushed a stool toward Eliza and said, "Here, lass, sit yourself down." As she spoke, her eyes were on the infant in the young woman's arms. George continued to sleep undisturbed.

Isabel raised her eyes to James and waited for him to speak. He pulled a stool near the one where Eliza sat slumped with exhaustion from the long walk. She kept her eyes on the floor.

He spoke. "As you can see, things are different now for Eliza. I thought she might be married since we came to Dalkeith, but that didn't happen. When I arrived at her family's cottage, her mother told me her father was killed in a ceiling fall, not long after we left.

Then I found Eliza with a bairn, and I came close to turning around and leaving, but something stopped me. I decided to stay and ask her and her mother to tell me what happened that she has a bairn without a husband. Her ma explained that with her pa dead, there was no one to defend her when the coal master became too . . ." Here he paused and then added, "friendly."

He continued. "Eliza begged him to leave her alone, but he said he would stop her mother and her sisters from working in the pits if she didn't do what he wanted. He knew they would starve if he did that. When he got her with child, he was the first one to condemn her and tell her she was going to hell. No one would believe her when she tried to tell them who the father was. The vicar at the church in Penston wouldn't allow the bairn to be baptized, and the Parish Poor Committee refused to help her."

James was quiet for a moment. Isabel stooped by the side of the stool and put her arms around Eliza, being careful not to wake the sleeping baby in her arms. She said, "Not ye nor the bairn should carry any blame for the sins of such a man. Ye both be welcome here in our cottage and in our family."

Eliza raised her eyes, and she looked at Isabel as a tear trailed down her cheek. "I thank ye for your kindness," was all she could say.

Isabel said to James, "Put some coal on the fire in the fireplace, so we can warm up the cabbage soup left from Sunday supper. Ye are both hungry, I am sure." As the soup warmed, Isabel asked, "What's the bairn's name?"

"'Tis a lassie, and her name is Eliza, like me. I call her little Lizzie."

Isabel's face grew serious, and she looked at James and said quietly, "Jamie, can ye bring yourself to accept the wee lass as your own? This is important." Her voice was firm.

"Ma, I been asking myself that all the way back from Penston. I have prayed that the Lord will make her part of my heart."

David smiled and teased, "If it was a laddie, I could play with him. Can ye take her back and get a laddie for me?"

With that, everyone laughed, and James ruffled his youngest brother's tousled hair. "This one is a month old, so 'tis too late to take her back. We'll have to keep her."

As James and Eliza ate the last of the Sunday soup, the plans were made for the Hogge family to go to the church the next evening, when the children normally went to school, and have the vicar marry James and Eliza. George was too weak to walk that far, so he suggested that James ask Richard Smith and Johnny to go with them to serve as witnesses. Richard Smith would have to give Eliza away, in the absence of a father.

But plans had to be altered when the Hogge and Smith families arrived at the Dalkeith village church. The vicar insisted that the banns for James and Eliza be posted for a week before he would marry them. To make the disappointment greater, he insisted that his fee for the marriage was five shillings, a difficult amount for them to pay. So they returned to the Hogge cottage, and as Richard Smith took his leave, he said, "We will be with you next Monday evening for the wedding. If ye need a shilling or two to pay the vicar, I might be able to find some—just a loan, ye know." With that he patted James's shoulder and walked away.

During the week, as they waited for each day to pass, Eliza stayed in the cottage and cooked for the Hogge family while she cared for little Lizzie. In the evenings, while the infant slept in a hammock suspended in a corner, James and Isabel took turns teaching Eliza to read from the Book of Mormon or the Bible, the only books in the cottage.

When the week had finally passed, the Hogge and Smith families again made the walk to the village church. Before they left, George took the hands of James and Eliza and gave them his blessing. "May ye always be good to each other and help each other all your days, and the Lord will bless ye both."

When they arrived, the vicar stood in the doorway of the church and challenged them. "I hear that some of you were baptized by the Mormon elders when they were here. Is that true?" he demanded.

No one spoke for several seconds. Then James answered, "Neither me nor Eliza were baptized into the Mormon Church. We were baptized into the Church of Scotland when we were wee bairns."

"What about you, Mr. Smith? Are you a Mormon?"

"Nae, Vicar."

Ignoring the others present, as if their spiritual condition was of no importance, the vicar turned on his heel and said, "Then follow me. Have you got my fee?"

"Aye, we have your fee," answered James.

While James and Eliza stood before him, the vicar pronounced them man and wife. He took his fee and then said, "If you want the child baptized, that will be two shillings more."

"Ah . . . ah, Vicar, we don't have the shillings to have the bairn baptized right now," James answered him.

"Then bring it back when you do." The vicar turned and left the group standing in the small sanctuary of the church. Isabel and Helen each gave Eliza a hug, and Isabel said, "Now ye are a Hogge, and it is time for us all to go home as a family."

Isabel continued to carry coal for Archie Kenny or Jack Kerr or any other miner who needed a fremit bearer but was not put off by her religion. After little Lizzie was weaned, Isabel stayed at home to watch her grandchild and stay with her dying husband. Eliza carried coal for her new husband to help support the Hogge family.

By early October, Helen knew she would have a child in the spring. When she told her mother, Isabel said, "I know that ye must continue to carry coal, but try to make the loads in your creel a bit lighter, for the sake of the bairn."

On a warm and bright day at the end of October when the sunshine covered the hillsides like a warm, golden blanket, George was laid to rest in the ground high on the hillside. James carved a wooden headboard for the grave which simply read: George Hogge 1806–1849.

CHAPTER 26
Baptisms

When the ventilation shaft for Pit Number Two was finished in early November, the miners and their families celebrated. The fire in the furnace at the base of the pit warmed the air and made it rise, the shaft acting like a great chimney, drawing fresher air into the main shaft. Two nine-year-old boys were hired to feed the furnace each day when they arrived at the pit at four in the morning.

At about the same time, Helen felt she had to lighten her loads, so she and Johnny paid Gwen, Johnny's eleven-year-old sister, to help carry coal. She came to live with them, just as Andrew had, to lessen the number of mouths Richard Smith had to feed. Since Johnny had married, the Smiths had missed his wages.

When the fire was started and the flames rose high, the air began to whistle through the main shaft, stirring the coal dust and making the miners cough more than usual. The first few days at their new job, the boys competed with each other to see how high they could make the flames rise. Then Ed Vickers, the new coal master, came down the main shaft of Number Two, which was something he seldom did, and yelled at the boys, "Ye will not use so much coal. When the fire is so hot, it makes the air move through the shaft too fast and stirs the coal dust." That took the fun out of the job for the boys.

As Helen and Johnny started their walk home from the pit on a Friday evening, the furnace boys walked just ahead of them. Johnny called out, "How do ye like your new job as furnace boys?"

One answered, "Not so fun as at first."

"Why not?"

"The coal master told us not to make the fire so big. He said it stirred up the coal dust too much."

Helen asked, "Do ye have to start a fire each morning when ye get to the pit?"

The boy responded, "Nae; the lads that work all night keep it going. Sometimes we meet as they are leaving and we are coming."

As the weather began to cool in mid-November, Helen asked Johnny, "What do ye suppose that great heap of lumber is that is being built over the ventilation shaft?"

"The word among the miners is that it's going to be the office of the coal master. They say he wants the warm air that comes up the ventilation shaft to heat his office." Within a month, the building had been enlarged to include a large coal-processing area where several big coal bins were located in which the coal would be washed before it was loaded into the freight wagons.

* * *

Robert returned to the pits before the late fall days grew excessively cold with enough money to pay down a portion of his family's debt and to preach again with Elder Brown as his companion. They received a commitment from James that he and Eliza would be baptized. After they had labored for an hour to build a little dam in the stream, the water gathered, and Robert removed his shoes and stepped into the little pond. He called to his older brother, "This is the most important decision of your life. Are ye still willing to become part of this new religion and be baptized?"

With only a brief hesitation, James removed his battered shoes and walked into the water. Robert raised his hand and after a short prayer lowered his brother fully into the water. Afterward, he shook his hand and then put his other arm around James's shoulder. "Ye will not regret this decision, Jamie," Robert said. Isabel gave her oldest son an embrace.

As Robert turned to invite Eliza into the water, several of the miners' children arrived at the stream with water buckets to fill. When they saw the small group at the pool, two of them dropped their buckets and turned and ran for the cottages calling out, "The Mormons are here baptizing, come and see."

Robert said to Eliza, "Come into the water quickly, lest we have some real trouble from some of the miners."

By the time the prayer had been said and Eliza had been lowered into the water, some of the children had run back to the stream with fathers and older brothers following. Robert looked at Richard Smith where he stood on the bank of the stream and asked, "Are you ready to make your commitment to the Lord?"

Smith stood for a moment and then said, "I plan to think on it a bit more."

Robert could hardly hide his disappointment, but David had taken off his shoes and splashed his way into the water saying, "My turn, Robbie." That brought a smile to Robert's face, and he offered a short prayer and lowered David into the water.

With that, Johnny and Helen stepped forward, and Johnny said quietly, "We have talked about this, and I think it's time to tell you that I have believed for some time now. I will be glad to be baptized." Helen smiled and squeezed his hand before he stepped into the water.

By this time, Eliza and James had begun their walk back to the cottage, hurrying to get into a warm room where their clothing would dry near the fireplace. Looking over her shoulder at the miners gathering near the stream, Eliza said, "Do ye think we ought to stay? I fear for Robbie and Elder Brown."

James answered, "Richard Smith is a big man and respected, so the miners will yell and ridicule Robbie, but Smith won't let anything happen to him. Of that, ye can be sure." James smiled to himself, remembering how Smith had plunged into the confrontation with the sheriff and the men that had accompanied him. "There are few men who would take on Smith," he added.

The little group had to listen to taunts and insults from some of the miners all the way back to the cottage. One miner had yelled, "Smith, 'tis a good thing ye are not wet, as ye would find your work at the pit much tougher."

He turned and responded, "Any man that tries to keep me or my family from our work in the pit because of religion will find himself dealing with me and a table leg. I am willing to take on any two or three of ye!"

Some of the miners scoffed at his words, but the group quickly fell apart, and they returned to their own cottages.

As the wet ones sat near the fireplace waiting to dry, Robert read from the Book of Mormon, beginning with the words, "'And it came to pass that he said unto them: Behold, here are the waters of Mormon (for thus were they called) and now, as ye are desirous to come into the fold of God, and to be called his people, and are willing to bear one another's burdens, that they may be light; Yea, and are willing to mourn with those that mourn; yea, and comfort those that stand in need of comfort, and to stand as witnesses of God at all times and in all things, and in all places that ye may be in, even until death, that ye may be redeemed of God, and be numbered with those of the first resurrection, that ye may have eternal life— Now I say unto you, if this be the desire of your hearts, what have you against being baptized in the name of the Lord, as a witness before him that ye have entered into a covenant with him, that ye will serve him and keep his commandments, that he may pour out his Spirit more abundantly upon you?'"

Robert then paused, and said, "This is the meaning of baptism. This tells us why it is wrong to baptize wee bairns, as they can't understand what it means."

Jamie and Eliza looked at each other and smiled. Isabel looked down at little Lizzie as she slept and said, "I think the vicar just lost two shillings."

Long after their clothing was dry, the small group, which included the Smith family, talked into the night about their new religion. The younger children sat in a crowded bunch on one of the old rope beds. Robert looked at Richard Smith and said, "Mr. Smith, can ye agree to baptism now?"

Richard Smith answered, "I am a long way from wanting to bear the burdens of some of those who ridiculed and threatened ye as ye were in the water this evening." With that comment, he stood and nodded his head at Effie. The two of them started for the door, and the younger children scrambled off the beds and quickly followed.

* * *

When the damp and piercing cold of late November set in, the coal master determined that the heat rising from the ventilation shaft was insufficient to heat the shabby, wooden building he used as an office, where he sat at a battered desk to complete the paperwork necessary for his weekly report to the laird. He waited until he saw the furnace boys from the day shift leaving and stopped them on their way home. "Ye can build a bigger fire now that winter has come. Tell that to the night-shift furnace boys when ye see them."

The furnace boys took to their assignment seriously to increase the size of the fire in the ventilation furnace and had a rollicking competition to see who could feed the flames the fastest with chunks of coal. The next several days were much more comfortable for Ed Vickers as he sat at his desk, but the coal dust churned in the pit shaft and tunnels.

As the daytime furnace boys made their way home on a Friday evening, they laughed and shoved each other as each insisted that he had contributed to the fire the most. They passed the night-shift furnace boys at the pithead and said as they passed, "The coal master wants fires bigger now that it is cold, but ye'll never beat the fire we had today. It was a big one."

They answered back, "Aye, we'll take a wager on that."

CHAPTER 27
"Fire!"

The great clang of the alarm bell cut through the dark night air. David sat up and asked, "What's that noise?"

James sprang up and said, "The fire bell! Bring a bucket and hurry. Everyone will be needed." He pulled on his shoes, grabbed a bucket, and ran out the doorway.

As Isabel stepped outside the cottage, she could see a great pillar of flame rising above the ground from the ventilation shaft. In horror, she whispered, "May God have mercy."

Stepping back inside the cottage she picked up the large pan used to do the washing. Eliza found a smaller pail and hurried after her husband. David grabbed a bucket and followed his mother. They became part of the crowd of people running and stumbling toward the pit. Johnny rushed down the path, and Helen followed him as quickly as her condition permitted her to move.

The clank of pails and buckets added to the noise and rampant confusion. The coal master tried to be heard above the roar of the flames. He finally resorted to grabbing each man or woman by the arm, and then he pulled or pushed each of them to a spot where he pointed at the ground and yelled, "Stay here. Don't move." When it became apparent what he was trying to do, the others stepped up and completed a line of people from the stream to as near the ventilation shaft as they could get, and then they began passing buckets and other containers of water down the line to the fire, where they were emptied and returned. The water only seemed to increase the appetite of the flames, as though it were a thirsty dragon.

The night was spent trying to put out the flames, but the task was impossible. The flames burned steadily for days, fed by the coal dust and the seams of coal that had caught fire. By morning, all realized that putting out the fire was impossible, and the miners and their families sat on the ground in exhaustion, some with their heads in their hands, many weeping. After the heat and flames lessened, the smoke continued to rise from the mouth of the pit as well as the ventilation shaft. After the heat no longer prohibited anyone from nearing the ventilation shaft, Laird Gray ordered that both the pit opening and the ventilation shaft be tightly boarded up in an attempt to smother the remnants of the fire, which continued to smolder.

The task of determining the number and identity of the dead began. Since entire families who worked on the night shift had been killed, some cottages remained silent and empty. In others, a lone survivor who had been too ill to work that night sat alone, staring into the distance.

The coal master finally called the remaining miners and their families together. "There were, as far as we can guess, thirty-nine men, women, and children who died in the flames."

Everyone stood in a cluster, huddled together outside the miners' cottages, watching their breath make steamy puffs in the cold air, reminiscent of the smoke that still somehow squeezed its way out of the pit openings. He read the names and then added, "If ye know of any others that are missing or dead, step forward and tell me." Then he continued, "One week from today, every ablebodied man and lad older than fourteen will report here in the morning to go down and bring up the dead. By that time, maybe the smoke will have cleared enough for us to get at the task."

A few present took note that it was Yule that day, and the day they were to descend into the pit to find the dead would be the first day of the new year.

Most were silent, but Jack Kerr said loudly enough for many to hear, "This is a sign . . . an omen. I say this bodes ill—that we will go into the pit on the first day of the new year to bring out the dead."

When that task began, even the hardiest of the miners came up from the main shaft coughing and weeping. When James could stop coughing from the smoke and soot, he said to those standing around him, "We found fathers and sons dead in each other's arms, mothers' bodies trying to protect their bairns. Some were kneeling in prayer—all black, all black as charcoal." James sat down on the ground, almost in a trance. "I would never have believed it if I had nae seen it with my own eyes."

Most of the bodies could not be identified, so they were laid in one mass grave on the hillside. Laird Gray furnished the wood for the coffins for the few who could be identified. He even insisted that the vicar be present to say the proper words at the grave. At the end of the short service, he spoke briefly to the coal master, and then he climbed into his regal carriage behind his four matched horses and rode back to his mansion.

The coal master left the colliery the next day to seek replacement workers and did not return for a week. After his return, more ragged Irishmen began to apply for work at the pit.

CHAPTER 28
Another Grave

Three weeks after the dead had been buried, late on the last Saturday evening of January, Helen shook Johnny awake. "Get Ma, quick. I hurt. Something is wrong, something is gai wrong," she told her husband.

After five hours of hard labor, a baby girl was born with the cord wrapped around her neck. She was perfect, but much too tiny and blue. She did not breathe or cry. Isabel wrapped her in a shawl and handed her to Helen. Helen held her against her own body as if she could give some of her warmth to the tiny form. She wept quiet tears.

Isabel gave Helen a kiss on the forehead and said, "Someday, ye will leave the pits, and ye will not have to carry coal. Then ye will have many strong and healthy bairns, but this one God took back to Himself."

Johnny stood with his mother-in-law in the doorway in the moonlight for a few minutes as they spoke quietly. He asked, "What should I do? I can nae stand to see her hurting like this."

"Just let her cry and rest. She will be much better in the morning, but don't let her carry coal for a day or two, even if the coal master gets angry, or she may never have any more bairns. Gwen can be your bearer for those days."

Two hours later, just before the sun rose, while Helen slept out of exhaustion and grief, Isabel, James, and Eliza met Johnny as it began to grow light and accompanied him as he carried the tiny body of the infant up the snowy hillside. Johnny had brought a shovel and in less than an hour had dug the small grave in the hard ground next to the grave of her grandfather. They laid the tiny body in it, wrapped in her grandmother's shawl. Johnny said a simple prayer. "We give back to Thee, our Holy Father, our firstborn. Please take her home and tell her we will meet her someday."

As they started back to the cottage, James asked, "Johnny, what name did ye choose for her?"

"Helen wanted to call her Isabel."

"Then I will carve a board for the head of the grave with her name on it, and when Helen feels stronger, we will bring her up here to see it."

When Johnny reached the cottage, he awakened his younger brother and sister, handed them an oatcake, then urged them to follow him to the pit without waking Helen.

Gwen asked, "Helen is nae going to the mine today?"

"She will be staying home from the pit for a day or two."

* * *

Robert read about the mine fire in the *Edinburgh Register* while he ate breakfast. Through the use of his abundant political power, Laird Ian Gray had managed to keep the information out of the newspapers for nearly two weeks after the burial of the dead. Robert looked closely at the names of the dead listed at the end of the article. He rose and hurried from the table in the warm kitchen to the print shop. Though he was relieved to find none of his family or friends listed, he said to Mr. McEwen, "I fear for my family, Mr. McEwen. I feel that I must be going back to see if they are all well."

Seeing his white face, Walter McEwen nodded and said, "Of course, lad; ye will need to go as soon as ye can." Robert left the next morning for Dalkeith, taking with him the shillings he had been able to save. Mr. McEwen gave him two pounds against his future service to take with him as well.

Upon his arrival, he sought out his mother to make sure that none of the family members had been caught in the fire. His relief was deep, but he quickly turned to the bigger problems facing the families. He asked the Smiths to join the Hogges in their cottage that evening. "It is time for us to make plans for some of ye to leave the pits. The pits killed my pa and his pa and his grandpa, and will kill all of you if we do not get some of you out so ye can go to join the Saints in America." After a moment of quiet, when no one spoke, he said, "I have brought enough shillings to pay off some more of the remaining debt of my family. James is the firstborn son, and he has a wife and a bairn to look after, so I think that he and his family should be the first to go, if they are in agreement."

Isabel spoke quietly. "If some of our debt is paid off at the company store, then they can leave the pits and no one can stop them. What debt is left will fall to me and Davy."

"Nae, Ma, we will not leave the two of ye here to continue in the pits without us. How will ye survive?" James's voice was firm. "Without me to dig, ye would come near to starving."

"Davy has started to dig coal. He is fourteen and has the strength to dig nearly as much as a man. I carry for him. We will help each other, and we will be all right." Isabel's voice was just as firm as her oldest son's had been.

James was immovable. "Ma, I will not leave ye to try to make it without me. Davy can dig, but not enough to support the two of ye. Ye would have to hire a coal pusher, and that would take too much of the pay."

Isabel could sense his resolve, but she was not deterred from the task of getting some of her family away from the pits. She looked at her daughter. "Helen, how much do you owe the company store?"

"I think we owe two, maybe three pounds."

Isabel was quiet a moment and then spoke. "Then this is the plan—if the Smith family all be in agreement." Isabel's determination showed in her eyes. "Robbie will take Helen and Johnny to

Edinburgh where they will find work and begin to save their money. Perhaps in a year or two they will have enough for a voyage to America to gather with the Saints there. There will nae be any more dead bairns because of her coal carrying." Then she looked at Robert and said, "What think ye, Robbie?"

At the thought of freeing his twin sister and her husband from the pits, he smiled broadly. "I will help in any way I can." This was something he had wanted since the night he ran away to Edinburgh without taking her with him.

Effie started to cry. Richard reached over and patted her hand comfortingly and said, "Ye needn't take on so, woman. This is a happy day for them."

"Oh, Mr. Smith, I know 'tis a happy day. That's what makes me cry. I can lie in my grave a little happier now, knowing that at least one of my lads has escaped the life of the pits."

Robert insisted that Johnny and Helen leave quietly in the early-morning dark, without any formal notice to the coal master.

By the time the young couple had finished eating their porridge the next morning, Isabel and Davy had knocked on the cottage door. When Helen opened it, her mother said, "Ye must be going with Robbie as quickly as ye can. I will tell the coal master after ye are gone. I fear that he may try to find some way to stop ye from leaving."

"Can he do that?" Helen asked.

"Aye, we hear that folks who try to leave the pits suddenly find their debt at the company store much greater than they earned."

James and Eliza stepped out of the darkness and into the cottage, and while James shook Johnny's hand, Eliza gave Helen a hug. "May the Lord watch over ye both," she whispered.

Helen had rolled her few belongings into one of the old quilts that had been used on their rope bed and put the other around her shoulders against the cold of the February morning. Johnny's parents arrived and gave them several oatcakes. Isabel pressed two shillings into Helen's hand and whispered into her ear, "I wish I had more to give ye, but this is all I have. Know that ye take my heart with ye." Then she hugged Helen.

Effie said, "Husband, ye need to show some affection to your son as ye may not see him or his wife for a long time to come." Richard shook Johnny's hand longer than was necessary and then patted Helen's shoulder, unable to say anything.

"When the company store opens," Robert spoke to Richard, "will ye please pay as much of these three pounds, four shillings as is needed against the debt of Helen and Johnny. Let no man who knows the whole story accuse us of being less than honest."

"Aye, I will do it."

Isabel stood next to David in the doorway as they watched the little group disappear into the waning darkness. "May the good Lord take care of ye," she whispered.

David answered with the faith of youth, "He will, Ma, He will."

CHAPTER 29
Haven in Edinburgh

Upon their arrival in Edinburgh that evening, Helen was exhausted even though they had been lucky enough to catch a ride in the vegetable cart of a crofter the last six miles. Robert presented Helen and Johnny to Mrs. McEwen and asked if they could board there.

Her face brightened as if she had lit a candle. "Sit down, and I'll put a good meal before ye. Ye must be starving. And to think that ye walked all the way. Ye must be tired as well. While ye eat, I will ready a room for the two of ye."

After she put a bowl of porridge and a pitcher of cream on the table, she hurried up the stairs to fix one of the rooms on the second floor at the rear of the house. As she did so, Robert told his sister and her husband about his first experience sleeping in a bed with a sheet and a blanket, and in a nightshirt. Helen said, "I once heard about such things, but we nae have such things like that to sleep in."

Mrs. McEwen was in her glory as she showed Johnny and Helen to their room. She took special pleasure in showing Helen a nightdress she had laid out on the bed. "Once this was mine, but God has blessed me so much I nae can wear it any longer, so it is yours now, and here is one of my William's nightshirts. 'Tis well worn, but it will keep Johnny warm."

Helen looked at Mrs. McEwen and said sheepishly, "I don't know how we will ever repay your kindness. What do we owe ye?

We have little money, but we want to pay a fair amount for our room and board."

Mrs. McEwen smiled and said, "Robbie pays me ten pence a day, but he is a young man with a bonnie appetite. As ye have few pence right now, I will ask fifteen pence a day for the two of ye. I know that ye don't have much to pay me with so ye can wait . . ."

At that point, Helen stopped her, and, taking both of the shillings Isabel had given her, she pressed them into Mrs. McEwen's hand and asked, "How long will this keep us?"

Mrs. McEwen smiled and said, "I don't want to take all ye have, lass."

Johnny responded, "Nae, we want to pay our way. We don't want to owe for our keep."

"Well, I'll allow that this will keep ye three days. If ye still don't have a position by that time, I can be patient."

"We will have a way to earn our keep by that time," Johnny answered. He did not feel as sure as he sounded.

Mrs. McEwen smiled and said, "The good Lord will help ye, I am sure. Now, since ye have walked so many miles, I suggest that ye lay down and get a good sleep. I will serve breakfast at about nine o'clock in the morning so ye have time to rest."

After putting on the nightdress, Helen lifted the quilt on the bed, and as she slid her feet between it and the flannel sheet she said, "If I lived a hundred years, I would never have guessed there could be such people in this world."

As Johnny pulled the nightshirt on over his head, he asked, "What people do ye speak of?"

"Kind people, kind as Mrs. McEwen. Do ye suppose we will meet other good people like her in this church from America?"

"I think we will meet many like her. Let us offer up a bit of a prayer for our good fortune and our new friend."

At nine o'clock in the morning, Mrs. McEwen climbed the stairs and knocked on the door. After she knocked a second time, the landlady called out, "Johnny and Helen, 'tis time for breakfast."

Johnny sat up, forgetting where he was. Mrs. McEwen called out again, "I'll expect ye down to eat in a minute or two." The kind landlady soothed their embarrassment at having slept so long as she set the meal on the table.

"Where's Robbie?" asked Johnny as he sat down at the table.

"He set off early to look for employment for the two of ye. He will be back when he has found something, I suppose."

As they were eating the porridge, Robert opened the door. "I have found two positions for ye to consider, Johnny, and maybe one for Helen." As he sat down to eat, he picked up a muffin, and with a knife he cut it in half as a subtle demonstration for his brother-in-law and his sister. Then he slathered on the butter. Johnny noticed and followed his example.

"Oh, Mrs. McEwen, I never tasted anything so good. Ye are a cook made in heaven." Johnny's comment was spontaneous. The pleased landlady radiated her pleasure. Then Johnny looked at Robert and said, "Robbie, tell us what ye have found."

Between spoonfuls of cream and porridge, Robert responded, "I found one for a man at a fish-market stall near High Street." Looking at Mrs. McEwen, he added, "I think it might be the one where ye get your fish. Then I found a brick maker looking for a strong man. He said he will take ye if ye would agree to serve as an apprentice for at least six months. The position will only pay seven shillings per week until ye finish your apprenticeship."

Mrs. McEwen offered her opinion without being asked. "Seven shillings per week be about all ye can get here in Edinburgh for a man new at his position. I know the fish monger, and I would nae want my worst enemy to work for him. He is a mean-spirited man."

"Well, I think then that I will talk to the brick maker, if ye can show me where he is," Johnny said to Robert.

Thoroughly involved in the plans for her new boarders, Mrs. McEwen spoke again. "What did ye find for Helen?"

"When I walked High Street, I stopped in a ladies' hat shop and asked if the lady there could use a girl. She said she could, but

Helen would have to learn the hatmaking trade quickly; she also said she could only pay three shillings a week until Helen learned the trade."

Helen smiled uncertainly and said, "I will be glad to try the position."

* * *

When Isabel and David turned in their equipment at the shed that evening, they found the coal master waiting for them with his fists on his hips and a scowl on his face. "Where's your daughter and her husband?" he asked belligerently.

Isabel stood unmoving and asked simply, "Why do ye ask?"

"Ye know why I ask! We lost over twenty good men in the pit fire, and I need every strong man."

"Well, ye will not have Johnny or my Helen any longer. They have left the pit and will never return."

Ed Vickers's face began to grow flushed, and his voice rose. "They can't leave the pit 'til their debt at the company store is paid."

Isabel answered simply, "'Tis paid."

"I will have your jobs over this," he fumed.

"That would seem foolish as ye just said that ye need every strong man, and my Jamie and Davy are strong lads." Her voice did not rise, and Vickers was too angry to notice the slight tremble in it.

The angry coal master turned on his heel and stormed away. Then he suddenly stopped and turned. "What would it take to get them back? I'll give him two more shillings a week."

"There is nothing ye can offer that will get them back!" This time her voice rose with anger and finality. She started up the path toward the cottages with a determined stride, her hands doubled up in fists at the end of her stiff arms. As she walked, several women caught up with her and asked about Johnny and Helen.

One asked, "Did they really leave the pits?"

Another inquired, "How did they get away? Did they pay off their debt at the company store?"

A third commented, "Bell, ye give us hope. Maybe some of our kin will someday leave the pits."

Isabel answered none of them, but as soon as David followed her inside the cottage, she closed the door, sat down hard on a stool and, putting her face in her hands, wept. "Oh, Davy, how we will miss them."

The coal master accosted Richard and Effie Smith later that same evening. With two men standing on either side of him, he stopped them in the path and started to poke Richard in the chest as he bellowed, "Your son and his wife have run away. He still owes the company store, and I will bring him back and make him go the round as an example to the others who think they can get away without paying their debt."

Richard, who stood two inches taller than the coal master, took hold of the hand Vickers was using to poke him and bent it upward, forcing Vickers to step backward to free himself from the grip. "Ye know that their debt is paid. Ye added to their debt just to keep them here. Ye are a thief and a liar," Richard said as he folded his arms over his chest.

"Ye have picked a fight ye will never win," Vickers yelled at him. "Ye will be responsible for the debt of your son if we don't bring him back." With that, Vickers and the two men who stood beside him separated and stepped around Richard, walking angrily back to the equipment shed.

Richard called after them contemptuously, "Ye can't get blood from a turnip."

As he and Effie started up the path again, she took his arm. He could feel her trembling. Even though neither the Hogges nor the Smiths would talk about how Johnny and Helen were able to leave the pits without being considered runaways, the rumor soon spread among the miners' families that somehow the "Mormons" had helped.

CHAPTER 30
Life in Edinburgh

Robert and Johnny said little as they walked briskly through the streets of Edinburgh, but Johnny examined the many new sights he had never seen before, such as the butcher's booth with the still-feathered but headless geese and chickens hanging by their feet.

The walk to the brick maker took more than half an hour, and at every turn Robert said, "Take note, Johnny, so ye can make your way home without getting yourself lost. We would nae find ye for three days in this city." Though Robert laughed, he meant his warning to be taken seriously.

"Pick up that apron over in the corner and follow me," the brick maker said to Johnny after shaking his hand. Robert left his brother-in-law to learn his new trade and retraced his steps until he turned the corner near the print shop and bindery.

Mrs. McEwen led Helen through the crowded streets to the milliner's shop on Church Street, just off High Street. There she introduced herself and Helen to Violet Cockburn, the mistress of the shop, and asked if she still desired an apprentice. The mistress of the shop answered in the affirmative. "And when can I expect Helen this evening?" Mrs. McEwen asked. When told the shop closed at seven-thirty each evening, she wished Helen well and left the shop.

Betty McEwen waited anxiously for the day to end so she could hear the news from her new boarders, and when Helen did not arrive by the time she had supper on the table, she grew worried. "Robbie, ye must go and find her. She may be lost." The landlady's voice was filled with worry.

He found her standing on High Street in the light of a gas street lamp, not far from the hatmaker's shop, wringing her hands and fighting back tears. "Oh, Robbie, thank goodness ye found me. I didn't know which way to go, and I have been standing here for nearly an hour." They arrived home in time to eat a late supper and quell the fears of both Johnny and the landlady.

"Tell us what your day was like, lass," the landlady asked her as she sat down at the supper table.

"Miss Cockburn said she might keep me, but I'll have to work in the back room as I am not presentable enough to be seen by the patrons." Helen dropped her head. Johnny put a kindly but awkward hand on her shoulder to comfort her.

"What did she say was the problem?"

She said my hair was untidy and my dress was shabby. I don't know what I can do about either."

"Well, I do. Now eat your supper." Mrs. McEwen had a determined tone in her voice. After the meal was finished, she rose and said, "Ye wait right here. I think I can solve your problem."

Mrs. McEwen disappeared into her room at the back of the house and reappeared with a dress of blue plaid with a white collar. "This was one of my favorites, but as I mentioned last evening, the Lord has blessed me so much I can't fit in it anymore. Now stand up, lass." She held the dress up to Helen and noted that it would be too big in the bodice for her and only a little too short at the ankle. "Never ye mind, I will have this fixed by morning." While her needle flew, the landlady sought and obtained a report from Johnny on his first day as a brick maker.

"The work is hard, but nae so hard as digging coal. I don't work in the dark, and the air is cleaner than in the pits. My job is to fill a big cart full of clay that I must dig from the hill behind the brickyard. I shovel it into a cart that is on wheels so it can be pushed to the large soaking pit, where it gets mixed with water. Then it can be molded.

"After the clay is softer, another lad carries it by buckets to the molding table where the brick molder fills the forms for the bricks. When the bricks have had time to dry, Mr. Duncan tells me we will stack them in the big kiln oven where they will be baked for more than a week. He says we will put near ten thousand bricks in the oven each time." He paused and then added, "I think he's pleased with my work."

"Praise God for such blessings," Mrs. McEwen said fervently. Then she added, "Morning will come early enough for us all, so off to bed with ye. In the morning the dress should be finished. Helen, have Johnny come down the stair and get it before ye get dressed."

Helen stopped on the stairs and turned. "Mrs. McEwen, the angels in heaven can't be as kind as ye are."

"Ach, 'tis a kind enough thing that ye say, my dear. Now off to bed."

In the morning, Johnny came down to find the dress on the little wicker settee where he had last seen Mrs. McEwen sewing the night before. He carried it carefully up the stairs. Helen put it over her head and smoothed the skirt with reverent awe as her husband buttoned the back. "I nae have seen such a bonnie dress in all my days," she said.

"Helen, 'tis your color, for sure," he responded.

When they came down the stairs for breakfast, Mrs. McEwen stood with her arms folded under her ample bosom and a broad smile on her face. "Now she will nae keep ye in the back room," she said triumphantly. "When ye have had time to eat breakfast, then I will put a crown of braids in your hair. She will not know ye." The landlady chuckled with satisfaction.

As Helen walked to the hatmaker's shop, she thought with pleasure that in her new dress no one on the street would ever guess that she had come from the mines. She made a special effort to note a landmark at each corner as she walked with the landlady.

"On your way back, remember to walk briskly, like ye have to meet somebody. If a man should approach ye, tell him ye are meeting your father, your husband, and your brothers at the next corner, and they would not like him. That should keep ye safe."

"Aye, Mrs. McEwen," Helen said with a smile.

As they entered the hatmaker's shop, Violet Cockburn looked up and said, "How may I assist you ladies?" as they entered.

"See, lass, I said she would not know ye." Mrs. McEwen beamed. Then she said to the shop owner in a slightly scolding tone, "This is Mrs. Helen Smith, your new apprentice. Perhaps now she will not have to stay in the back room."

Oblivious to the disapproval in Mrs. McEwen's tone of voice, Miss Cockburn walked in a small circle around Helen and then said, "Indeed, you are right presentable today, Helen. I have increased expectations for you." With that, the little landlady left the shop with a smile and a light step.

At the end of the week, Johnny and Helen sat at the kitchen table and counted the shillings they had earned. Together they separated out the shillings they would pay Mrs. McEwen for room and board. Then Helen added another two for the landlady. "She has been so kind to us, and I want to pay her for the dress." Johnny nodded his agreement.

As the days were cold, Mrs. McEwen sought and found a cap and a seaman's jacket for Johnny and a cape for Helen for a few shillings in a second-hand shop off High Street. Each day she moved around her kitchen, singing in a nearly tuneless way under her breath, "By yon bonnie banks and by yon bonnie brae . . ." as she prepared the meals for her boarders. As she took her bread out of the brick bustle oven with the long, wooden paddle, she finished her breathless solo, "And me and my true love will never meet again on the bonnie, bonnie banks of Loch Lomond." After she set the long paddle holding the two loaves of hot bread on the table, she brushed the flour from her hands and apron with satisfaction.

* * *

The little group of four made their way to the "Mormon" meetings in a rented hall on Sundays, regardless of the weather. Each sermon finished with the admonition for those present to make plans to gather to America and join the other members of the Church in the Valley.

In February Elder Franklin Richards returned to preach again in Edinburgh and asked Johnny if he was willing to be ordained an elder like his brother-in-law, Robert, had been. Johnny was nearly overwhelmed. "'Tis a privilege to accept such a call. What would be my responsibilities for such a thing?"

"You will assist with the blessing and passing of the Lord's supper at each Sabbath meeting, and at every opportunity you will bless the sick and you will preach the gospel to those who are willing to listen."

CHAPTER 31
Renewed Hope and Renewed Loss

In the late spring when Helen, Johnny, Robert, and Mrs. McEwen sat around the supper table, Helen took a big breath and said, "I must tell ye all that Miss Violet told me today that I must quit the hat shop."

All three looked at her with grave concern. Robert asked, "Why would she do such a thing, Helen? Ye have given her satisfaction in every way."

"Today I told her that we would have a new bairn in a few months. She said it was not proper for a young woman with child to be working in a shop. I am happy to think that God will send us another bairn, but I am worried about having no position to bring in some shillings."

Johnny gave out a whoop and said, "What does it matter if ye cannot work for Miss Violet. I am making enough each week to feed us both, and we will have a tiny lad or a lassie to take the place of our first one."

Mrs. McEwen smiled and said, "There are some months before the bairn arrives. I think I can find ye an easier position where ye can still bring in some shillings. Would that please ye both?"

Helen nodded and smiled. With the assistance of Betty McEwen, within a week Helen was serving as a housekeeper for Catherine McEwen, the wife of Walter McEwen. The landlady was happy to take another one of her outgrown dresses and remake it for Helen, putting tucks in the bodice so it could be expanded as Helen grew.

Walter and Catherine McEwen lived in the flat above the print shop, so Helen walked to and from her position each morning and evening with Robert. She chattered nearly every day about the coming event. "Do ye think it will be a lad or a lassie, Robert? What shall we name him—or her?"

Finally, after a week of such questions, he answered, "I think it will be either a lad or a lassie—and ye will know what to name the bairn when it arrives." Helen's happy enthusiasm was not dampened by her brother's mild exasperation.

Catherine was the second wife of Mr. McEwen and at least twenty-five years younger. She had no children of her own, so she fussed over Helen's expectant condition. After the first week, Helen said, "I should not take any payment from Catherine McEwen."

"Why do ye say such a thing?" Johnny asked.

"Because she nae will let me lift or carry anything, and today she taught me to make pound cake. She says she will show me how to make shortbread tomorrow. I do not see that I am of any help to her." But Catherine insisted that Helen be paid three shillings a week, and Betty McEwen knew it was for her companionship that Helen was appreciated.

When Helen gave birth in late November, it was to twins. They were named William and Allison. Little Willie, named for the dead son of the well-loved landlady, was a strong boy with a lusty cry, but Allison was tiny and weak. Catherine insisted that she and her husband, Walter, be named the godparents for the children, but Helen and Johnny explained that there would be no baptism into the Church of Scotland for the children and thus no official godparents. A surprised Catherine asked why not.

Johnny explained, "Wee bairns do not need baptism as they cannot sin." That discussion led into many others. When Catherine insisted that Walter give her one of the extra copies of the Book of Mormon that he had remaining from the printing he had done for Orson Pratt some years earlier, he was speechless. Within the month, Catherine was baptized into the new American church and joined the others in their walks to Sabbath meetings in the cold of December, while Helen remained at home with the babies.

On a Sunday in mid-January, the sun warmed enough to melt the snow on the streets into slush, and when Helen saw the sunshine, she asked Johnny, "Do you think that we could take the bairns to Sabbath meeting? 'Tis nae so cold as it has been."

Johnny answered, "Aye, I would like the folks there to see our two beautiful bairns." So the proud parents each carried an infant and walked with the landlady, Robert, and Catherine McEwen to meeting.

After the meeting ended, Helen stood at the door of the meeting-house and said with concern, "The sun has gone, and the snow has returned. Our beautiful day is fading away."

The carriage traffic in the streets had increased greatly as the wealthy citizens of the city made their way home from church services. As the little group walked back toward the boardinghouse, they were sometimes forced out into the street to avoid the deepest piles of slushy snow, puddles of water, mud, and the filth dumped from the second-story windows of the big houses of the merchants. As they talked happily, Helen carried Allison wrapped in a shawl against her right shoulder. Occasionally she would take Johnny's arm as they stepped around the puddles. Catherine McEwen had coaxed them into letting her carry little Willie.

As they stepped out into the street to avoid another pile of slush melting into a large puddle, a beggar woman in rags approached Johnny and asked, "Sir, have ye a half penny or a farthing for an old woman? I ain't had nothing to eat in two days."

As Johnny tried to step around her, she blocked his way, preventing both him and Helen from getting out of the street. Taking hold of his jacket front, she asked more desperately, "Won't you take pity on an old beggar woman? Ye look like a good Christian man. Sure, and ye have a good, charitable heart."

Johnny looked at her guiltily and said, "I may have a coin or two." With that he started to search his pockets. As he did so,

Helen and the others watched him intently. None of them noticed the great carriage pulled by four matched chestnut horses rolling swiftly toward the little group. As Johnny pressed two farthings into the old woman's hand, Betty McEwen suddenly cried out, "A carriage is coming, get out of its way."

Looking up, Helen screamed, and Robert tried to pull her out of the way, but the old woman was standing between them and safety. The horses bore down on them swiftly, so Johnny pushed Helen hard before he leapt out of the way in the opposite direction. The great carriage rolled over the old woman as if she were no more than a small bump in the road.

Helen screamed as she fell to the ground, and Johnny ran to her, calling, "Helen, are ye all right?" Pulling her to her feet he said with relief, "Are ye all right? Are ye hurt?"

In a frantic voice she answered, "I'm all right, but where is Allison?" She pushed past Johnny and ran back into the street.

Several tradesmen, who had witnessed the incident, ran out into the road where they grabbed the harness of the horses and brought them to a stop. Another man ran beside the carriage and pounded on the door. He called out, "Stop the carriage. Ye ran over an old woman."

The carriage came to a stop about fifty feet beyond the body of the old beggar and the form of Helen who was kneeling in the street, huddled over the crushed body of little Allison. Helen picked her up and cradled her against her body as she rocked back and forth, sobbing.

Johnny and Mrs. McEwen rushed to Helen and lifted her to her feet. Continuing to sob, the young mother said, "I dropped her. I dropped her when Johnny pushed me out of the way. I dropped my little Allison, and now she's dead." She leaned against Johnny's shoulder, and the grief poured out of her like water from a bucket tipped at a well.

The carriage door opened and a large man in a velvet suit with a ruffled shirt stepped down from the carriage as the driver said, "Sir Isaac, I did not see them in the street until it was too late to stop the horses. Ye were in such a hurry . . ." His face was white, and he pulled on the reins to quiet the horses.

As Robert ran toward the gentleman, he yelled at him, "Did ye not see us standing there in the street? Your carriage has killed the bairn and run over the old woman." He was shaking as he reached the carriage, where he stopped short. He found himself looking into a face he knew, older but still familiar. Robert was looking directly into the eyes of Laird Isaac Keith from Penston. He put out his hand to steady himself against the carriage as a flood of old memories and new grief washed over him. Once again, Sir Isaac was a source of pain for him and his family.

Sir Isaac pulled a small leather pouch from the pocket in his vest and took what amounted to ten pounds out of it. He pressed the coins into Robert's hand, folding his hand shut over the money. Robert stood as still as if he had turned to stone. In a voice accustomed to giving commands, Sir Isaac stated, "This should take care of any expenses associated with the funerals. It was really not my fault nor that of the driver. Why were all of you in the street? Intelligent people know to keep out of the way of the carriages."

With that, the laird climbed into the carriage and tapped the roof with the head of his walking stick. The driver slapped the reins against the horses' rumps, and the carriage rumbled away. Robert continued to stand in the street like a statue. After a minute, he slowly opened his hand and looked down at the silver coins, then turned and made his way to his sister, who was surrounded by her husband's arms. Catherine, the little landlady, and the tradesmen formed a small group around them. Helen held Allison's tiny body clutched against her.

When Robert reached the little cluster of men and women, one tradesman said to him, "We knew old Bess. She's been in this neighborhood for years. What do ye plan to do for her funeral?"

Robert put several of the silver coins from Laird Keith into the man's hand and said with a voice that could hardly be heard, "Ye will see that she gets a Christian burial?"

The man's face lit up, and he said as he respectfully pulled at his forelock, "Aye, sir, we'll give her a great sendoff with this."

During the week that followed the loss of little Allison, Helen refused to leave the landlady's home. Her grief was doubled as it combined with the loss of her first child—a grief that had been stored away since the stillbirth. Helen would not eat and could not sleep. Johnny often found her sitting in the dark in their little bedroom, holding Willie and weeping.

When Johnny tired to comfort her, she would shake her head and say, "I should not have taken them out into the cold that day. I should have stayed here with them. This is my fault."

"'Tis no one's fault, Helen. We still have little Willie, and there will be other bairns for us. We have many years ahead to welcome more lads and lassies." But Helen would not be comforted.

The others walked to Sabbath meeting without her. On the way, Johnny said, "I fear that if we stay here any longer, Helen will never cease to grieve. I think it's time for us to plan to go to America." Robert quietly nodded in agreement.

When they arrived back at the boardinghouse after Sabbath meeting, Johnny sat with Helen in the dark of their bedroom and asked, "Helen, we finally have enough money saved for the voyage to America. Will ye come with me?"

"Of course, as I am your wife." Her voice was flat and almost a whisper.

"But I mean will ye come with me—and bring your heart?"

She looked at him as if seeing him for the first time in many days, and after a moment said, "Aye, I will try." From that day forward, she began to heal.

CHAPTER 32
Leaving

As people leaving the meeting churned past the three men, Elder Richards stood wrapped in thought for a moment and then responded to Johnny's question. "The Church agent in Liverpool has made arrangements for a group to travel on a ship that leaves toward the end of March. It will be the last ship we will send any Saints on, as the others will arrive too late in the season to make the journey west. It will dock in Baltimore. If you can be ready to leave by then, he should be able to obtain steerage passage for you."

Johnny responded, "That would be a great blessing for us, President Richards."

"You are sure you do not want to wait for the ship our agent will charter that will leave next January? It will dock in New Orleans, and the journey from there to Kanesville would be much easier."

But Johnny shook his head and added, "Nae, I think my wife and I need to be on our journey to Zion as soon as possible. We have recently lost a bairn, and I fear that my wife will nae cease to grieve until we are long away from here."

Elder Richards turned to Robert and asked, "Will you be going as well, Robert?"

Robert had dreamed of the day he would be able to sail to America, his "promised land," from those first days of reading the Book of Mormon. He had often pictured himself and his family on that ship sailing westward, but he knew his answer. "As much as

I want to go to America, President Richards, I feel that I must try to free more of my kin from the mines and see that those who desire to go are able to make the journey. Then I will make the journey to the Valley."

So the plans for the voyage for Johnny and Helen were made.

Within two weeks, one of the missionaries traveling from Liverpool to Edinburgh received a letter from the Church agent telling Johnny and Helen that steerage passage for them had been obtained on the ship *Flora Macdonald,* which would leave Liverpool on the twenty-eighth of March.

As soon as their landlady learned of the plans for her little family of boarders to emigrate to America, her smile faded and her tuneless singing grew quiet, but she helped in every way she could. They were given a handbill that listed the things they would need to take, including a kettle, a pot, a few tin cups, plates, a few clean cloths, soap, water containers, quilts, and warm clothing.

"Mrs. McEwen, come with us. Ye have nae reason to stay here," Helen said.

"I think I am too old for such a journey."

"But the Church leaders have asked us all to gather to Zion. Ye must come too," Helen said earnestly.

"Perhaps someday," the landlady said unconvincingly.

When it came time for Johnny, Helen, and little Willie to leave the boardinghouse, the landlady rode with them in a hired wagon to the great canal that connected Edinburgh and Glasgow. There, before they carried their limited possessions onboard the shallow-bottomed barge, they paused and each gave both Robert and Mrs. McEwen a great hug.

"Oh, Robbie, how I wish ye were coming with us," Helen said, fighting to keep back tears. "But ye will remember in the spring to put flowers on little Allison's grave at St. Cuthbert's?" Robert simply nodded; the knot in his throat made it difficult for him to speak.

Having fully given in to her tears, Mrs. McEwen said, "Now ye must take good care of little Willie on that great ship. I will miss the three of you more than ye can guess—and I fear for all of ye on that great ocean. Say your prayers so the good Lord will keep watch."

After Helen and Johnny walked up the gangplank, they carefully stepped onto the deck of the old barge and turned to wave. As Helen held Willie, she pressed her cheek against her husband's shoulder and asked, "Oh, Johnny, is this the right thing to do? I am so scared."

He answered with more confidence than he felt. "Aye, we are doing the right thing, and time will tell us so."

Mrs. McEwen wiped her eyes with a corner of her apron, while Robert waved his cap. He had a determined smile on his face, even though he already felt the loss of his sister's presence. "They are beginning a great journey. May the good Lord see them safely to the end of it," he said.

"We will all see our journey to the end, Robbie. We just don't know which side of the veil we will be on when we do," the landlady responded.

* * *

After they disembarked from the canal barge in Glasgow, Johnny found a man with a wagon for hire. "We must go to the train station where we can buy tickets to Liverpool. Will you take us there?"

The man nodded and said, "Climb in. It'll cost ye ten pence for your bundles and the three of ye." The wagon rattled and bounced for more than two miles from the canal to the train station on roads sometimes paved with cobblestones and sometimes rutted and muddy. The warehouses and tenement houses on either side of the streets rose two and three stories above the street, some with smoke streaming from the chimneys. The smoke soiled the sky, cutting off much of the sunlight. When they arrived, the wagon driver pointed out the ticket office of the bustling train station.

The next train did not leave for Liverpool until nearly eight o'clock that evening, so they located a wooden bench by the ticket office and sat down to wait. By the time the train arrived at seven o'clock P.M., a group of nearly a hundred and fifty had gathered, waiting to board. The great hiss made by the release of the steam from the engine as the train came to a stop made Willie cry and the other small children cling to their mothers. The steam churned around the engine and drifted over the waiting passengers like the breath of a dragon.

Only a few of the waiting passengers climbed aboard the first-class railcar. The others, along with Johnny and Helen, boarded the third-class cars. The railcars were dirty, smelly, and stained with chewing tobacco. The wooden benches were hard and backless.

The passengers tried to get comfortable, but the windows were open for ventilation and permitted smoke and cinders to drift in. It was evident that it would be a very long and tiring night.

Within a few minutes, the uniformed conductor came through the train car and said to everyone, "Have your tickets ready. We will leave in thirty minutes. This train is going to Liverpool by way of Gretna Green, Carlisle, Penrith, Lancaster, and Prescott." He repeated the names of the towns and villages with a rhythm born of experience. "The trip will be ten hours, with stops in each town on the way, so ye will arrive in Liverpool, if that be your destination, by about six o'clock in the morning." With that, he stepped up to the first family group and took their tickets.

When the steam in the boiler had reached sufficient pressure, the train lurched forward and within a few seconds lurched forward again. Eventually it began to pick up a more steady speed, and soon the sideways motion and the clacking of the wheels on the rails added to the discomfort of the night. With Willie sleeping on her lap, Helen leaned her head on Johnny's shoulder and tried to sleep. Occasionally she wiped a tear from her cheeks. "Too late to turn back, too late to turn back," the wheels of the train repeated as they clacked over the miles of track. Oh, how she would miss Robert, Mrs. McEwen, and the rest of her family. Would she ever see any of them again? She was suffused in loneliness, even though she sat by her husband with her child on her lap.

CHAPTER 33
Setting Sail

Upon reaching Liverpool the next morning, the train began to brake, and the sound of the escaping steam from the engine boiler awakened the passengers and frightened the children. Helen lifted her head from her husband's shoulder and asked, "Johnny, now what should we do?"

"Elder Richards said there would be a man to meet us. He will take us to the ship, and I must not get tickets from anyone but him. I think his name is McCoy."

The train finally came to a jerking halt. When they reached the station platform, they set their bundles down and looked around for Brother McCoy. A man with a very red beard and a great shock of red hair poking out from under a battered hat was sitting on the seat of a wagon in the muddy road. Johnny said, "Wait here. I'll see if that could be him."

As he approached the man, he called out, "Your name McCoy?"

The man nodded and responded, "Aye, Matt McCoy. And your name?"

"I'm Johnny Smith. Me and my family are going to the ship *Flora Macdonald* at the wharf. Do ye have our tickets?"

"Aye, I got tickets for the Smith family. Any other Saints on that train?"

"None that we met."

After settling themselves and their meager belongings in the wagon, the noise of the wagon wheels made it impossible for them to talk without raising their voices, but they watched in wonder as they rode through the city. Liverpool was more noisy and dirty than Edinburgh or Glasgow and seemed to be a crowd of tenement houses and factories blackened by the smoke of decades. The streets were busy with carts, wagons, carriages, and people of every description and occupation.

By the time they arrived at West Waterloo Dock, the noise had increased to a level requiring anyone trying to communicate to speak in a near shout. The area was a mass of docks, wharfs, and piers, which were filthy and crowded with pickpockets, peddlers, women of questionable occupations, and ragged street urchins. The great warehouses that lined the streets were tall enough to keep the streets in the shadows most of the day. When they finally saw the masts of the great ships come into view, Helen and Johnny looked on in relief and amazement.

Finally Helen spoke. "Which is the *Flora Macdonald?*" she called to Mr. McCoy.

"That one over there," he said as he pointed. "The one with the figurehead that looks like a wooden lady with not enough clothes on—see her under the bowsprit where she's decorating the prow of the ship." He pointed as he spoke, and Helen followed his pointing finger as his nautical words meant nothing to her. "Your ship won't be officially leaving until early tomorrow, but everyone must board tonight. Sometime after all are onboard, the government medical examiner will come to make sure there are no diseases among the passengers. In the evening, the ship will be towed out into the river where she will be anchored for the night. Then in the morning, weather and all things cooperating, she will probably set sail. Ye better be on it as soon as the captain lets the passengers board. Now here are your tickets. That will be five pounds for the two of ye, no cost for the bairn. Ye'll need to pay me for them now, so I can buy more for the next group of Saints going to America."

As they started up the gangplank, Johnny looked around and commented, "I think this will be the adventure of our lives, Helen."

"I think ye speak the truth," she answered quietly.

While climbing the gangplank, they were met by a rough-looking crewman in a red-and-white horizontally striped shirt who asked, "Names?"

Johnny told him, and then he asked, "Ye with the Mormons?"

They nodded and answered, "Aye."

He turned his head and spat a large wad of tobacco juice over the side of the ship, wiped his mouth with the back of his hand, and said, "Well, I guess this ship be carrying about twenty-five of ye. The other passengers be regular folk. The rest of the ship be loaded with freight for the Fogg Mercantile Company. I hope the Mormons be no more trouble than the freight. At least the freight won't keep us up at night singsongin' a bunch of hymns." He spat again. Then he called after them as they reached the deck, "Ye'll be traveling in steerage amidships. Go down the hatchway by the mainmast."

They made their way carefully down the narrow, spiral stair into a dark area below deck where they could not stand upright. There they met a sailor, and Johnny asked, "Where's the steerage place?"

He did not answer but just pointed toward another spiral staircase. They carefully made their way down another level.

Stooping to avoid hitting their heads on the beams that supported the deck above them, they made their way through the semidarkness lit only by an occasional kerosene lantern hung on a nail to an area where a few adults were quietly talking while several children were sleeping.

"This place is near as dark as a cave," Helen commented. The entire steerage area was a series of berths, many joined at the head or side with others in groups of four, each large enough to sleep three or four adults. At one end of the steerage compartment were two large tables with benches on four sides. All were bolted to the deck. There were no provisions for privacy.

"If this is where we will live while we are on the ship," Helen said, "I hope we don't grow daft in the darkness. It feels so much like being back in the pits."

As the late afternoon sunlight waned and the darkness crept upon the city, the passengers began to arrive in a steady stream. Some were loaded with many boxes and bags, while others had little more than the clothing on their backs. They all put as much of their baggage under the bottom of the lowest berth as they could. What would not fit under the lower berths was put in wooden foot lockers bolted to the bulkhead.

As each family descended into the steerage area, Johnny noticed that they were almost equally divided between those with a Scottish burr in their speech, and those who were from County Down and spoke with a soft brogue, as the ship's port of origin was Belfast.

At six bells a man descended the staircase and in a loud voice called for the attention of the group. "My name is Elder Jonathan Stephens, and I have been appointed as the branch president of those who are members of the Church. This is my third crossing, so I will promise you that as we are all headed for Zion, the Lord will bless and protect us to the same degree that we are obedient to His laws and commandments."

He continued, "These are the rules for the Saints, and we invite all other passengers to join us in obeying them. Each morning at eight bells, we will gather on the deck as long as the weather will permit and sing a morning hymn and offer a prayer for the day. Each evening at seven o'clock, which is six bells, we will do the same, followed by spiritual instruction. It is important that you have your evening meal finished by eight bells. If there are any disagreements between members of the group, they will be brought to me if they are not settled peaceably. You will come to me with your illnesses, births, deaths, and other problems. There are seven families of Church members on this ship, which amounts to nearly one-half of all the passengers. As it will be some weeks before we reach Baltimore, we must work together and care for each other as did the Saints in the New Testament. Is that understood?" The members of the group nodded and quietly assented to the new organization.

After evening prayer, a steam tug was attached to the bow of the ship by a long hawser, and as the passengers stood on the deck in the early twilight, it towed the *Flora Macdonald* out into the Mersey, River, where she dropped anchor. The channel was cluttered with arriving and departing ships at anchor with sails furled. The health inspector was rowed out to the ship, and after looking over the passengers' manifest, he perfunctorily signed off on it and returned to the dock.

Before some of the passengers lay down to sleep that night on their hard berths, those who could hung one of their precious quilts for privacy on the two or three old nails which had been pounded into the beam above their berths for that purpose. The gentle rocking of the ship in the current of the Mersey River and the sound of the ship's bells as they rang the hour and the half-hour eventually intertwined with the dreams of a new land and a new life for most of the passengers.

At six bells in the morning, the sounds of the sailors calling to each other and the noise of the great hawsers lifting the anchor made the entire ship shudder, awakening everyone. As they turned the bars in the great capstan, the sailors sang together in a chant that kept them moving in unison.

"Oh, Johnny, let's go up and watch the sailors," Helen said.

As Johnny started up the narrow hatchway, almost everyone else in steerage followed. The captain stood near the helmsman at the great wooden wheel on the quarterdeck and watched another steam tug pull the ship into the Irish Sea with the help of a following wind and the current of the river. The passengers stood almost spellbound as they watched the process of setting sail. As the sailors swarmed barefooted over and up the shrouds and ratlines to the top of the mainmast and the mizzenmast, one of the children called out, "Look, Pa, look, Ma! They're climbing to heaven."

As the crewmen moved out along the top gallant and freed the sail to catch the wind, the children cried out in pleasure. A small girl said excitedly, "See, now the boat has wings, just like a bird."

"Captain," Elder Stephens spoke loudly enough to be heard above the wind, "this is the finest and smoothest departure I have ever experienced. May I credit it totally to you and your crew?"

The captain laughed but answered modestly, "A perfect wind is ours today, Elder Stephens. I could not have arranged it better if I had spoken to the great Creator Himself."

"Some of us have already done that for you," Elder Stephens called back with a smile.

As the sails filled with wind, the ship moved swiftly and smoothly westward, and the English shoreline began to slip away. Helen and Johnny stood together with Willie in his mother's arms as they watched the process. "I will surely never again see such a beautiful sight in all my days," Helen whispered as she looked at the billowing sails.

"Aye," he answered in quiet awe, "I think we move on the breath of God."

As the wind from the sea reached the passengers on deck, Helen said, "We are leaving a whole life behind, Johnny, and we nae can know what our new life will bring."

As the passengers gathered around to watch the old world slip away behind them, they began to sing "O God, Our Help in Ages Past," and Elder Stephenson offered a fervent prayer for the safe crossing of the ship and a safe arrival in America. As the passengers bowed their heads in prayer, the captain doffed his cap and stood respectfully silent. Each of the sailors on the deck followed his example, some more willingly than others.

* * *

For the first several days, the ship was never out of sight of land. The captain identified the Isle of Man and the coast of Scotland for interested passengers. Despite the cold wind, the children were thrilled to see a great school of porpoises as the ship sailed around the north of Ireland. They leaped out of the water and played about the bow of the ship.

On the evening of the fourteenth day, lightning shot across the sky, followed by thunder with a sound like a cannon shot, and the wind freshened rapidly. The captain called out, "Passengers, go below." To the crew he called out, "Clew up the canvas on the main topsail!" Then calling out in the other direction, "You, clew up the fore topsail, and you, lower the main topgallant." Some of the sailors were not working fast enough to please him, so he called out again, more urgently, "Lower the topgallant, spill the wind, spill the wind! Quick's the word, make sharp the action." His powerful voice carried over the sound of the coming storm.

As the barefoot crewmen clambered up the mainmast and the foremast, Johnny called out to Helen above the wind, "We must get ourselves back down inside the ship. 'Tis getting bad." As they made their way down the hatchway past the second deck, Helen had to hold on to the railing with both hands to stay on her feet. Johnny held on with one hand as he carried Willie with the other to keep from being washed away by the water that began to pour down the hatchway with each great wave that was driven onto the deck by the increasing wind. By the time they had reached steerage, they were soaked with seawater, and the bow of the ship was repeatedly rising and falling, shaking everything loose. As soon as all passengers had climbed down into steerage, the hatch was secured, preventing the passengers from going on deck until the storm was over.

The night was long, and the noise of the creaking timbers and the heaving of the ship kept everyone awake. The small children cried and clung to their mothers throughout most of the night. Those who did not eat any supper fared better than those who did.

In the morning, the storm continued unabated, and the seasickness of the passengers reached severe proportions.

On the third day of the storm, the wind quieted enough for the captain to send the first mate down to steerage with advice for the passengers. "Ye will all fare better," he told them, "if ye eat only boiled rice and drink rice water; or if ye brought lemons onboard, suck one."

When the ship was clean and orderly once more, Elder Stephens stood on a barrel on the deck and preached to all within hearing the basic principles of faith, repentance, baptism, and the need for the guidance of the Holy Ghost. He read portions of the Bible and the Book of Mormon. Within three days, several of the crewmen asked about baptism. Two of them, boys of about fourteen, Georgie Barber and Ben Richie, proceeded to be baptized on the afternoon of the fourth day. The captain permitted a narrow, short platform to be built by the ship's carpenter which was extended from the ship as near the water as possible. Elder Stephens had himself lowered by a rope along with the two young men with ropes tied around their waists. There in the ocean, they were baptized, with the baptizer being as immersed in water as the candidates for baptism.

That evening, a small celebration was held by the Saints to welcome the two young men into the faith. One of the passengers played a fiddle, and the passengers danced until they were ready to drop.

On the forty-ninth day they sighted land, but it was three days more before they entered the Chesapeake Bay and sailed northward. The sea-weary passengers celebrated. By this time, much of the hardtack had become wormy, and the drinking water was green and had an unpleasant smell.

The captain dropped anchor when Sparrows Point was sighted and waited for a steam tug to take the ship into the wide mouth of the Patapsco River to the Baltimore wharfs. The evening before they were to disembark, Johnny spoke quietly with Helen. "I fear that we don't have enough money now to get to Zion with the other Saints. We only have three pounds, four shillings. I have spoken with Elder Stephens, and he says that there are others who have the same need for funds and that we will have to find work here so we can save enough to go to the Valley in a year or two. I know that this is a disappointment, but I can't think of any other way to fix our situation."

"Johnny, we will trust in the Lord. He will help us find a position here for awhile."

He nodded in agreement and then said, "We have survived the pits and the weeks on the water. Now all we can ask is that our lives be spared again to see the Valley."

CHAPTER 34
Mine Collapse

Robert continued to wave his cap at his sister Helen and her husband and infant son as the barge grew smaller and finally passed out of sight, moving west on the Union Canal toward Glasgow. As he turned away from the canal he said quietly, as though he were thinking aloud, "Helen and Johnny have begun a great adventure. I hope we will see them again someday. May God watch over them on this journey."

The landlady answered, "We know He will."

The two of them climbed into the rented wagon that had taken them to the canal to return to the boardinghouse. As they rode, Robert raised the question again that had been asked of the landlady before. "When will ye make plans to gather to the Valley with the Saints, Mrs. McEwen?"

"Robbie, I think on it often, but still something tells me that I may never make the journey."

As Robert was setting type the next morning for the last page of a pamphlet ordered by Orson Pratt entitled *Divine Authenticity of the Book* of *Mormon,* Elder Pratt entered the print shop and bindery. He shook Walter McEwen's ink-stained hand and asked, "How is the printing coming, Mr. McEwen?"

"Mr. Pratt from America, I can tell ye that Robbie has been working hard on it."

As Elder Pratt examined some of the finished pages, he stopped and said to the owner of the print shop, "We're having another meeting at your sister-in-law's house tonight, Mr. McEwen. When will we see you there?"

"I wouldn't count on seeing me, Mr. Pratt, but I must say that I admire your unwillingness to give up on me. I am sure Robbie will be there, as well as my wife, Catherine. Robbie never misses a chance to preach or be preached at." With that, he chuckled and turned back to his work.

Robert smiled and nodded. "Of course I'll be there."

That evening as had happened many times before, another group of people sat around the small kitchen-sitting room of the boardinghouse of Betty McEwen. At the conclusion of the evening's discussion, two of those present consented to baptism.

On Saturday, those desiring baptism rode in a rented wagon with Elder Pratt and Robert to the Firth of Forth. Robert was tremendously pleased that Elder Pratt had asked him to perform the baptisms. As they rode through the bumpy streets, Robert said, "Mrs. McEwen has told me that this is your second mission to the British Isles. The Saints are grateful that ye were willing to return to Scotland to preach again, but ye must miss your family greatly."

"That is true, but I always try to remember that the work of the Lord must go forward." Elder Pratt continued, "I will not be able to remain here in Edinburgh any longer than is necessary, as I must return to Liverpool to direct the missionary activities in these islands."

Throughout the following weeks, Robert continued his work in the print shop, where he set the type and printed several thousand copies of the pamphlet ordered by Elder Pratt. When Elder Pratt returned to the print shop to get the finished copies of the pamphlet and the hymnbooks previously ordered, he said, "Robert, I have just received a notice that President Brigham Young has made great progress in establishing the Perpetual Emigration Fund to aid the Saints in their gathering to the Valley. It may take some time before there are sufficient funds available for the Scottish Saints to make the journey, but I urge you to tell your family members to prepare themselves to go to America."

Robert said, "'Tis good news, Elder Pratt."

* * *

As Robert sat reading the *Edinburgh Register* in April he read of another mine collapse in Dalkeith, this time in Pit Number Three. The news appeared in a small article on page four with no listing of the names or numbers of the dead. He would never know that once more the laird of the Cowden coal pit, Sir Ian Gray, had used his abundant political power to suppress and minimize the story.

When the landlady saw his white face, she said, "What is it in that newspaper that has upset ye so, Robbie?"

"Mrs. McEwen, there has been another mine cave-in at Dalkeith." With that, he rose and moved closer to the fireplace as if an increase in light would make more information appear in the article. "There is nae information about the dead." His hands had begun to shake slightly.

In her practical way, the landlady put her hand on his to calm him and said, "In the morning ye will go to Walter and tell him that ye must travel to Dalkeith to see if the members of your family be safe. He has a good heart. He will not object. Why, he may even offer ye a small loan to pay toward their debt." Then she turned and took down a small clay pot from the lintel above the fireplace and dumped several coins into her hand.

"I will help ye with the debt as well. Here, let me give you what I have saved." She turned his hand up and put two pounds and six shillings in it.

"Mrs. McEwen, I nae can take your money."

"Of course ye can. This is a loan and I know ye will repay me when ye can, but for now, ye must think of your family."

Robert left on the journey to Dalkeith very early the next morning after speaking with his employer, who gave him two pounds and five shillings against his future labor to pay against his family's debt. He walked, then begged a ride in the jolting vegetable cart of a crofter, and arrived that evening at the Cowden coal pit as the sun was setting. The Hogge cottage was empty. White-faced with fear and worry, he knocked on the door of the Kerr cottage and asked where he might find his family.

Jack Kerr pulled him into his cottage in his hurry to tell Robert all that had happened. "Then ye have only just heard about the pit collapse in Number Three?" he asked. Without waiting for an answer, he continued, "The laird blamed Vickers for the collapse and fired him. Said he was fed up with ceiling falls, drownings, and cave-ins that were killing too many of the miners, keeping him from meeting his quotas. 'Poor management, that's what it has been for too long.' That's what the laird yelled as he left Vickers's office. Vickers had a right to be angry as he was being pressed to work the men in weak tunnels that should have been closed. It was the only way to meet his quota, but he was out of a position just the same." Jack paused for a moment and grinned. Then he added, "The laird gave the position to James."

CHAPTER 35
Disappointment

For a split second, Robert was dumbfounded. Then he asked in disbelief, "Ye are saying James is the new coal master? Are ye daft? How can that be?"

Jack Kerr began to laugh at Robert's reaction. "Aye, I'll say it to ye again. James is the new coal master."

"But why would Sir Ian make James the coal master? There are older men with greater experience here—like yourself."

"But the laird has nae forgotten my involvement in that little darg that turned into a strike. He will nae choose any of us who led that strike to be coal master." Jack grew serious and continued, "Look, lad, this is a real blessing for your family. They have all been moved into the coal master's cottage across the way. Be glad for them."

All Robert could bring himself to say as he turned to leave was, "I have my doubts that this is a blessing. It may be more like a curse."

Robert made his way across the little valley, past the equipment shed, and up the hillside a short way. When he reached the coal master's large, two-story stone cottage, out of habit he took off his hat. Then he knocked on the front door. When a young woman of about twelve answered his knock, he stated hesitatingly, "I am seeking James Hogge. I have been told he is here."

She bobbed a small curtsey and asked, "And who shall I say is here to see him?"

"I am his brother, Robert Hogge."

"If ye will step into the sitting room, I will tell him that ye are here." With that she pointed to a chair in the main room and slipped out of sight.

Robert heard a child's voice call out, "It's Robbie! Papa, Mama! It's Robbie come to see us." With that, Lizzie ran into the room and threw herself at Robert. The soon-to-be four-year-old chattered as steadily as water poured out of a pitcher. "Robbie, ye have come to see us in our new house. Isn't it grand? Come see my room." With hardly a pause for a breath she added, "But I was afeared to sleep there all alone for a while, so Ma let me sleep with her and Pa. Now I'm not afeared to sleep alone in my own bed anymore." With that she started to pull him out of the room. "Come and see it."

At that point, James entered the room and shook his brother's hand. "Robert, we are so glad ye have come to see us. We did not know how to let ye know of our good fortune."

Isabel entered the room behind James. She hurried to Robert and, putting her arms around him, said, "It is an answer to prayer that ye are here, Robbie. Come, sit by me and we will talk. Have ye had something to eat for supper?"

When Robert shook his head, she called to the little servant girl, "Jane, have cook fix Robbie some supper." Then she coughed hard into a handkerchief. The cough was all too familiar to Robert.

The girl that had answered the door bobbed another curtsey and hurried away. Soon Eliza and David entered the room, and everyone began to talk excitedly to Robert at the same time.

Robert finally spoke. "How is it that ye are here in the coal master's cottage, James? Jack Kerr said that ye had been made coal master. Is that true?"

James smiled broadly and answered, "Aye, that's true. I know ye are wondering why he would choose me, but I think it is because we were never much involved in that brothering and strike that Joe Moffatt and Jack Kerr led."

At that point, the servant girl appeared with a tray that held a bowl of cabbage and beet soup, a large piece of fresh bread, and cheese. As intent as he was on learning what had happened since the mine collapse, Robert's hunger overcame his curiosity, and for a few minutes he ate hungrily. When he had emptied the bowl his mother asked, "Can we get ye some more to eat, Robbie?" With that, she coughed again, hard.

His smile of thanks was mixed with worry as he shook his head. "Nae, Ma. That was more than enough."

Looking from James and Eliza to his mother he said, "Now ye must know that I have been saving my money to come back to pay off the debt of our family at the company store, so ye could leave the pits. I have come to tell ye all that it is time to come to Edinburgh with me so we can make plans to gather to Zion with the Saints."

Isabel was racked with a siege of coughing. When it was over, James answered, "Robert, when I became the coal master, our debt was forgiven. Not just the debt of Eliza and me, but of Ma and Davy, too. We have left the pits. I made Davy a tag man yesterday, so he doesn't have to go down in the pit anymore, and Ma and Eliza will never carry coal again. The good Lord has answered prayers we never dared ask."

"But Jamie, we have been planning to go to America and gather to the Valley with the Saints for a long time. Don't let this change that dream," Robert pleaded.

As if to reassure Robert, James responded, "Robbie, I have talked with Sir Ian, and he has given me the authority to sink another pit, not far from Number Three, and he said he would allow the installation of a waterwheel with a steam engine to keep the pit dry. I can make the lives of the miners so much better. And the missionaries can come and preach, and no one will be permitted to throw rocks at them or mock them when they do any baptizing."

Robert said in concern, "James, don't let this cottage and an easier life take ye captive. I would rather go the round than see ye choose this life over gathering with the Saints to the Valley."

James quickly tried to justify himself. "I am in a place where I can do some good things, Robbie. Be happy for me." The last statement was almost a plea.

"But ye and Eliza will nae be going to America." Robert's voice was low and quiet with disappointment. Then he looked at his mother and asked, "Do ye feel the same, Ma? Or will you and Davy come with me?" He turned and looked at his younger brother. "Ye always wanted to go to America."

Isabel answered quietly, looking down at the handkerchief she had clutched in her hands. "Robbie, as ye can see, I am sick with the black spit like your father was—too sick to make such a journey. It was always in my heart to go to America and gather with the Saints, but that time has passed for me." Then she raised her head, and, looking at her youngest son, she said, "But if he still wants to go, Davy has my blessing."

"Will ye go with me, Davy? Will ye come to Edinburgh and prepare to go to America with the Saints?"

"Let me think on it, Robbie. If ye will stay with us tonight, we can talk about it in the morning."

Robert was quiet for a moment and then added, "I wish ye would all think and pray on it tonight. It was always our dream to get away from the dangers of the pits."

James answered, making light of Robert's urging, "We are nae in danger any longer, Robbie. We have left the pits and will work at the pithead, out of the dark and the danger. Have no concern for us."

"But Elder Pratt and Elder Richards have told us that the Lord wants us to gather to the Valley. Ye are choosing another path." Robert's voice trailed off in disappointment.

James had no more to say about the matter, but was obviously unhappy that Robert would not take satisfaction in his new position.

Though Isabel tried to draw Robert into the conversation that continued well into the night, he said little more. When Isabel's coughing grew worse, Eliza said, "It's time for us all to sleep.

Robert, let me show ye to your room upstairs." Silently, he followed her.

In the morning, as they ate breakfast, Robert asked David, "Have ye made a decision? Do ye desire to go to America with me, or do ye wish to remain here at the pit?"

"I have thought on it much during the night, Robbie, and I think I will stay here—for now. Maybe I will go to America in a year or two."

"I can nae change your mind?" David shook his head, so Robert rose from the breakfast table and said quietly, "Then I had best be getting on my way."

As Isabel bid her son farewell, she made every effort to maintain her composure. James shook Robert's hand and said, "We will see each other again." With that he lifted Lizzie high enough for her to give him a big hug.

As Robert started down the path to the pithead, he turned and waved to the little group standing at the front door of the cottage. His mother was weeping. Robert knew that this was the last time he would see her and perhaps the last time he would see the others. That thought hurt so much it made it hard for him to breathe for a moment. He turned his steps toward the miners' cottages to find the Smith family. He had not felt so sick and cold for a long time—not since Laird Keith had found him visiting Victoria and made him go the round.

When he reached the Smith cottage, he knocked, and the door opened quickly. "Come in, come in, Robbie." Effie's voice was full of genuine pleasure at seeing the young man.

As he was invited to sit at the old table, Effie asked, "Did ye have any breakfast? I will fix ye some porridge if ye are hungry."

Robert shook his head and said, "Nae, I have eaten. I am here to tell ye that none of my family is going to America."

Effie said sympathetically, "I thought as much. Perhaps James and Eliza can nae bear to leave the big cottage."

"And Ma is too sick," he continued. "I have brought enough shillings to pay the debt of my family, but as they are staying here I am offering to pay down your debt so some of you can come with me." He looked at Richard and Effie Smith as he asked, "Are ye willing to leave the pits and go to America to gather with the Saints?"

Richard shook his head. "Maybe someday, but not right now," was all he said.

Robert stood and moved his stool over beside him and as he sat, he quietly asked, "Do ye believe what we preached to be true? Do ye believe the gospel as we have taught it to your family?"

"Aye, I believe it to be true."

"Then why are ye not willing to go to America to be with the Saints?"

"Because I can't be one of ye."

"Why do ye say a thing like that?" Robert asked in surprise. "Why would ye not be baptized if ye believe this religion is true?"

"I carry too many hard feelings toward those who have kept me and my family in the pits for so many generations. Maybe someday my heart will be softened, but right now, it is full of anger and unforgiveness. How can I ask God to forgive me if I can't forgive others?"

Robert had no answer. Richard sat silent.

No one said anything until fifteen-year-old Katie spoke up, "But Pa, I want to go to America. I want to go to the Valley."

Everyone was quiet for a moment. Effie's face reflected the surprise everyone felt at Katie's statement. Then Effie said timidly, "What do ye think, husband?"

Richard shook his head and said firmly, "We have nae heard from Johnny and Helen since they left the pit. They may be dead, drowned in the sea, or in the ground. We know nothing of where they are, or even if they are still alive. I don't want to lose Katie or any of the others in my family."

"But, Pa," Katie continued to plead, "I don't want to carry coal all my life. I want to go to the Valley. Please don't make me stay here if I can go with Robbie."

Richard was quiet for several seconds. Then Effie reached out and put her hand on his shoulder. "Husband, it is wrong for us to keep Katie here if she wants to go to the Valley. We must let her go. 'Tis the right thing to do."

"But for a young lassie to go with a young man who is nae relation to her will bring shame upon us all."

Effie looked at her husband and said, "Husband, ye know that we can trust Robbie. We have known him all his life. He brought us the gospel."

Richard nodded and said, "Aye, I know he can be trusted."

"Then I will put part of the money I brought into your hands to pay down a portion of your debt at the company store, so no one can try to keep Katie here." Robert spoke with urgency. With that, he stood and took some coins from his pocket. As he offered them, Richard Smith said gently but firmly, "Nae, keep your money. None of my family will go to America until I learn what be the fate of my oldest son. Put your money away."

Seeing the resolve on the face of Richard Smith, Robert returned the coins to his pocket and said, "Then I had better be going. I need to get to Edinburgh before dark. I ask God's blessing on all of you—and may I someday see you in the Valley."

Effie rose and gathered the oatmeal cakes which she had made for their breakfast the next day, wrapped them in a clean cloth, and handed them to Robert. The Smiths stood in the doorway of the cottage and waved as Robert made his way toward the cart path.

About two miles west of the village of Musselburgh, he came upon a crofter by the name of Gibb with a hay wagon being pulled by two horses. Robert asked him if he could give him a ride. He offered to pay the man who said, "Aye, climb in. I will take ye as near to Edinburgh as I come for a ten pence." Despite his disappointment and the feeling of emptiness inside, Robert lay back on the hay and fell asleep.

After about five hours of riding, the old horses began to stumble and snort and finally stopped. "I fear that old Will and

Bruce will go nae further with such a heavy load. Ye will have to walk from here."

About eight o'clock that evening Robert arrived at the boarding-house of Mrs. McEwen. He knocked at the door and waited, hearing nothing. He knocked again, this time much louder. After several minutes, a light moved past the window, and the stout figure of the landlady with her dust cap awry on her white curls opened the top of the divided door. She held a candlestick. "Robbie, is that ye?" she asked as she held the candlestick high above her head.

Robert spoke. "Aye, Mrs. McEwen, 'tis me, Robbie."

She smiled and swung the bottom of the door open and said, "Are there no others with ye?" He shook his head. She gave him a motherly hug, almost setting his hair on fire with the candle. "I will fix some porridge, and ye can tell me why ye are alone."

As she stirred the oatmeal, Robert explained that the circumstances of his family had changed so much that none of them were willing to go to America with him. By the expression on her face, it was evident that she understood his disappointment.

As he slept that night, the dream of the great ship on the ocean recurred, but this time he stood alone on the deck.

CHAPTER 36
The Mines of Maryland

Elder Stephens spoke with Captain Sisson about the financial situation of some of the families who would soon be disembarking from the *Flora Macdonald* and asked his advice. "The tradesmen can probably find work in Baltimore; for those who cannot find a position in the city, there are positions in the coal mines in the western part of Maryland or eastern Kentucky," he responded.

As the passengers gathered for their last hymn and prayer on the deck, Elder Stephens shared the comments of the captain with the group. Then he added, "There is a bank not far from the dock where all of you can exchange your British money for American dollars. I will remain here in the city for two more days. When you know where you will be, tell me of your plans so I can let the leaders of the Church know. That way, none of you will be forgotten."

As the members of the Church disembarked, they were met by members of the small branch in that city and asked what help they would need for their journey westward. Several families, including Johnny and Helen, were taken into the homes of the members for a day or two until they could make other plans or find employment. Others who had sufficient funds asked to be pointed toward the train station, where they planned to purchase tickets on the Baltimore and Ohio Railroad to begin their journey to Chicago. From there they would purchase a wagon and supplies to start for Kanesville, Iowa, to join with the other wagon trains going west.

After being fed a meal by the Williams family, Johnny sat at the kitchen table in the two-story frame house and talked with Herb Williams. "What kind of a position are you looking for to support your family?" Herb asked.

"I have been in the mines all my life, but for the last while I was apprenticed as a brick maker. Do ye think there might be a way I can find a position with a brick maker here?"

"I know of none, though I am sure there are some in the city," Herb responded. "I do know my wife's brother who works in the Big Vein of the Georges Creek coal field. He lives in Gilmore on the west side of the state and has worked in the mine there for about ten years. He does well by his family."

Johnny shook his head. "I don't want to go back into the mines. I could do it myself, but I don't want my Helen carrying coal anymore. I don't want her in the pits ever again."

Herb Williams looked shocked and a bit self-righteous. "We don't allow women in the mines here in Maryland. I never heard such a thing—women in the mines! No, no, here in America we wouldn't permit it."

"If that's true, Brother Williams, then I would not object to going back into the mines until we earn enough money to gather with the Saints in the Valley." Johnny was silent for a few seconds, and then he continued, a bit embarrassed. "I don't know how much that will be, as I don't know where the Valley is that the elders talk so much about."

"Well, Brother Smith, I have been told that it will take about 340 U.S. dollars, maybe 350, to get my family to Sioux City, Iowa, by train and from there, to outfit a wagon to go the thousand or so miles to get to the Valley. I would guess that it will cost you the same."

As the men sat speculating at the kitchen table, Helen sat with Willie on her lap in the small parlor where she answered Mrs. Williams's questions. "Where did you come from?" was the first question. Her eyes were such a dark blue they were almost black.

"We came most immediately from Edinburgh," Helen said. Then Helen asked, "How long have ye been here?"

"About two years. We hope that we will have enough money saved in another year to go west."

"Oh," Helen said in disappointment, "I didn't think it would take so long."

In the morning, Herb Williams took the Smith family to the bank, where they exchanged their British coins for U.S. bank notes. When the teller at the window offered Johnny paper money for his British coins, he objected. Herb reassured him that the paper money was of equal value, but Johnny shook his head with skepticism and accepted it hesitantly.

From there Herb walked the two miles with them to the railroad station, where they were able to purchase tickets to Gilmore, Maryland, where Herb's brother worked. That left them with only a few bank notes and even fewer coins, part of which they spent on apples and bread for the long train ride. Herb insisted that there would be work in Gilmore, and that his brother would help them find it. Facing the train ride with only faith that there would be work at the end of it, they climbed onboard and waved their thanks to Herb. "Please tell Elder Stephens where we are going," Johnny called from the open window of the train car. Herb nodded his assent.

They arrived at Gilmore in the late afternoon. After getting off the train, Johnny asked the first man they met where they could meet the coal master so he could apply for work.

"Coal master, you say?" was the response. "I think you mean the mine foreman. He's up at the tipple, but I doubt he's hiring right now, as a large bunch of African slaves were brought in just a few days ago. If you want work, get back on that train before it leaves and go on to Lonaconing. They're hiring there at the Eckhart Company Mine."

"How far is it to Lonaconing?" Johnny asked.

"Oh, about an hour and a half, I reckon. Not more."

Following the advice of the man, they got back on the train. When the conductor had been paid for the tickets, Johnny was not sure how much money he had left, as he did not understand the conversion from British pounds to American dollars, but he knew it was not very much.

When they arrived in Lonaconing, the sun was low in the west, about to dip behind a mountain crest. It was a small community, lying in a long valley between two mountain ridges. They were the only people to get off the train. "Johnny, what will we do?" Helen's voice was filled with worry.

"We start asking people or knocking on doors 'til we find someone to help us," he answered. "But first, let's say a prayer." He put his arm around his wife's shoulders as she held Willie and said simply, "Dear Lord, night is coming on and we need shelter and work. Please help us." With that, they walked to the ticket window in the little station, where a tall, blond young man about Johnny's age was beginning to close up for the night.

"Sir, can ye tell us where we can go to find work in the mine, or where we can find a place to stay 'til we can get a position?"

The man stopped what he was doing and looked them over thoroughly. "I can tell from your speech that you are new in the country."

"Aye, we got off the boat yesterday morning in Baltimore, and we are almost out of funds. We were told there would be work for a miner here."

After a short hesitation, the man put out his hand and said, "My name is Vic Hansen. I'm the stationmaster. What's your name?"

"I'm Johnny Smith from Scotland, and this is my wife, Helen, and our little Willie."

"I'll tell you what I'll do. Your speech reminds me of my wife's father, who was from Lanarkshire. He was as good a Scotsman as you'll ever find. You come with me, and we will take you in for the time being. My wife will enjoy hearing you talk since you sound so much like her father."

They walked about a half-mile to a two-story, white frame house. As he entered the front door, Vic Hansen called out, "Hope you're dressed, Della, as I have brought home some company."

A woman as short and dark as her husband was tall and blond came through the door from the kitchen, with a dishtowel in her hand. She patted a few loose curls of her dark hair into place and said, "Well, Victor, and who is this little family ye have brought home with ye?" The Scottish burr in her speech made Johnny and Helen feel at home immediately. "Sit down, sit down, and tell me all about yourselves."

While Johnny and Helen recounted their experiences of the previous few weeks, both Vic and Della listened. Then Della spoke. "So ye have come so far and have no place to lay your heads this night. We can't have such a thing happen to a nice Scottish family. Ye will stay here with us until we find ye a place of your own." She laid her hand on her husband's arm and added, "Victor will take ye to the tipple tomorrow and get ye a position in the mine if that be what ye want. Now ye must excuse me, so I can put on our supper."

As she left the room, Johnny asked embarrassedly, "Mr. Hansen, what's the tipple?"

"That's what we call the buildings where the coal is washed, cleaned, weighed, and loaded into railcars to be taken to the iron furnaces or to the barges on the Potomac. The foreman has an office there. Tomorrow morning, we will go find someone who can hire you."

After a pleasant supper with the Hansens, Johnny and Helen tried to express their gratitude for the kindness shown them, but both of the Hansens seemed to feel that it was no more than anyone else would have done.

Early in the morning, Johnny accompanied Vic Hansen to the tipple, which was about a mile from the Hansen home. It was about two hundred feet up the mountainside near the mine opening, reached by a road that zigzagged up the mountain. They found the foreman's office, and Vic put his head in the doorway. "Mr. Sacksby, I've got a good man for you here. He has mining experience and can go to work right away."

The mine manager looked up from a cluttered desk and said, "Bring him in." He pointed at two straight-backed chairs, and they sat down. "Since you're the station master, what makes you a good judge of miners?" Johnny was not sure whether the mine manager was joking or not.

"I know he will do well for you here, because he's a Scotsman, like my father-in-law was."

"On your word, then, I'll give him a try."

With that, Vic Hansen put out his hand and shook the mine manager's hand vigorously. Then he added, "He has a wife and a child, so he needs a small cottage right away. Do you have an empty one they can rent?"

"Yeah, I've got the one your wife's father used until his death. It still has the furniture in it. That ought to do."

With that, Johnny's new friend left the office. He turned and grinned just before he closed the door, and said, "For supper, come back to our place tonight."

"Well, what do we call you?" the mine manager asked.

"Smith. My friends call me Johnny Smith."

And thus, a new life in a new country at an old job began for Johnny. At the end of the first week of working in Lonaconing, he brought his pay home, and he and Helen asked Della to explain its value. Della explained that the pay was more than the sixteen Scots shillings Johnny had been earning in Scotland each week. "Ye are making a bit more than ye would in Scotland, maybe four or five shillings more."

Helen looked up into Johnny's face and smiled broadly. "Husband, we did right to come to America."

"Aye, indeed we did."

CHAPTER 37
The PEF

Robert returned the money his landlady and his employer had loaned him and again took up his work at the print shop. After the new year arrived, Elder Franklin Richards addressed the Edinburgh Saints and told them of the establishment of the Perpetual Emigration Fund: "There will not be funds enough to take every Church member to America immediately, but each person may apply for assistance from the fund, and as it increases, selection will be made based upon the usefulness of the occupation of the head of the family in building up Zion in the Valley and the length of membership in the Church."

The meeting ended at that point as the excitement of those in attendance increased. Elder Richards stopped Robert as he was leaving the meeting and said quietly, "Robbie, I did not see your name on the list of folks who have signed up for help from the PEF. I want you to put your name on the list. We need men like you in the Valley."

* * *

In the fall, after a Sabbath meeting had ended, a printed handbill sent by the Church agent in Liverpool was passed out, listing the names of those who had been accepted as participants by the Fund for the next voyage to New Orleans. When the list was read aloud by the elder conducting the meeting, Robert heard his name.

When she heard the news, Mrs. McEwen asked, "When will ye be leaving?" Her voice was quiet.

"In January," he responded.

* * *

A week before the date for departure, as they sat and ate supper in the landlady's kitchen, Robert said quietly, "I have something that I must do. I have thought much about it, and I must do it." With no more explanation, he said to Mrs. McEwen, "I would be in your debt if ye could fix me some oatcakes or something to eat that I can carry in the morning, as I will have a long walk ahead of me."

"Of course, laddie; I will be glad to do it." Robert would say no more about his self-appointed errand.

In the morning as he stepped out of the cottage door, he folded the collar of his jacket up and pulled his cap down to protect his ears from the cold. Then he examined the coins he had in his pocket. He counted two pounds and five shillings and hoped fervently that it would be enough. The balance of the money in the jar under the bed was for the trip. He stuffed his pockets with the pieces of bread, cheese, and the oatcakes Mrs. McEwen gave him. With that, he left her warm kitchen with the words, "Keep me in your prayers, Mrs. McEwen."

As his figure disappeared down the street, she said quietly to her dead husband as she stood in the doorway, "Oh, William, if he is going where I think he is going, he needs our prayers. It has been a long time. He does not know what he will find."

Robert walked all day in the chill air, and he longed for a warmer coat. He steadily retraced the steps he had taken so many years earlier as he made his way back toward Penston Grange. When he arrived in the village, it was early evening. He had eaten the food Mrs. McEwen had sent with him, and he was hungry, tired, and anxious.

He found a boardinghouse in the village and knocked. When the landlady opened the door, he asked, "Do ye have room for one more boarder this evening?"

She nodded and opened the door wide so he could step in. As he sat down at her kitchen table to eat, he asked tiredly, "What day of the week is it?"

She looked at him strangely, and answered, "Today is Saturday. Tomorrow is the Sabbath. 'Tis strange ye don't know that."

He responded, "I have been traveling a long way, and 'tis easy to lose track of the days."

As he had hoped, she pursued the matter and asked, "Where ye been traveling and what brings ye here?"

"I come to Penston to talk to the laird of the mines here or at least to speak with the coal master, to see if he might be interested in the installation of a waterwheel to pump the water out of the mines." Robert fervently hoped that he would be forgiven for his stretching of the truth. He continued, "Do ye know the laird or the coal master here in Penston?"

"Well, I don't know the laird, but I can tell ye a little about the coal master. His name is McBride, and if ye want to see him tomorrow, on the Sabbath, ye might attend church services. He's always there, sitting by the laird."

"And when are church services?" Robert asked.

"Morning meeting begins at ten and usually lasts two hours. I am sure ye could meet the laird there too, if Mr. McBride wants to give ye an introduction."

"I thank ye, ma'am, for that information. Now, if it is possible, could ye show me to my room so I can rest, and would ye wake me by eight in the morning?"

When she showed him to his room, Robert took off his coat, shoes, and pants and laid them across the foot of the bed. Then he slid under the blanket and was asleep almost immediately. In the morning, the landlady knocked on the door at eight and said, "Breakfast is ready, sir."

After he had dressed and eaten, he excused himself and said he would take a brisk walk around the village before church services. He paid her the ten pence she asked for.

"Will ye be spending the night again?" she asked.

"I think not," he answered. With that, he put on his cap and stepped out of the doorway.

He walked casually around the village and then made his way down the cart path he remembered well, toward the cluster of miners' cottages. He made his way as unobtrusively as he could past the cottages and toward the buildings that contained the offices and coal-processing equipment for the mines. On the far side, he could see the two-storied, stone cottage that belonged to the coal master. He stood in the shadow of the equipment shed, choosing a position where he could see the house. Despite the cold, his palms were sweaty with nervousness. He waited for what he thought was about an hour before seeing McBride come around from the back of the building driving a dogcart pulled by one of the big draft horses used in the gin. He watched as the trap with its solitary figure made its way along the cart path to the village.

Suddenly Robert was immersed in memories. In his mind he could see the smiling and laughing face of Victoria Keith, whose father's big house was just over the hill, but it was quickly pushed aside by the memory of the long, humiliating walk behind the dogcart as he was forcibly dragged back to the mine to be put in shackles. Washing over him like a great wave he could not escape was the memory of the horror he had felt when the carriage of Sir Isaac had run down the little group in the street in Edinburgh.

He shook his head, wiped perspiration from his forehead with the back of his hand, and decided it was time to do what he had come to do. He tried to walk with confidence, as if he had business where he was going. When he arrived at the front path that led to the coal master's house, he could see no movement inside the house, only a thin trail of smoke from the chimney in the kitchen, so he made his way around to the back. There was a stable made of the same stone as that from which the house was made, with the double door standing open. Inside was the other draft horse used at the gin. Entering, he looked around and found what he was looking for—a bag of oats. He took a handful and offered it to the horse. The animal snorted and gladly took the offered grain. Robert patted its neck and spoke quietly to it, until it ceased to show any nervousness.

He found a bridle hanging on a nail on the wall. He had never put one on a horse, but he had seen it done when he had watched the horses changed at the gin. He offered another handful of oats, and as the horse lifted its front lip to eat the grain, he slid the bit into its mouth. He said aloud, "Nice old horse; see, that was nae so hard." He fitted the bridle over its ears and patted it again.

He left the stable and walked around to the front door of the large house. He knocked hard. No one answered, and his heart skipped a beat. He knocked again, harder, and listened for some sound. After a few moments, the door was opened by the house-keeper.

"I seek the master of the house. Is he at home?" Robert asked respectfully.

"Nae, he is at church services," she said flatly.

"When will he be home?" he continued.

"And what business would that be of yours?" she responded belligerently.

With that, Robert pushed his way past her and asked, "The lady of the house is home?" He stepped into the sitting room and looked around the room.

"And what is that to ye? Ye got no right being here. The master won't like it."

"Well, I have come to see the master, and since he is elsewhere, I need to see the lady of the house."

She started to push him out through the open doorway, saying, "The lady of the house never sees nobody. Now be on your way."

Robert stepped past her and took the stairs to the second level two at a time. He called out, "Janet, Janet, it's Robbie. Are ye here? It's Robbie."

The housekeeper started laboriously up the stairs, insisting, "Ye must leave right now." Instead, he started down the hallway on the second floor, opening each door as he came to it. There were bedrooms, a sitting room, and one room appeared to be a child's nursery, unused.

He continued to call out, "Janet, Janet, are ye here?" As he neared the door at the end of the hall, it began to open slowly. Robert stopped. Looking at the woman standing there, he recognized her as his sister. "Janet, don't ye know me? It's Robbie."

With that, she threw the door open with a force that made it thud against the wall, and rushed to him. "Robbie, I can't believe it's you. Oh, Robbie, it's good to see ye. Robbie, Robbie, Robbie." She leaned into his arms and held on so tight it hurt his shoulders. "It's been a long time. I though ye had forgotten about me."

Robert loosened her arms and stepped back. "Nae, Janet. None of us have forgotten ye." It was apparent that she was expecting a child. Old bruises showed green and yellow on her throat, and one large, red welt stood out on her forehead. Dark blue bruises left by a large hand were evident on her wrists.

By this time, the housekeeper had finally reached the top stair, panting with exertion, and leaned on the railing. She said between breaths, "I don't know who ye are, but the master will nae have strangers in the house. Now get out."

Ignoring the housekeeper, Robert said, "Janet, I've come to take ye away. Ye must come with me now. Get a cloak and bonnet and come with me."

"I can't go with ye, Robbie. I'm married to Mr. McBride. I am no longer a free woman."

"That is true enough. Ye are a prisoner, Janet, but now ye are coming with me. I will not have my sister beaten by anyone, not even her husband. Now let's get your cloak."

He hurried into the room she had come out of and found a woolen cloak and a bonnet in the wardrobe. He put the cloak around her shoulders and said, "Do ye have any money?"

"Nae, he sees that I never have any money. He has always been afraid that I might run away."

"Well, his fears are right. Ye are going away with me right now. Are ye willing?"

"Aye, but we will not get far before he finds us, and then he will drag ye back and give ye ten lashes, Robbie." Her face was white with fear.

"We will get away. The great God of heaven will help us." With that, he pulled her toward the stairs, and after the two of them descended, Robbie urged her into the kitchen and out the back door. While the housekeeper was laboriously making her way down the stairs, panting and wheezing, they hurried to the stable. There he pulled the horse nearer to the gate across the stable entrance and helped Janet step up onto the horizontal bars of the gate. She climbed to the second bar, and Robert helped her to turn and sit on the back of the old horse. He climbed onto its back behind her, and, pulling the reins, he turned it and gave it a kick to get it moving out of the stable. It did not want to hurry, so Robert gave it another kick in the flank.

The animal started to trot, and Janet said, "Oh, Robbie, I can't ride this way. Make it go faster or slower. I can't abide a trot."

Robert gave the old draft horse another kick in the flank, and it began to move more quickly. Its movement would never be described as a canter and certainly was not a gallop, but at least it was faster and not as jarring as a trot.

He spoke loudly in Janet's ear, "How long do ye think it will be before McBride comes home from church services?"

"Cook always has his dinner ready at two o'clock. He never comes before then."

"Good. That gives us more than three hours before he puts up the alarm."

"Robbie, ye have stolen a horse. He will try to get ye hanged for that."

"When we are near to Edinburgh, I will turn the animal loose, and it will probably find its way home in a day or two."

The old horse had slowed to a walk, but in less than three hours they were skirting Musselburgh, taking a southerly cart path to avoid being seen as much as possible. The old horse was tiring, so they paused near a small stream and a sheep fold with a low rock wall that Janet could use as steps to get on and off the horse. They allowed the horse to get a long drink and graze for a few minutes while Janet rested on the wall.

After about ten minutes, Robert said, "Janet, let me help ye get back on the old beast so we can be on our way again."

For the next half hour, Robert allowed the horse to walk while they rode slowly west between the sheep pastures in silence. Finally he spoke. "About three miles from here, there's the cottage of a crofter by the name of Bert McOrmie who was baptized a year ago. We should be able to rest there for the day and let the horse go. From there, we will only have a few miles left to go, and we will walk that after it gets dark. Can ye walk that far in the cold?"

"I think so. Robbie, where are we going?"

"To the boardinghouse of a good woman in Edinburgh who will help us. I've lived with her since I ran away from the mines. She's been a second mother to me."

When Robert reached the crofter's cottage, they were welcomed by Mrs. McOrmie. She clucked her tongue when she saw Janet's condition. As Robert turned the horse loose and slapped it on the rump, she said to her, "Ye come right in here and lie down on the bed and rest 'til I can get ye something to eat. Ye must be exhausted." Janet smiled wanly and thanked her.

Robert sat down in the warm kitchen, and as Mrs. McOrmie prepared the cooked cabbage, turnips, and beets, he said, "I hope I have nae put ye and your husband in danger. There are some folks seeking us that be nae afraid to use the law against us."

"Ye say the lady is your sister?" Mrs. McOrmie asked. Then without waiting for an answer, she continued, "I am nae so blind as to overlook the bruises on her neck and wrists. She's been ill used, and ye will have my sympathy and help, and that of my husband in keeping her from him that has been using her that way." She looked up from slicing a beet and asked, "What is it that ye need from us?"

"A place to rest until it is dark enough for us to start the walk to Edinburgh. There we have friends who will help us."

"We will not hear of ye walking to Edinburgh. My good man, Bert, will drive ye in the wagon. 'Tis too far for a woman in your sister's condition to be walking."

When Bert came in from the field, Robert awakened Janet, and the four of them sat at the kitchen table to eat. Mrs. McOrmie asked Janet, "When is your time?"

Janet smiled tiredly and said, "The village doctor said it would be early in April, but I fear that this one will be like the others and come too soon."

Robert looked at her and asked, "There were others?"

"Aye, two others, two lassies. Both are buried in the churchyard in Penston Grange."

"Do ye know why ye lost them?" Mrs. McOrmie asked sympathetically.

Janet was silent for a long moment. Then she took a big breath and said, "I believe that each one be hurt beyond help by Mr. McBride when he hit me."

Mrs. McOrmie put her hand over her mouth in horror and then said, as she lowered it, "What kind of man strikes a woman with child?"

Janet answered with a sad little smile, "The kind of man who drinks too much."

Robert said quietly almost under his breath, "He is a lucky man that I never knew, as I would have waited to strike him down when he came home."

Janet put her hand over her brother's and said, "Robbie, nae, ye must never feel so much hate. 'Tis a heavy burden. I chose my own bed. 'Marry in haste, repent at leisure.'" She quoted the old proverb sadly. Then she sat up more straightly and, smiling, asked Mrs. McOrmie, "Do ye have a family?"

Glad to have a change of subject, Mrs. McOrmie answered warmly, "Aye, we have two grown lads with bairns of their own and a lassie expecting her first any day now. All tolled, we have five grandchildren, soon to be six, and what a joy they are to us in our old age."

After the meal, Janet rested until dark, and then Mr. McOrmie hitched his horse up to the wagon, and Mrs. McOrmie put a quilt over a thick layer of hay so Janet could lie down as they traveled over the rutted cart path. They arrived in Edinburgh before midnight and thanked the good farmer for his help. He looked at Robert and said, as they shook hands, "I sure wish ye would stop by and visit awhile when ye are out our way, as it has been a year since we seen ye." Then he winked and added, "And that's what I'll tell anybody who asks." Then he turned the wagon around and started back to his farm in the moonlight.

Robert took Janet's hand and led her through the narrow streets to the familiar boardinghouse and knocked firmly on the kitchen door. After about five minutes, a light could be seen as a candle brightened the kitchen. The top of the divided door opened, and, holding up her candlestick, Mrs. McEwen could see Robert and his guest.

"Come in, Robbie, come in. I see ye have brought me a guest, and if I be a good guesser, I think this must be your sister. Ye share the same eyes. Come in out of the cold." With that, she opened the lower portion of the door and welcomed them into the still-warm kitchen where they could sit by the remnant of the fire in the fireplace.

CHAPTER 38
Lonaconing

"There are nae lassies in the mine, none at all. And the lads are at least twelve years old. I like that," Johnny told Helen with enthusiasm after his second week in the mine.

Johnny brought home more money each week than he had in Scotland, but many of the things at the company store were more costly, so as the time passed only a little could be saved toward the completion of the journey to the Valley. At times, Helen grew discouraged. "Johnny, I think no one knows we are here—and maybe no one cares."

Then her husband would gently remind her, "We have come to America, and we have a strong, healthy lad who will never work in the mines of Scotland. We must be grateful—and patient." Then she would smile again.

In the fall, when Johnny had been in the mines a little more than a year, a pair of men in black suits and worn shoes, dusty from walking, came into the village. They stopped at the train station and asked Vic Hansen if he knew John Smith and his wife. He smiled, and said, "I do, indeed I do, and they are good friends. What is your business with them?"

Both men shook Vic's hand, and one said, "We are missionaries on our way to England to preach the new and everlasting gospel of Jesus Christ, but we have been asked to locate John Smith and his family. It was reported to the leaders of our Church that they had immigrated to this country from Scotland and had found work in the mines in this area. We have been seeking them for some days."

"Well, your search is over. Step out here on the platform, and I will point you to their house." Vic Hansen led them to the edge of the train station boardwalk and pointed up the rutted and dusty street.

Both visitors tipped their hats and started up the road. When Helen opened the door, she cried excitedly, "Oh, ye are missionaries! Come in, come in. We feared that no one from the Valley knew we were here." She pointed at the two straight-backed chairs in the little sitting room and said, "Johnny is on his way home, I'm sure. Please join us for supper. Tell us how ye found us here."

The sun was beginning to set behind the hills to the west where the maples and oaks were aflame with autumn colors. When the meal was ended, Helen excused herself to clear the table, and the three men sat and discussed the difficulties the young couple had faced on their journey from Scotland.

As Helen began to wash the dishes, one of the elders told Johnny, "The main reason we have come this long way to find you is to tell you that there will soon be help for you and your family to go west to the Valley. We do not have sufficient funds with us, but now that we have found you, we will send a letter back to Salt Lake City, and the next pair of elders to come this way may be able to bring enough funds to aid you in your journey west."

Johnny called out to Helen, "Wife, do ye hear what the elders are saying? They came to tell us that we can soon go to the Valley to join the Saints in Zion."

Helen came to the kitchen doorway and, beaming, said, "Aye, I am listening to everything they are saying. I'm so glad to hear it."

One of the elders explained further, "This will only be a loan, and when you are settled in the Valley, you will be expected to repay it to the Perpetual Emigration Fund so others can be helped in a like manner." He continued, "You will have to take a steamboat down the Ohio River to St. Louis, and then you will need to travel up the Missouri River to Kanesville, Iowa. From there you will join a wagon train to go the rest of the way."

In the morning, the elders began to seek out anyone interested in hearing the message of the gospel by knocking on each door in the little community. Their reception was usually cool and occasionally hostile.

A few weeks after the elders had left for England, the priest from the Orthodox Church in the community came to the Smith cottage to tell Helen and Johnny that they were damned for being part of the "Mormon" Church, and he warned them both that the only way to save their souls was to renounce their religion.

"Why are you so full of hate for a religion that preaches faith in Christ and repentance and good works?" Johnny asked respectfully when the words of the priest had begun to slow down. The priest sputtered in anger and finally turned and stomped away.

The priest repeatedly spoke against "Mormonism" from the pulpit in his homilies, and by the turn of the year, many of the people in the little community would cross the street to avoid speaking with Helen when she walked to or from the company store.

As he entered the kitchen one evening with a cut on his chin and an eye swollen shut, Johnny said, "I think the time is coming when some of the men in the mine will see that I lose my position. Let us pray that the help from the elders comes before I have no more work. There are some very angry people here in Lonaconing because of our faith."

Then he said quietly, almost to himself, "In this great country where we believed that we would be free to practice our religion, 'tis strange to find the same unbending hard-heartedness toward our faith that we faced in Scotland."

CHAPTER 39
Freedom for Janet

Mrs. McEwen made a late supper for Robert and Janet. The solicitous landlady fed them some porridge, fresh buttered bread, and milk. In the morning, at breakfast, Mrs. McEwen fussed over Janet. "Ye poor dear, 'tis plain to see that ye have been ill used. 'Tis a good thing your brother went to get ye to take ye away from that vile man."

The landlady would not hear of Janet staying alone. She said, "We know she can't be seen in public, and 'tis not safe for her to be alone even here, not with an evil man seeking to drag her back to a life of ill use. I'll not hear of it." Robert went to church services by himself.

After the meeting in the Carpenters Hall, Robert spoke at length with President Edward Martin, who had recently been called to serve as the president of the Glasgow conference of the Church. He had come from Paisley to address the Saints and make a final count of those who were prepared to take passage on the *Kennebec.*

"Those of you sailing on the *Kennebec* are to travel to Glasgow by January eighth and be prepared to take the steamship *Loch Lomond* from Glasgow to Liverpool with the other Saints by January ninth," he explained. "The tickets for the boat have been purchased through the Perpetual Emigration Fund, as have the steerage tickets for the voyage on the *Kennebec.* The ship is scheduled to depart on January tenth. I warn those planning on the trip that arriving in Liverpool any earlier than the ninth will require that you rent rooms in that city near the docks, which would be costly, of poor quality, and poorer safety. To arrive any later may possibly cost you a place on the ship."

When Robert arrived back at Mrs. McEwen's boardinghouse, he shared the instructions with the landlady. She tried hard to smile but finally said with a quivering voice, "Oh, Robbie, when ye go it will be like losing my little Willie all over again. Ye have been a son to me for these few years." With that, she turned her back and put her hand over her trembling lips.

"Mrs. McEwen, 'tis time for ye to make plans to go to America. If ye sell the boardinghouse, ye will be well provided for, and ye can join us in the Valley," he responded.

She shook her head and said, "For the time being, my boarding-house is a friendly way station for Saints making the journey. Even with ye gone, there will be others who will make their way here on their journey to America. Ye must know that this is my part in the gathering of the Saints."

During the remaining week, clothes were mended and a few replaced. Another quilt was made for Janet's use on the voyage. Mrs. McEwen went to her closet and took the last of the dresses she had been too blessed to fit into for the last several years and remade it for Janet. Additionally, she gave Janet a long roll of soft muslin to make nappies for her new baby, which would be born during the voyage.

"Are ye nervous about this voyage?" the landlady asked her.

Janet answered, "Nae. No matter what the future holds, I am grateful that I have left a house of hurt and anger to be with my brother."

On January seventh, Robert gave his farewell to Walter McEwen and wished him well. "Ye have nae been anything but kind to me in the years I've worked for ye. May God bless ye in times to come, and soften your heart so ye may recognize truth when ye hear it—or print it." With that, they both laughed and shook hands.

As Robert walked back toward the boardinghouse through the familiar streets, he looked at everything as if to seal it in his memory—

the buildings, the people, the shops, and stalls. He murmured to himself, "Since I arrived in this city it has become my home. Now it is time to prepare to find a new home." With that, he shook off his melancholy and started to walk with long, determined strides toward the future.

As they ate supper the evening before they were to leave, Janet shared her concern with the landlady and her brother. "Mr. McBride will stop at nothing to get back what he believes to be his," Janet told the others. "I fear that he will have the canal, the train stations, and the docks in Glasgow and in Liverpool watched. What will we do? How will ye get me onto the barge on the canal without anyone recognizing me?"

Mrs. McEwen expressed her solution. She said, "Ye will wear the dress I made over for ye, and ye will put your golden hair up in one of my bonnets so as to hide it. Ye will take Robbie's arm, and if ye are asked, ye are his wife."

Robert said, "I think Mrs. McEwen is wise. We will follow her advice." Then he said, "I also think a name change would be a good idea, at least until we are on the ship. What name would ye like for the journey?"

"I think I would like to be Agnes, like the little sister we lost so long ago," Janet said quietly.

In the morning, both of them put all of their belongings, which had been bundled in their quilts, into a rented wagon, and before they climbed in for the ride to the Union Canal, Robert and Janet both gave Mrs. McEwen a hug. Robert then took her hand and said, "Ye have been like a mother to me for these past years, and I will miss ye—and your cooking—as much as any son could." With that he gave her a little kiss on her cheek where her tears wet his lips.

As she waved to them, she called out, "May we all meet again, if not in this life, in the one to follow." Robert waved his cap as a farewell as they started down the rutted road. Then they settled in their seats to watch the city pass by. Only Robert guessed the loneliness the little landlady would feel as she returned to her empty kitchen.

CHAPTER 40
Escape

When the wagon reached the canal, Robert and Janet discovered that they would have to wait for an hour before the barge arrived. Other members of the group of emigrating Saints began to arrive, and soon the crowd swelled to thirty. Robert noticed a rough-looking man slouching in the shadows of the canal office, watching them closely. As Robert helped Janet from the wagon, he said loudly enough to be heard by the man, "Agnes, do take care. Take good hold of my hand."

After the barge arrived, they waited impatiently to climb aboard, as the man in the shadows had begun to show too much interest in Janet. When he neared her, she began to sneeze, holding a kerchief to her face. Robert asked consolingly, "My dear Agnes, are ye coming down with a fever or the ague? 'Tis a long journey, and ye need to be well."

Robert guided her through the crowd while Janet continued sneezing and coughing into a kerchief that almost covered her face. The watcher appeared frustrated in his plans. When the signal to board was given, Robert took her up the gangplank first.

When the barge arrived in Glasgow, the darkness had arrived as well, but five hired wagons waited for the Saints who disembarked from the barge. Each family piled their belongings into one of the wagons, filling them almost to overflowing. The children climbed into the back and found a place to ride on the bundles. When the wagons stopped in front of a rented hall, the driver of the first wagon called out, "Everybody out. Get your belongings. Ye will be staying here tonight."

There they were greeted by Edward Martin, who invited them into the large hall lit by a few kerosene lanterns, which cast flickering shadows. Lining the walls were wooden, straight-backed chairs and benches where at least thirty other people were already making their temporary camp, grouped as families. "You will have to make do here tonight, and in the morning the wagons will return and take you all to the dock to meet the steamship. Be ready by eight o'clock in the morning. There will soon be someone here with bread and soup for your supper."

Robert grew solicitous of Janet, and as the members of the group tried to make themselves comfortable on the floor or the benches in the large room, he asked, "Janet, do ye think ye will be able to sleep on such a hard bench? Can I put my coat behind your head?"

Janet smiled and said, "I will sleep the sleep of a free woman, no matter the hardness of the bed."

In the morning, the wagons arrived, and after each person was given a piece of fresh bread and cheese for breakfast, the families loaded the wagons again and climbed in for the ride to the wharf, where they would board the steamship to Liverpool.

At the wharf, while the tickets were passed out by Edward Martin, Robert and Janet noticed another disreputable-looking man lounging in the shadows, watching everyone as they arrived. Janet quietly but fearfully said to Robert, "I know that man. He works for Mr. McBride."

The steamship was sitting at the pier, which jutted out into the River Clyde, while crewmen carried freight onboard. It was nearly four hundred feet long and at least fifty feet in the beam. The two great, black funnels were belching steam in preparation for starting the journey. After a few minutes, the captain pulled the chain on the whistle, and the belching steam and sound made the passengers jump and the small children cry with alarm. Robert pushed his way through the crowd and said, "I must get ye onboard. I will go onboard and ask the captain if we can come on before the others."

With that, Robert took her up the gangplank and onto the deck, passing under the rope that closed the deck off to the public. They walked around the boat until they found the captain. "As ye can see, my sister is with child and is feeling weak and ill. Can we put her on the boat right now so she can sit?"

The captain was silent for a minute and then said in a brisk English accent, "I should not make any special exceptions, but my wife is expecting shortly, and I can sympathize with your sister."

He led Janet to the upper deck and forward to the large, inside passenger cabin, where those on the wharf would have difficulty seeing her. The crowd had to wait for another thirty minutes, but the captain finally stepped onto the gangplank and, facing the crowd, called out, "All can board now. Please make your way courteously onto the boat."

The captain permitted Janet and Robert to remain there in the inside cabin, which was one large room with water- and salt-stained windows on three sides and hard, wooden benches inside, facing the bow of the boat. The windows were closed, and the cabin was stuffy. As the boat began to move away from the pier, the motion of the current and the waves made Janet grow pale and bite her lower lip. To make matters worse, one of the men sitting in the cabin lit a cigar.

After a few minutes of trying to tolerate the cigar smoke, Janet begged Robert, "Oh, I am going to be sick. Please ask the gentleman to put out his cigar."

Robert stood, and, walking unsteadily as the boat moved over the water, he slowly made his way to the man with the cigar. He said, "Sir, I regret to tell ye that your cigar smoke is making the lady sick. Would ye please put it out?"

The man looked up at him and answered rudely, "If the lady does not like the smell of a good cigar, perhaps she can find a seat somewhere else."

Robert said again firmly, "Ye have been asked nicely to put out the cigar, as it is making the lady sick. If ye choose not to, then I will help ye off this ship, and ye can swim to Liverpool. If ye don't like that choice, ye can move out onto the open deck." The man rose and with a surly expression moved through the door and out onto the deck.

The trip on the steamship took twenty-four hours, and some passengers were mildly seasick by the time the vessel reached the mouth of the River Clyde, but the motion of the water made Janet severely ill. When they got off the boat in Liverpool, she begged for something cool to drink and a place to lie down, but the wagons that were to take them to the Bramley-Moore Dock were waiting. She tried to make herself comfortable on the baggage in the back of the wagon.

When she was finally settled in the wagon, the driver drove to the *Kennebec's* berth at the dock. As the emigrants climbed out of the wagons, President Franklin Richards arrived in a carriage and shook the hand of every man and tipped his hat to each woman.

He spoke to those in the wagons or waiting to unload their belongings, saying, "The captain has said that you can board at eight bells this evening, so you will have to wait until then. I regret the delay, but the captain appears to be inflexible in his decision." A collective groan arose from each group as he spoke with them. "I suggest that you unload your belongings there on the pier and appoint two or three strong men to watch them. The rest of you can wait with them there or you may explore the docks, but if you choose to do that, be careful of the pickpockets."

Robert and a man by the name of Ralph Rowley were appointed to stay with the emigrants' belongings. Most of the women, including Janet, chose to find a place on a box or a bundle to sit, wrapping their cloaks around them against the cold.

"Hold on to your tickets as there is no other way that you can board the boat," Elder John Higbee said loudly as he gave each person a steerage ticket. Elder Higbee had been assigned to act as president of the group on the voyage.

As nearly two hundred and fifty passengers milled about, seeking established friends and making new acquaintances, Robert took note of a rough-looking man who stood near the gangplank of the ship berthed nearest the *Kennebec*.

"See that ruffian watching us? Do ye think he holds ill motives toward the Saints?" Robert leaned toward Elder Higbee as he spoke and nodded in the direction of the man in question.

Elder Higbee said, "We will find out." With that, he approached the man.

When the coarsely dressed man was approached and asked his intentions, he exploded in abusive language and threatened to strike Higbee. He ended his tirade by saying, "My business is none of yours. I came here because it is well-known that ye Mormonites be quick to steal young girls and women. In fact, I come to take back a married woman that a Mormon elder stole from Penston Grange."

Elder Higbee, looking shocked, turned around and walked back to the group waiting to board the ship. He said to Robert, "Do you know anything of what this man says?"

Robert answered, "I know there are no women in our group here against their will, but I need to speak more with ye about the matter. Can we step away from the group?"

When the two men had finally made their way across the street filled with carts, wagons, and peddlers, Robert began. "I think my sister is the woman that man says was stolen from Penston. Her husband is a vile, harsh, drinking man who has beaten her 'til she had to bury two stillborn bairns. When I found her, she was covered with bruises, and her third unborn bairn be threatened by his temper. He is so violent that her arm has been broken more than once, and she fears for her life. Surely we can't send her back to such a man."

Elder Higbee said, "I must meet your sister." The two men made their way back across the street and through the crowd until they arrived at the pile of bundles and boxes waiting to be put onboard. Janet was nervously sitting there, waiting to board.

Robert introduced his sister and said to her, "Elder Higbee will be leading our group on the voyage, and he wants to speak with ye."

Elder Higbee looked at Janet closely and said, "I have been told by your brother that you desire to leave your husband and travel with the Saints to America. Is this true?"

Janet only nodded, white-faced and worried.

"Your brother tells me that you have been ill-used by your husband. Is that true?"

Finding her voice, she answered quietly, "Aye, I've been ill-used from the very day I married the man and have buried two stillborn bairns because of it." With that, she undid the buttons at the wrists of both sleeves on her dress and pushed the sleeves up to her elbows. Her arms were covered in bruises of several colors, in different stages of healing. Just below her right elbow was the scar of a large, badly healed burn. Pointing to it, she said, "That he did one night while he was drunk. In the morning he said I fell into the fireplace."

Elder Higbee's face grew grave, and the muscles in his jaw hardened. She continued as she took off her bonnet and shook her hair out, "There are many other scars that I can't show ye, but ye can see this." With that, she bent at the waist and threw her long hair over her head. There, those standing close could see several bald patches, where the hair had been pulled out at the roots.

Elder Higbee's face softened, and he said, "It is obvious that you have been ill-used, and no husband has the moral right to treat a wife in such a manner. Since you go of your own free will, you are welcome to travel with us to Zion."

At that, she leaned her cheek against his shirt front and said, "May God bless ye for your charity." Then she tucked her long hair back into the bonnet and put it on her head again.

Elder Higbee bowed to her, turned, and walked up the gang-plank. He spoke to the sailor standing guard there, and with a nod was permitted to pass. After about ten minutes, he returned to the group, and climbed onto a barrel that stood with the other bundles and boxes, and motioned for the group of passengers to gather around him. He spoke loudly, "I have spoken to the captain, and, calling upon his charitable feelings, I have convinced him that the women and children should be permitted to board immediately with their belongings. He has asked that they remain in the steerage area for the rest of the day, to keep them out of the way of the crew as they prepare the boat for sailing. At eight bells, the men of the company may board." A cheer went up from the group.

As the women sorted through the pile of bundles and boxes to locate their own things to take onboard, Janet was escorted toward the gangplank by her brother. As she started up the gangplank, the roughly dressed watcher pushed his way through the crowd and tried to grab her by the arm.

As she turned to see who was reaching for her, he yelled, "Ye will be coming with me. The coal master claims ye as his wife."

Robert stepped between him and his sister and said, "Hurry! Get aboard."

She hurried up the gangplank. Brother Ralph Rowley, who had been watching, rushed to assist Robert. As the man tried to force his way onto the ship, Robert threw himself at him, dropping him in a heap. As the two men struggled, Brother Rowley took hold of the man, and with the help of Robert, they lifted him above their heads and threw him into the water. He thrashed about in the water, yelling curses.

For the rest of the evening, the men and boys among the passengers stood guard and prevented anyone who was not a crew member or a passenger from boarding the boat. By eight bells, another two hundred passengers, largely latecomers of all genders and ages, boarded the ship along with the men who had been standing guard.

CHAPTER 41
The Kennebec

After a steam tug pulled the *Kennebec* from the dock out into the Mersey River, the ship remained anchored there for the night, along with a variety of other ships, all with sails furled. On the morning of January tenth, the tug returned, and while the passengers stood on the deck, it towed the ship into the Irish Sea. The passengers, who had gathered to watch, marveled at the sight of sails filling with the wind as the shore of England slipped away. There were three hundred and thirty-three Saints onboard and another one hundred and twenty-five Irish passengers. Additionally, there were nearly fifty crewmen on the *Kennebec*.

When supplies purchased by the Perpetual Emigration Fund were distributed, the English passengers expressed dissatisfaction with the oatmeal they were given, and the Scots found the pork unfamiliar, so an exchange was made, which made both groups happier.

During the first day at sea, Elder Higbee stood on a barrel on the upper deck and organized the Saints into four wards, appointing an elder over each. Robert was appointed to preside over the Second Ward. "Worship services will be held twice on Sunday and twice during the week. Each morning, the quarters are to be cleaned, and school classes for the children will be established," Elder Higbee announced. He continued, "Despite the cold wind, each of you is urged to wrap up warmly and take a brisk walk about the deck each day, for the sake of health."

When the wind and spray were too cold to tolerate on deck, the Saints would gather in the steerage compartment by wards, and as the small children quietly played near the feet of their parents, the adults and older children were given the opportunity to hear from those who were willing to talk of their conversions to the gospel of Jesus Christ and of their missionary travels.

Robert's remarks were always greeted by applause when he finished his stories by saying, "And then Elder Leishman and I rose from our bed in the haystack and ran like the wind—and the vegetables the crofters threw at us made for a good dinner that day."

A storm came up swiftly and tossed the vessel about until even a few of the crewmen were too sick to keep to their feet and took refuge in their quarters. After the first fifteen hours of the storm had passed, the wind eased slightly, but the heavy seas kept all but the heartiest passengers in their berths. A few rose to find a pot or a pan. Even after stomachs were empty, the passengers held the containers closely, as if they were precious.

To add to their discomfort, one of the Irish women repeatedly insisted, "This ship will surely sink. Just listen to the creaking and groaning of the timbers. I know we will die in the depths of the sea."

One of the men answered her in a groan, "Death would be a kindness to us now."

After nearly three days of seasickness that left many extremely weak from dehydration, the seas calmed enough that the elders could make their way throughout the steerage area to check the condition of those in their care.

Samuel Lyons, a Presbyterian minister, went about telling anyone who was willing to listen that God was punishing those on the ship because they had tolerated the Mormons. "Not only have ye tolerated the Mormonites, but many of ye have joined with them in their worship services. We shall be lucky if He does not send us to the bottom of the sea with these accursed Mormonites!"

As if to prove him wrong, Robert asked all who could to kneel with him to ask God to calm the sea. "If the Savior could calm the

Sea of Galilee, then surely He will calm these waters," he said as he knelt to lead the prayer.

Within the hour the sea grew calm, and the ship made headway again with a fair wind in the sails. "I wish I had thought to seek divine help sooner," Robert earnestly whispered to Elder Higbee. "It might have saved us all much misery." With that, he smiled, but he meant what he said.

That evening at worship services, attendance of those who were not part of the group of Saints doubled. The Reverend Lyons sat sullenly, silently watching with folded arms and refusing to join the group. When approached by some who invited him to join with them, he replied, "'Tis a coincidence, a coincidence— that's all."

By evening of the third day, all aboard appeared to have regained their well-being, except Rebecca Allen, a young woman from England. She continued to be too ill to eat or drink or even stand.

Mary Ann Rowley, her friend, sought Robert out and asked him to come with her to give Sister Allen a blessing. "I fear that she cannot continue this ill without suffering extreme consequences," Sister Rowley said. "Please, give her a healing blessing," she pleaded.

A small group gathered around as Robert knelt at Rebecca's side where she lay on her berth. He recognized the young woman as he and Elder Higbee laid their hands on her head. He had taken notice of her on more than one occasion as the passengers had walked the deck in good weather. She had deep blue eyes and long, richly auburn hair. At times, he had heard her deep and throaty laugh reach him on the sea breeze. The few freckles on her cheeks stood out against her white skin, which presently was clammy and cold. She opened her eyes. Robert asked her, "Sister Allen, do you believe that through the holy priesthood which we hold that the Lord will heal ye?"

She weakly nodded her head. As Robert prayed, he asked that she be healed and that she be freed from the illness that had brought her down at that time. Further, he asked that she continue to be free of illness for the balance of the voyage. As he closed his prayer, she weakly smiled and asked for something to drink. Within a few minutes, she sat up and said, "I am very hungry now. Sister Rowley, would you be so kind as to boil some rice for me?"

Those who had gathered around the sick woman smiled, and many nodded. One man, not a member of the group of Saints, said quietly with satisfaction, "This ship is in no danger of sinking. That minister can be damned for all the attention anyone will pay him now."

Robert called upon Rebecca each day to see how she was feeling, and within a week they were taking a walk together each day on the deck. On one of their walks she explained, "I was living with my grandparents in Manchester after the death of my parents, but when I listened to the Mormon elders and was baptized, my grandfather sent me away. He said, 'We will have no Mormonites in this house.' I left with my hair still wet from my baptism. Mary Ann and Ralph Rowley took me in, and the three of us made plans to go to the Valley with the assistance of the Perpetual Emigration Fund."

By the time the *Kennebec* had been at sea for a month, the number of Saints had grown by twenty-five. The first mate, several crewmen, and eight of the Irish passengers were baptized in a large barrel of seawater. That evening two passengers removed their violins from their cases, and many of the passengers danced until midnight.

Janet had been quiet and withdrawn from the social activities of the group from the beginning of the voyage. When Robert commented on it, Rebecca told him, "I think maybe she's worried about what others think of a woman in her condition leaving her husband."

But the second Saturday in February, after the evening meal was finished, Janet came to Robert and said quietly, "I have nae felt the bairn move for nearly a week. I fear that this one be as dead as the others were before birth." She continued, her face gray with illness. "But with each of them, they came within one or two days of becoming so still."

Robert asked worriedly, "How are ye feeling in other ways?"

"I don't feel so good. I can't tell ye any more than that. I just don't feel so good."

Robert put his hand against her forehead. "Janet, ye are burning up. Why didn't ye say something sooner?"

"I didn't see that anything could be done about it."

"Ye must lie down. I will put some quilts on the berth, so it will not be so hard. Then Rebecca and I will put some cold cloths on your forehead."

By the time Robert had made Janet as comfortable as could be expected on the hard berth, Elder Higbee approached and asked, "What is the matter with your sister? She looks so pale."

Robert answered, "Go and find the ship's surgeon. I hear that there is one." By the time the doctor arrived, Janet's contractions had begun.

The men were pushed away by Rebecca and Sister Rowley, and another quilt was hung to give Janet more privacy. She lay still, whimpering with each contraction. Rebecca could do little but keep her brow cool with water and hold her hand.

The ship's surgeon admitted immediately that he had never delivered a baby. "You ladies know as much or more about this than I do. I just left a naval warship, and we never had any infants birthed on it."

After four hours of contractions, Janet opened her eyes and, looking at Rebecca, said weakly, "If the bairn lives, please raise him—or her—for me."

Rebecca grew alarmed and said, "Janet, ye are talking foolishness. Ye'll be fine. Ye will live to raise this child yourself."

With that, Janet shook her head slowly back and forth and said, "Nae, I think not." Then, with the next hard contraction and all the strength remaining in her weakened body, she pushed, and

Mary Ann Rowley wrapped the tiny, cold, very blue body of the infant in a clean cloth.

Rebecca stood and lifted the hanging quilt. She said in a frightened voice, "Robert, get Elder Higbee to come so you can give her a blessing. You mustn't let her die."

As soon as Robert returned with Elder Higbee, they stepped inside the quilted partition and laid their hands gently upon Janet's head, and Robert began to pray. He started to ask that she be healed, but stopped midsentence. After a lengthy pause, during which he struggled to regain his self-control, he started again, and through quiet tears, said, "The Lord wants to take ye home to Him, Janet. And in accordance with His will, we give ye permission to go and leave this mortal body. Though we want to keep ye here, we know that ye will go to a better place and to a loving God." His voice trailed off to a whisper. "As the Savior said, 'Be ye not afraid.'"

Then Robert stood, wiping his eyes with a kerchief. He stepped away from the berth. Mary Ann stepped forward and laid the small form in Janet's arms. She gave a weak smile, and, looking at the little, blue face, she asked in a whisper, "Is it a lad or a lassie?"

Mary Ann answered, "A laddie, my dear."

"Then his name is Robert, after my brother who came to save me," she said as she closed her eyes. Robert leaned over and gave her a kiss on the forehead. At that, the ship's bells rang, marking the midnight change of watch.

Robert and Rebecca spent the rest of the night alone with Janet's body, and in the early morning, at four bells, when the captain came with sailcloth for the shroud, he found that they had carefully wrapped a roll of muslin around her like a wide shawl, as she held her baby in cold arms.

He offered the help of the sail maker to make the shroud, but Robert told him, "We thank ye, but we will not be needing his help. This is something we must do." With clumsy fingers, Robert followed Rebecca's instructions as he sewed the shroud, wiping an occasional tear as he labored to push the needles through the stiff canvas.

"Do ye think that if I had nae gone back to get her, that maybe she would have lived?"

"Robert, do not blame yourself." Rebecca put her hand on Robert's and added, "God took her home. It was His decision." When it came time for Janet to be taken up the hatchway to the upper deck, Robert carried his sister as if she were a child, her cold arms holding her infant.

At six bells, an hour before the normal time for morning prayers, the passengers gathered for the short farewell service. Elder Higbee read from the Bible, "'But now is Christ risen from the dead, and become the first fruits of them that slept. For since by man came death, by man came also the resurrection of the dead. For as in Adam all die, even so in Christ shall all be made alive.'" He continued, "'Blessed are the dead, which die in the Lord from henceforth: Yea, saith the Spirit, that they may rest from their labours; and their works do follow them.'"

The two forms, wrapped as one in the white sailcloth, rested on the long plank that was supported on a sawhorse at one end and by the side rail of the main deck at the other. As Elder Higbee finished his remarks, the ship's bell began to toll. Robert and Ralph Rowley lifted the end of the plank off the sawhorse, and Janet and her babe slid quietly into the sea with nothing more than a small splash, and disappeared into the dark water. Elder Higbee concluded by saying, "We all await the day when the sea will give up its dead."

A unified "Amen" arose from the passengers.

Robert turned and stared out at the sea with unseeing eyes, saying nothing. In his mind he watched his sister, his childhood playmate, laughing and playing in the stream with Helen in Penston Grange, her golden hair streaming in the wind. Those memories were pushed away by the mental picture of her at eleven, dragging a heavily loaded slype through a mine tunnel. He remembered her as a sixteen-year-old, stooped and heavily loaded with a creel on her back, and lastly, he saw her big with child with bruises on her wrists, chin, and neck. After a few minutes, Robert said quietly to Rebecca, "It was good that she was here with us when it happened, and not with him. She would have wanted to be with us at the end."

CHAPTER 42
Deep Creek

Johnny had arrived home from the mine the first weekend of March with a black eye. "Today, on my way home from the pit, three miners stopped me and told me that I must give up my religion or leave the pit. I told them that my religion was nae business of anyone but me and mine, but they disagreed, and ye can see the result." He sat quietly while Helen got a cold, wet cloth. As she pressed it onto his eye he asked, "How much money do we have saved?"

Helen answered, "We have twenty-nine dollars and fifty cents saved, but we owe the company store about four dollars."

"We can't wait any longer for help from missionaries that may be passing this way. Do ye think we can get to St. Louis with what money we have?"

Helen answered, "I don't know, but I think we will have to try."

"Then we will work through Saturday evening, and after we get paid, we will pack our things and buy what we need from the company store. On Monday morning we will hire a wagon to take us to Westernport, and there we will hire a flatboat on Deep Creek and make our way to Parkersburg. From there we can get on a steamboat to St. Louis."

Helen's voice was full of worry. "But how long do ye think it could take us to get to St. Louis?"

"Maybe ten days or more," he answered. "I know that sounds like a long journey, but we have nae other plan."

The preparations were simple, as they had little to take. On Saturday and Sunday Helen baked biscuits and boiled two dozen eggs. She obtained a small wooden box from the store and packed the few remaining garden-grown squash and potatoes that she had been able to keep through the winter; she also added flour, sugar, oatmeal, salt, cornmeal, and molasses. Then she bundled their few belongings in a rag rug she had made for the floor and made a second bundle with the quilts. Each bundle was tied with a rope, which could be put over the shoulder of the one who would carry it. On Monday morning, instead of going to work, Johnny walked to the company store and paid the four dollars and seventy-five cents they owed.

"You folks going somewhere?" the storekeeper asked.

"Aye, we're going to St. Louis," was Johnny's terse reply. "Do ye know anyone who would take us to Westernport?"

The clerk nodded. "Al Yocum will probably take you."

Johnny had to call on their friendship to get Al to lower his rate to something fair, but he promised to bring his wagon by the cottage about ten o'clock in the morning.

On his way back to the cottage, Johnny looked around at the little community of whitewashed houses with the dogwood and redbud trees that were soon to bloom in anticipation of warmer weather. It had been a pleasant home until the issue of religion had made things difficult.

After many hours of rumbling over a rutted road, the wagon reached Westernport. James paid Al two dollars for the use of the wagon, and then he unloaded it near the little pier on the river. A rough-looking man was sitting cross-legged on the pier about twenty feet in front of a dirty tavern. He was dangling a fishing line in the river, looking out from under the battered rim of an old straw hat. Johnny approached him and asked, "Where can we rent a flatboat to take us to Parkersburg?"

The man rubbed the unshaven stubble on his chin and spat a brown gob of tobacco into the river. "Well, I think I might know someone who might have an open scow for hire." He stressed the word *might* each time he said it.

"Can ye point us in the right direction, as we would like to get on the river right away?"

"I might find him for the right price," the man said, and then spat again.

Aggravated with the man's unresponsiveness, Johnny turned and went into the tavern, leaving Helen with Willie and the bundles. He came out in about two minutes and walked back to the man on the pier. "Why didn't ye tell us that ye are the only man with an available flatboat right now?"

"What's the hurry?" the man said with a grin that exposed stained teeth. "A little conversation never hurt nobody."

Johnny was growing impatient. "Will ye take us to Parkersburg, and what will ye charge?"

"Well, how many of you be going?"

Johnny answered tiredly, "Ye can see there is me, my wife, and our bairn. What will be your price?"

"Any stops on the way?"

"Nae, we be going directly to Parkersburg."

"Am I feeding you, or are you feeding yourselves?"

Helen answered, "We will feed ourselves. What will you charge to take us there?"

The man was quiet for a few seconds and then said, "How soon you want to get there?"

Johnny's frustration was increasing. "As soon as possible."

The man scratched his chin and answered, "Twenty dollars."

Johnny answered, "That's robbery, and ye know it. We will wait until another flatboat becomes available. In the tavern they seem to think that will happen in a day or two."

"Well, you gotta remember that this is a trip for three, four— maybe five days. But—as you'll be feeding yourselves, I guess I could charge less. What do you propose to pay?"

Johnny decided that he would have to bluff his way through this bargain. "Five dollars for all of us."

"Ha, you take me for a fool? Twelve!"

Johnny shot back, "Six!"

The man responded, "Eleven!"

Johnny countered, "Seven!"

"Eight."

"Done." Johnny put out his hand to shake the other man's hand. Then he said, "My name is Johnny Smith, and this is my wife, Helen, and our laddie, Willie. And your name would be?"

"Bo," was his response.

"Bo?"

"Yep, jus' Bo."

"When do we leave, Bo?"

"Gimme an hour. I'll be back with the scow. I'll take my pay right now."

"Nae, five dollars when we start down the river and the balance when we reach Parkersburg." Johnny's voice was firm and his expression even firmer as he folded his arms over his chest.

"All right, all right," Bo said, and he sauntered away down a path by the river. He was back in an hour, using a long pole to control a flat-bottomed boat floating with the current. It was about eight feet wide, three feet deep, and ten feet long. It had a large rudder in the middle of the back that was controlled by the tiller, and an empty oar lock on each side. The matching oars were laid inside, along the sides of the boat. Bo pushed the tiller to one side with his leg and poled it to the narrow wooden pier that ran out into the river for about ten feet. Johnny helped Helen into the scow and handed Willie and the bundles to her. Bo simply watched.

After the little family was settled in the flatboat, Bo said to Johnny, "If you want to get this flatboat movin' I better see five dollars now—in gold. None o' that paper stuff."

Anticipating just such a request, Johnny took a five-dollar gold piece from his shirt pocket, rose to his feet, and handed it to the boatman without comment. With that, Bo put the coin into a small leather pouch hanging from a thong around his neck, tucked it into his worn and tattered buckskin shirt, and started to pole the flatboat out into the current.

As the current took hold of the boat and pulled it swiftly out into the middle of the river, Willie squealed with delight. Bo was adept at keeping the scow moving bow first with the current, but when it started to slip sideways, he yelled, "Johnny, grab an oar and get us straight with the current."

When twilight had come to the river, Bo continued to find the middle of the current with the tiller. After about an hour, he said to no one in particular, "It's about time for some supper. Better fix it now. We will float all night since we got a full moon and smooth water." Helen got into her box of provisions and distributed a hard-boiled egg and a biscuit to each member of her family. Then she asked, "Is there any way we can cook up some oatmeal in the morning for breakfast?"

He answered, "Yep, I'll build you a little fire you can cook over if the river is still smooth."

After the eggs and biscuits had been eaten, Bo said to Johnny, "Here, take the tiller while I light my lantern. Just keep it in the middle of the river and watch for snags." As Johnny took the tiller with some uncertainty, Bo laughed and said, "Don't be scared of it. You'll be expert at it before we reach Parkersburg. Did you think I was going to hold the tiller all the way? I gotta get some sleep sometime."

He picked up a jug from the corner of the flatboat, then putting it over his elbow and lifting it, he took a long drink. Johnny said, "If that is what I think it is, I must hope you will nae drink in the presence of my wife."

"This? You can't be against a bit of weak grog now and then for a man who's taking you and your family four days down the river."

"It had better be only now and then," Johnny said, shaking his head in exasperation.

Bo's response was to begin to share his flatboat experience. "You can see that this river looks smooth and quiet right now. After a rain, there's lots of snags—dead tree trunks and branches that will hang us up or even tip us over, so when you take the tiller, you gotta watch for shadows cast by the snags if they're above water. When they're under the water, the current will flow 'round them, and you gotta watch for that. The next day or two, the current won't be so bad, as the river is only middlin' high right now and we ain't had a rain in a week, so when I give the tiller to you, Mr. Smith, it won't be so difficult to handle. I suggest that the little one be put down for the night. On this kind of a trip, when you can get some sleep, take it." With that, he took control of the tiller again, much to Johnny's relief.

Helen untied one of the quilt bundles and wrapped herself and Willie in a quilt, and within a few minutes the motion of the water had rocked them to sleep.

CHAPTER 43
The Savannah

About midnight, Bo nudged Johnny with his foot, waking him. "Your turn to navigate while I grab a few winks of sleep," he said. "Just remember to watch for the snags and go 'round 'em." As Johnny stood up, Bo pushed the tiller into his hands. "You think you can do it?"

He nodded his head, rubbed his eyes, and answered, "As long as the river is calm and the moon bright, I guess I'll be fine."

Bo sat down on the boat bottom, leaned against the side of the boat, folded his arms, and pulled his straw hat down over his face. Within two minutes his snores could be heard from one shore of the river to the other.

Johnny tried to navigate the river carefully, but the light the lantern cast on the water was shallow, and the trees on either side of the river sometimes prevented the moonlight from penetrating. On two occasions he bumped a snag in the river. The first time, Bo's voice came from under the hat, "That weren't bad enough to count. We only count the ones that get us wet." The snores began again in another minute. The second time was just a scrape, and Bo didn't seem to notice.

In the early-morning light, Bo pushed the hat off his face and stretched and yawned mightily. He took the tiller from Johnny and told him, "You better get an hour's sleep, as we're gonna pull into Oakland for fresh water in a little bit. Then your woman can make some breakfast."

The stop in the little village of Oakland was brief, just long enough for Bo to fill two jugs with spring water and collect enough wood scraps for a little fire. Then he poled the scow back out into the current, and the journey continued. While Johnny handled the tiller, Bo showed Helen how to set up the little tripod from which they could suspend a pot of water over a rusted, flat piece of metal about three feet square, which was elevated above the deck about two inches by an iron collar and attached with screws. "Keep the fire on that piece of metal, or we'll burn a hole through the boat, and she don't float so good that way," Bo told Helen. "This here is my own invention. So far, I've only had one boat burned out from underneath me." Helen looked at her husband in alarm. Bo laughed as he started the fire with one of Helen's precious matches.

After the oatmeal was made, Helen put a big dollop on a tin plate and passed it to Johnny. When she offered one to Bo, he responded, "No, sweetie, I don't eat that stuff." Then he took a drink from the jug he had used the night before and said, "This here will be my breakfast."

During the afternoon, Johnny handled the tiller again, and Bo poled the boat through shallow water to increase the speed of their journey. After about two hours of that strenuous work, he sat down for another nap. An hour later, when Bo stood up from his nap and took the tiller, Johnny said, "How did I do?"

Bo said, "We didn't end up in the river. That means you did fine."

Two more days passed in similar fashion with Bo poling the boat past sandbars and shallow water spots and having Johnny use the oars for greater control in the swift places.

When the scow entered smoother water, Helen asked, "How much longer before we reach Parkersburg?"

"We ought to get there by sometime tomorrow," he reassured her.

By morning, the chill of the night air gave way to the sight of the morning sun, and by midday, the air was warmer. Helen passed the last of the hard-boiled eggs and biscuits around, and by late afternoon Bo began to hoot and wave his hat. "There's Parkersburg; get your stuff ready." The river had begun to widen quickly, and the current was growing slower.

As he pushed the tiller to one side, the boat drifted near a wooden pier. Bo pulled out the pole and pushed the scow until it bumped the pier, and then he leaped out and tied it to a post. "And I got you here before suppertime. I'll take the rest of my pay now," he said as he held out his hand to Johnny.

"After you help us unload," Johnny said.

"That weren't part of the deal," Bo responded.

Johnny started to laugh and said, "That's right, Bo. Ye got us here without losing any of us or our belongings. And ye proved that ye are a good man at heart."

"I'll have none of that kind of talk," Bo responded. "Next you'll be telling me I ought to be a church-going man. Heaven forbid," Bo said as he spat a wad of tobacco into the river. "When St. Peter calls me, I'm gonna tell him that I'm bringin' my jug and my tobaccy, and if he says I can't, then I ain't goin'."

By this time Helen had lifted Willie out of the flatboat and was standing on the levee. Johnny handed the bundles to her, then offered the remaining three dollars of the fee to Bo and shook his hand. Then he asked, "Where do we go to get passage on a steamboat to St. Louis?"

If you stand here long enough, the steamboat will stop right at your doorstep, so to speak. You see where the river gets much wider? Just beyond that bend is the mighty Ohio."

"When will the steamboat be here?" Johnny asked.

"A packet boat comes sometimes on Friday—if I remember right. What day is it?" Bo scratched the stubble on his chin as he spoke.

"Today is Thursday, I think," Johnny said. "That means we will have to find a hotel or boardinghouse for the night," he said to Helen.

Bo leaned closer to Johnny and said, "Let me suggest to you that you find a boardin' house. The hotel in this town ain't no fit place for ladies." At that, he raised both of his eyebrows twice for emphasis. "You need to take a walk along the main street and ask the first refined person you meet where there's a respectable boardin' house. I wish you safe journey." With that, he put his straw hat on his head, turned, and started up the street toward the two-story building with the sign that read "Parkersburg Hotel."

Johnny and Helen picked up Willie and the bundles and started to walk down the main street of the village. There, they found a small frame house with a little wooden sign over the front window that read, "McCarthy's Boardinghouse." After spending a pleasant evening there, the Smith family took deck passage the next day on the steamboat *Savannah*.

The lower deck was heavily loaded with stacks of cargo, and they discovered that at least a dozen deck passengers had remained onboard to protect their belongings. The fewer the possessions, the more fiercely their ragged owners guarded them. They finally found a place on the starboard side where a few passengers had left the boat, taking their belongings with them.

Three hours after the Smiths arrived in Parkersburg, the captain and other crewmen returned to the boat after a visit to the Parkersburg Hotel. The captain yelled, "All male deck passengers off to load wood." About a dozen men made their way off the boat and walked over to the freight wagon as if they had done this before.

Johnny followed the other men off the boat and over to a large wagon. There each man was handed, one or two pieces at a time, an armload of wood that had been cut to feed the boiler of the boat. Johnny followed the other men back onto the boat, where they dropped the wood into the bin near the boiler. That process took about an hour. The crew filled the boilers with water and stoked the fire under them. Finally, the captain climbed to the pilot house and pulled the rope on the steam whistle, which echoed across the river. After ten more minutes, the captain sounded the whistle again, and the passengers who had disembarked to visit the bar at the hotel returned to the boat.

After the passengers had boarded, the boat pulled out into the middle of the Ohio River. Johnny and Helen were amazed at the broad expanse of water that shimmered in the early twilight. "I've never seen so much water except in the River Clyde and the great ocean," she whispered. When the late afternoon had darkened into twilight, the reflections of the lights from the boat that seemed to float over the water were the only real measure of the speed with which they were traveling. The river was high, and the boat moved swiftly with the current.

As Helen sat on the deck holding her sleeping son in her lap, she and Johnny could hear laughter and the sound of feet on the deck above them. Then they heard the sound of music: a banjo, violin, and guitar.

Johnny looked at Helen, and without saying anything, rose and walked toward the stairs where they had seen a sign prohibiting deck passengers on the second deck. Slipping under the rope across the staircase, he made his way quietly up the stairs, and, keeping in the shadows as much as possible, he found the double doors on the second deck where some of the cabin guests were entering. He stepped up to the doors and pushed one open a few inches. Inside was a two-level salon carpeted in red with large, round tables and a small platform at one end of the room where three black musicians played. The lights above the round tables trembled with the motion of the boat as the men under them played cards and smoked cigars. Women in full-skirted dresses and bare shoulders gathered at one end of the room where they chatted and sipped from wine glasses held in white-gloved hands. Johnny had never seen anything like it in his entire life. He stood still for a few minutes until he looked up and saw the captain coming. He stepped into the shadows, and after the captain had entered the salon, he made his way back down to the lower deck.

When he got back down to Helen, she said, "What were you doing?"

"Helen, ye would never believe what I saw up there," he said. "There's a big room with a red rug, and bright lights, and men playing cards and drinking. The women wore bright-colored gowns and white gloves, and the musicians were playing. It was amazing."

After he had again described everything he had seen, Helen could only shake her head. "That sounds like something God would not want us to be doing," was all she said.

Following the stop at Cairo, Illinois, the boat left the Ohio River and started up the Mississippi, its speed slowed by the river's strong southerly current. At Cape Girardeau, several deck passengers disembarked, and several well-dressed cabin passengers boarded. Helen said to Johnny, "What kind of men dress like that?"

He answered, "I think they play cards for a living. See the gold watch fobs and the beaver-skin hats on two of them?"

"Aye, and the ladies are dressed in a fashion that says they are no one's wife or mother," Helen added. After a few moments of watching, she added, "We are going to a worldly place, I think."

CHAPTER 44
A Wedding at Sea

As the *Kennebec* sailed westward toward what Robert thought of as his promised land, he and Rebecca continued to spend time together, usually walking and talking on the deck, no matter how cold or windy the conditions. They watched the icebergs off the starboard bow and the great seabirds as they circled the ship, diving and soaring in the air. For the morning and evening prayer and hymns, Robert stood near Rebecca and enjoyed watching others in the group turn and look with approval at her as she sang without self-consciousness in her rich voice.

After six weeks at sea, a baptism was held, and four passengers and two crewmen were immersed in the big barrel on the deck. Later that evening, with lamps hung in the rigging and before the entire ship's company, the captain united Rebecca Allen and Robert Hogge in holy matrimony.

That evening, with the violins playing vigorously, the passengers and a few of the crew danced and made merry well into the night. Robert and Rebecca stood on the quarterdeck, near the helmsman, and watched. He spoke after some time and asked, "Sir, and ma'am, why don't ye join in the merrymaking? Ye have good reasons this night to celebrate."

They were silent so long that the sailor began to think that they had not heard him. Then Robert answered quietly, simply speaking out loud to himself, "This voyage is like life."

"Aye, sir?"

"It has proven itself to be full of grief and joy—and joy and grief. Perhaps the two must always come together." With that the couple stepped into the darkness at the ship's rail and said no more as they watched the stars.

When the lookout sighted the lighthouse at the mouth of the great Mississippi delta, the captain dropped anchor where the great muddy stream that flowed down from the north made a brown, swirling path through the blue of the sea. In the morning, a steam tug appeared. The crew attached a long hawser to the bow, and the tug began the process of towing the *Kennebec* for twenty-two hours up the river to New Orleans.

As they watched the land pass on both sides of the river, Rebecca said, "I had forgotten how beautiful the trees and grass can be. It rests my eyes to look on them. But see how different they are from home. The trunks lean out over the water with those great gray-green veils hanging from the branches. They look like a painting. And the air is so heavy."

The sixty-nine passengers from the *Kennebec* who had been traveling with the aid of the Perpetual Emigration Fund were housed in several boardinghouses and hotels near Lafayette Square with many of the other passengers. After five days, they received word from the Church agent in New Orleans that the steamboat *Pride of the West* had been chartered for some of the *Kennebec* passengers, but because it was a small steamboat, only families with children, the aged, and the infirm would be traveling upriver to St. Louis aboard it. All other *Kennebec* passengers would need to plan on staying in New Orleans for at least another week or ten days.

Robert looked at Rebecca and said worriedly, "We will soon be out of money if we do not find work. We must feed ourselves for a week or ten days and still be able to purchase supplies for the trip to St. Louis when the agent for the Church is able to find us a boat."

That evening, as they sat in the dining room of the small hotel where they were staying, a group of the *Kennebec* passengers began to sing some of the hymns of the Church as the dinner ended.

Rebecca's voice filled the room with its rich timbre as she sang along with the others. After the group had sung three hymns, the hotel owner stepped out of the kitchen, and, removing the apron tied about his round middle, he wiped his hands on it and stepped to the front of the room.

Raising his hand to quiet his twenty guests he said, "I have seldom heard such sweet music. Please continue to sing as long as you desire." As one of the men led the next hymn with his voice, the others joined, and the hotel owner walked between the tables until he determined that it was Rebecca he was seeking.

After some of the diners stood and began to separate to return to their rooms, he approached Rebecca and said, "Is this gentlemen your husband?"

"Yes, he is," she responded, taking Robert's arm.

The man turned to speak to Robert and said, "Your wife has a particularly pleasing voice, sir, and I would like to invite her to sing in my dining room each evening for both the early dinner and the late supper for as long as you board here, if you would not consider such a request to be impertinent."

Robert smiled proudly and nodded toward Rebecca. "Such a decision must be made by my wife."

The hotel owner turned to her and said, "If ye would consider the invitation, I would be willing to pay you one dollar each evening if you would sing for each sitting of diners. The first is at seven P.M. and the second at nine P.M."

Rebecca blushed somewhat and said, "Oh, Robbie, I don't know if I could do such a brazen thing."

The hotel owner responded, "Oh, ma'am, with as lovely a voice and as refined a presence as you have, no one would consider a song from you to be brazen."

"Robbie, what do you think I should do?" she asked as she looked into his face.

"I would love to have the world hear your voice, my dear. And we could put the money to good use."

Turning back to the owner, she smiled and said, "Then I will try to please your diners. But I have no dress fit for such an occasion." With that, she looked perplexed.

"My wife may have one you could wear. She is about your size and has one or two evening dresses for formal occasions."

That night, when Robert and Rebecca answered a knock at the door of their room, the wife of the owner stood there with a wine-colored dress in her arms. "My husband thinks this dress may suit you. I look forward to hearing you sing tomorrow evening." With that, she was gone down the hall.

Though she sang unaccompanied, the diners applauded with vigor the next evening after Rebecca had sung "Loch Lomond," and they called out for another song. She followed with "Annie Laurie," and was applauded again and asked for another song.

The next day Robert asked Mr. Mueller if there was any kind of work available for men in the area. He responded, "If you are not afraid of physical labor, you might try offering your services loading the steamboats at the levee. I hear the stevedores are some-times paid a dollar if they work all night."

So Robert walked to the levee the next evening and located a boat being loaded and asked if he could be hired. When the boat captain nodded, he took off his coat and spent the night loading cotton bales. In the morning as the sun rose, the boat captain handed him a silver dollar. He returned the next night and the night after that.

The Church agent finally sent word that the steamboat *Natchez* had been hired to take the rest of the passengers from the *Kennebec* to St. Louis, as well as some of the passengers from the *Ashley* and the *Chaloner* who were still in New Orleans. Rebecca laughed and said to her husband, "I am so glad we will not be staying in this city any longer. I can hardly understand some of the people here when they talk. I don't know if I could ever learn the language."

CHAPTER 45
Steamboats to Kanesville

"More Mormons Arrive in St. Louis" the article read. "Recently upwards of 1,000 Mormons have arrived in St. Louis since spring, not more than 600 of whom have been able to leave. There are at this time in St. Louis about 3,000 English Mormons, nearly all of whom are masters of some trade, or have acquired experience in some profession, which they follow now. As we said they have no church but attend divine services twice each Sunday at Concert Hall, and they perform their devotional duties with the same regularity, if not in the same style, as their brethren in the Valley.

"We have witnessed the congregation as it issued from the hall and at religious meetings on Sunday, and certainly we think it does not compare unfavorably with other congregations."

After the steamboat *Savannah* arrived in St. Louis, Johnny and Helen had found a small room to rent near the St. Louis levee. As Helen cleaned the kitchen the second evening after they had arrived, she picked up the newspaper that had been wrapped around the fish they had purchased. As she prepared to put it in the stove to burn, she saw the article, which was in a month-old copy of the *Missouri Republican*. Helen called out excitedly, "Johnny, come see this article about the Mormons in the newspaper." The next Sunday they joined the other Saints who met in the Concert Hall on Market Street. There they were introduced to Elder Abraham Smoot, who had been assigned to assist in getting a large group of Saints to the Valley with the help of the Perpetual Emigration Fund.

The following Wednesday, about two hundred Saints crowded into the upstairs room of a public house on the levee, where they met with some of the members of the Church who had arrived earlier by steamboat from New Orleans. There they were introduced to Elders Eli Kelsey and David Ross, who had come down from Kanesville to act as temporary agents for the Church. Elder Kelsey had chartered a steamboat to take part of the group to Kanesville.

It was determined that those from the *Kennebec* who had come up the river on the *Pride of the West* several days earlier and who desired to leave immediately would be given the opportunity to board the side-wheeler *Saluda* in the morning. Elder Kelsey, who was conducting the meeting, had made arrangements for the deck passage of one hundred of those *Kennebec* Saints.

Elder Kelsey stood on a chair and spoke after quieting the noise in the room. He explained, "The Missouri River is full of late ice this season, and many of the boat captains have been unwilling to make the trip up to Kanesville. But we have been lucky enough to receive a commitment from Captain Francis Belt of the steamboat *Saluda,* a man of good reputation, who will take one hundred of those Saints desiring passage up the river tomorrow."

"When will the rest of us be able to go up the river?" one of the men called out.

Elder Kelsey responded, "Elder Abraham Smoot, who is standing right here, will book passage as soon as he can for the rest of you desiring to go to Kanesville. It will surely not be more than a day or two before he can obtain a commitment from a steamboat captain to take the rest of you who desire to go up the river at this time. Tell him where you will be staying so you can be notified when he obtains a boat."

When the meeting ended, those seeking passage on the *Saluda* crowded around Elder Kelsey and Elder Ross, and when all one hundred positions had been filled, others who had been waiting and hoping there would be room enough for them turned away in disappointment.

After the meeting ended, Johnny stepped up to Elder Smoot and said, "Our funds are getting low. Is there no chance we might find a way to go on the *Saluda*?" Helen anxiously watched Elder Smoot's face.

"We will find another boat to take you to Kanesville, and I can promise you that you will be grateful that you were not on the *Saluda*," Elder Smoot said.

Helen asked, "What do ye mean?"

His answer was brief. "I do not fully understand exactly what I am feeling in this matter, but I am uneasy for those going on that boat, and I feel impressed that it will prove better for those who go on another boat."

Johnny and Helen joined the Saints who were remaining behind as they waited on the levee the next day and watched the big side-wheeler begin its journey. It was nearly one hundred and eighty feet long and twenty-five feet in the beam, with two stacks forward of the pilot house and two great paddle wheels, but it looked like an old and tired boat.

After several strong crewmen had poled the boat away from the levee, the steam belched from its smokestacks, and the starboard wheel began to rotate in reverse as its port wheel rotated in a forward direction, giving the captain a swift and efficient way to maneuver into the main current of the river. Then both paddles stopped, and for a few seconds the boat drifted with the current, and then both began to turn in a forward rotation. The boat began to move northward against the current. Waves of farewell were exchanged between those on the crowded lower deck and those who remained behind.

CHAPTER 46
The Saluda and the Isabel

Standing on the levee, Helen and Johnny watched the *Saluda* until it was out of sight. Then he took the printed handbill out of his pocket that he had been given at the meeting and looked at it again. "It says here that we need to have enough supplies to take care of ourselves for the ten days it could take to get to Kanesville."

Helen looked at the list once more and said, "It will take most of the money we have left to buy the things we need."

"It must be done," Johnny responded, so they spent much of the balance of the afternoon making purchases on Market Street.

After they had returned to the boardinghouse in the early evening, they found another handbill, this one tacked on the door. It read:

> To all Saints waiting for passage to Kanesville, you will need to report to the levee the morning of April 1, for passage on the steamboat *Isabel*. Captain William Miller. Departure time, twelve o'clock, noon. Deck passage available for two hundred and fifty.
>
> Signed, Elder Abraham O. Smoot.

"I am so glad to see we won't be staying in this city any longer, as our money is going fast." Helen's voice reflected her relief. "And with a name like the *Isabel,* this boat will surely bring us good luck."

The morning of April first, as the Saints began to board the *Isabel,* Johnny said, "This is a much newer boat and in better condition than the *Saluda.*"

"Aye, I said this steamboat would bring us good luck," Helen said and laughed.

A few of the passengers were rough Missourians, and several others were on their way to the California goldfields. When the Missourians discovered that there were Mormons on the boat, one of them laughed boisterously and said, "Don't they know that ol' Governor Boggs put a bounty on all of 'em? Maybe we ought to have a contest to see who can shoot the most of them after we throw 'em overboard, before the current carries them away." Then he and his companions laughed loudly. "We should get more points for the little ones than the big ones. They're harder targets to hit."

Even though Elder Smoot asked them to stop frightening the women and children, the loud and crude threats continued.

During the nights, Helen and Johnny fell asleep to the sound of footsteps and laughter on the decks above them, as well as the music that came from the great salon on the second deck.

On the evening of the seventh day of the trip, the *Isabel* docked at Lexington, Missouri, where the captain told the passengers and crew that they would take on water and wood. The boat was docked at the lower landing, about two hundred feet down current from another steamboat. "That looks like the *Saluda,*" Johnny called out as they waved to those on the deck, hoping to see friends and acquaintances.

That night both boats remained docked. In the morning, many of the passengers on the *Isabel,* including Johnny and Helen, watched as the crew of the *Saluda* took in the lines cast off on the shore. Many townspeople had come to watch the *Saluda* from the bluff above the river, as was common practice. Some of them had placed bets as to how long it would take the captain to navigate the river bend. As the boat slipped stern-first into the river, the captain began to ring a big black bell with the Full Speed Ahead signal. Before the great paddlewheels had turned three times, a sound greater than any firedamp explosion blasted the forepart of the *Saluda* in every direction, throwing wooden planks, iron pieces, cargo, and the bodies of passengers into the river and onto the shore.

The women watching from the *Isabel* screamed, as did many of the townspeople. Helen cried out, "'Tis the firedamp. Oh, Johnny, 'tis the firedamp that got them." Then she began to sob and shake as memories of explosions in the pits rushed into her mind.

He put his arm around her and held her. "Nae, Helen, ye know it can't be firedamp. Must have been too much heat for the boilers. 'Tis a terrible sight, a terrible sight." His voice broke.

The remaining wreckage of the *Saluda*—comprised of the stern, a portion of the bow, and portions of the paddlewheels—drifted a short distance and began to sink into the river, its bow against the shore. Elder Smoot waved to the men on the *Isabel* and yelled at them, "Come, help us find the survivors."

Johnny said, "Ye stay here with Willie. I will help where I can."

The men from the *Isabel* along with many townspeople spent the next several hours trying to find the living under the wreckage of the boat, digging wherever they heard cries for help or the sobbing of children. When Johnny returned to the *Isabel,* he was covered with dust, blood, and slivers of wood. When Helen saw him she cried out, "Oh, Johnny, ye look like ye have been digging in the pits after a cave-in."

"'Tis just as bad—nae, 'tis worse, as there are so many small bairns hurt or killed," he responded. He talked while he washed off the blood and dirt, using a small washtub of river water. He said, "It was not all bad. We uncovered a little two-year-old lass who found her mother. That was a happy sight." He continued to wash. "The dead have been laid out on the shore—covered with sheets and blankets from the folks of the town. I think Elder Smoot said there were twenty-eight dead of all ages, but more than double that number can nae be accounted for. Maybe they were swallowed up in the river."

After several hours had passed, Elder Smoot came to the *Isabel* and told the captain to continue his journey to Kanesville. "The good people of Lexington will do all in their power for the dead and injured." He continued, "The injured have been taken to a warehouse near the river; it has become a makeshift hospital. Captain Belt, the two pilots, both of the engineers, and many of the other crew members are among the dead. Other victims, both living and dead, have floated down the river." He remained behind to continue to direct the rescue efforts when the boat started up the river again.

Among the lucky ones were the dozen passengers who had boarded in St. Louis and had disembarked at Brunswick before the *Saluda* reached Lexington. This included Elder Eli Kelsey, who had gotten off to purchase cattle, which he planned to drive overland to Kanesville.

Captain Miller encouraged any passengers from the *Saluda* who were able to come aboard the *Isabel* and they would be taken to Kanesville without charge. About thirty-five did, making the decks of the *Isabel* more crowded. The *Saluda* passengers sat silently staring at the water for hours, unresponsive to questions or offers of food. They were without belongings or baggage, and some without loved ones.

For five more days, the *Isabel* made its way up the river against the current, with the original passengers offering to share what provisions they had with those from the *Saluda*.

Before the steamboat arrived at its destination, the news of the disaster in Lexington had reached the people in Kanesville. Frantic friends and family members searched the face of every passenger who left the boat, looking for those who had been on the *Saluda*. They crowded around and asked for information. Occasionally a cry of joy could be heard as family members were found and reunited. But many approached the *Isabel* passengers with questions that could not be answered.

"Have you seen William Dunbar and his family?"
"Can you tell us what happened to Henry Ballard?"
"Is George May or his wife, Mary, alive?"
"I'm here to meet Duncan Campbell. Did he survive?"
But no one had any answers.

CHAPTER 47
Kanesville

When the passengers had disembarked from the *Isabel* in Kanesville and made their way through the crowd of those who were waiting and hoping for news of loved ones, they found an agent for the Church who was waiting with a wagon.

Elder Isaac Bullock recommended one of three hotels or boarding-houses in the town to the new arrivals and said, "After each of you have settled your families, you can come down to the Big Pigeon Tabernacle on any Monday, Wednesday, or Friday night of the week, at six o'clock, for services. We have too many Saints here in Kanesville to fit everyone into the meeting hall at once. There we will determine what assistance you need to help get you west."

Johnny asked, "Where's the tabernacle? How will we know it?"

Elder Bullock said, "You will know it when you see it. It is the biggest log building in town, down on East Broadway."

After everyone had loaded their belongings into the wagon, it was piled high and had no room for anyone to ride. Several men said, "You lead the way, and we will follow."

The first stop was the Kanesville House Hotel, and when the wagon stopped, several families unloaded their belongings. Each family gave the driver ten cents. The second stop was the Iowa Hotel. Johnny said to the driver, "We'll stop here." The sign outside said that each room was fifty cents a night.

They ate supper that night in the hotel dining room, and when they paid for it, Johnny said, "We need to find another place to get our meals, someplace that will not cost so much. And we need to find some work, or we will be out of funds very quickly."

That night, for twenty-five cents, the manager of the hotel arranged for a tub of water to be brought to the Smiths' room. The water was cold, but each one of them took a bath. After the baths were finished, Helen spent the next hour washing everything that they had worn for the last several weeks except the underwear they were sleeping in. Then she tried to find a place to hang the wet clothing to dry. While Willie and Johnny slept, she unrolled one of the bundles and took the rope that held it together and tied it to the straight-backed chair in one corner, opened the window in the room, and then closed it on the other end of the rope. Then she undid the other bundle and took the rope from it and tied it to the chair and to the doorknob to keep the weight of the wet clothing from tipping the chair over. Then she hung the wet clothing on the rope and hoped everything would dry by morning. Then, and only then, did she climb wearily into bed.

In the morning, they selected those things that were the most nearly dry, dressed, and set about to see the town. Late in the morning, they found a small frame house badly in need of paint with a sign in the window that read *Meals Available,* so Johnny knocked on the door. When the spare, tall, gray-haired lady wearing gold-rimmed pince-nez answered the door, he took off his cap and asked, "Do ye feed strangers here?"

She answered abruptly, "That's what the sign says. If you want some breakfast, come in and I will feed the three of you for fifteen cents."

Helen and Johnny exchanged a look of gratitude and entered the little house. Mrs. Collins showed them to the kitchen where two other travelers were finishing their meals. In a few minutes she had wheat mush and cornbread on the table. As they ate, she asked what had brought them to Kanesville.

"We are coming from Edinburgh, Scotland, on our way west to join the Saints in the Great Salt Lake Valley," Helen stated.

"Hrump," she snorted. "More Mormons. Well, at least you won't be here long. If all the Mormons that came through Kanesville were to stay, there would be some real trouble. We don't need you or your gold Bible."

Helen and Johnny were startled by her hostility. "Why are ye so angry with the Mormons? What did they do to make ye so angry?"

Mrs. Collins sat down at the table, and suddenly her stern face began to soften and her lower lip began to quiver. "My daughter ran off with one of them." She dabbed at her eyes with her apron. "He proposed to her, and she went with him. I haven't seen her since. I don't even know where she is now."

Helen impulsively put her hand over that of Mrs. Collins and said, "If she loved him and he loved her, then wherever she is, she is happy."

With that, Mrs. Collins permitted herself a small, thin smile, and said, "Forget my harsh words. You are welcome to come back here for all your meals while you are in Kanesville." When they returned to Mrs. Collins's house for supper, they told her that they would need to find some other place to stay soon and asked if they could offer her address as a place where messages could be left for them.

"I hope that does not offend ye," Helen said.

Mrs. Collins was very quiet for a moment, biting her lower lip. Then she said, as if following an impulse, "I have an extra room. It was my daughter's, but if you do not object to staying with a woman who has sometimes spoken against the Mormons, you are welcome to stay here."

"We thank ye, Mrs. Collins. What would we pay ye for board and room?" Johnny asked, worried about his diminishing funds.

"The three of you can stay here and have two meals for seventy-five cents a day. Would that be acceptable to you?"

Johnny was slow to answer, as he was thinking about the three dollars and sixty cents in his pocket, which was all the money they had. Then he took a big breath and said, "That will be fair for as long as our money lasts. We hope that I can find a position before we run out of funds."

She asked, "What is it that you do to support your family?"

"I was a brick maker and before that a coal miner."

"About three miles farther up the river, there is a clay pit run by a brick maker. Tomorrow morning, you walk up the river and tell the owner that Mrs. Collins sent you. Now, when will you be leaving that hotel?"

"Tomorrow morning," Helen said.

On Sunday, they walked to the great log tabernacle on East Broadway, which the Saints had built a few years earlier for a meeting-house. Upon arriving and entering the large building, Johnny started to laugh. It was suddenly apparent just why it had gained the nickname Big Pigeon Tabernacle. There were more birds in the rafters than there were people on the benches.

After Sabbath worship services, those gathered there were asked to separate into companies, depending on their financial situation and the date they planned to go west. Those dependent on the Perpetual Emigration Fund were told to gather in one corner of the large room, where they would be instructed. The group of nearly two hundred men, women, and children stood around, trying to keep fussing children quieted. After about half an hour, Elder David Ross stood on a chair and motioned them to come close enough to hear him.

"You are all likely to be assigned to the wagon train that will be under the direction of Abraham Smoot." In response to questions called to him, he responded, "Yes, that is correct, he is still in Lexington, but when the dead have been buried and the living provided for, he will be joining us here."

Someone called out, "When will that be, as some of us have nary two pennies to rub together?"

"It may be a few more days." At that, several men were heard to groan. "If you don't have funds to support your families while you wait, I recommend that you seek employment."

In the morning, Johnny walked up the river and found the clay pit without difficulty. He was hired immediately. When Helen asked Mrs. Collins if there was some way she might be able to earn money, perhaps by doing laundry, Mrs. Collins said, "Yes, Helen, there is always a need for a laundress in this town. I will put a small sign in my window, and in a day or two you will have more than you can do."

The next weeks passed quickly, with Johnny earning a dollar a day at the clay pit, and Helen able to earn nearly as much doing laundry. The constantly steaming tub of water on the stove sorely tested Mrs. Collins's patience, but each evening after supper, the three of them would sit at the kitchen table, and Johnny and Helen would talk about their new religion and read to Mrs. Collins from the Book of Mormon.

Finally, a message came in the form of a printed handbill, which was left at the door. It read:

> To those traveling with the assistance of the Perpetual Emigration Fund: Elder Abraham O. Smoot will be leaving on June 1st by riverboat for Atchison, Kansas, where he has arranged for cattle and wagons for a group of three hundred and fifty. Those who want to be considered for inclusion in this wagon train must notify Elder Smoot by May 25th.
>
> Signed, Abraham O. Smoot, Wagon Master.

That Sunday, Johnny carried Willie on his shoulders even though the child would have preferred to use his strong little legs, and he and Helen walked to the tabernacle an hour before meeting time was scheduled, in the hope that they could find Elder Smoot and officially put their names on the roster of those who would be part of his wagon train.

CHAPTER 48
Reunion

At the hotel in New Orleans, Robert and Rebecca sat at a table in the empty dining room and talked cheerfully about the anticipated nine- or ten-day trip up the Mississippi. They counted the money they had earned between them. Rebecca said, "We have enough to travel as cabin passengers, but I think we can save some money if we travel as deck passengers."

Robert said, "Are ye sure ye want to travel that far as deck passengers? I hear it can be cold and wet and very uncomfortable." She would not change her mind.

The next day was spent purchasing the provisions that would be needed on the journey upriver to St. Louis. That evening, Rebecca sang for the dinner guests for the last time. After the dining room was empty, Rebecca and Robert approached the hotel owner and Rebecca said, "Mr. Mueller, it's time we told you of our plans. We have talked it over and decided that it is time for us to move on. We have obtained deck passage on the *Natchez* for tomorrow morning to go upriver to St. Louis." She added, "We thank you for the hospitality you have extended to us, but we need to be on our way."

The face of the hotel owner began to redden, and he said angrily, "You mean to just up and leave me, just like that? And after the good wages I've been paying you?"

"We are sorry, Mr. Mueller," Rebecca said sympathetically. "But we need to get on with our journey. We will be joining a wagon company going west as soon as we can."

Mr. Mueller was quiet a short moment, and then said contemptuously, "It's the Mormons and the gold-seekers that are taking their wagon trains west right now, and you folks don't look like gold-seekers. Are you Mormons?" Without waiting for an answer, he continued with increasing anger, "I've been paying Mormons here in my hotel?" By this time his face was scarlet and his voice at the level of a shout. "You get yourselves out of my place early in the morning, or I'll call the constable."

Rebecca said placatingly, "We wish you well in your future business efforts, Mr. Mueller." As they started up the stairs, Robert added under his breath, "And I think we best be leaving very early in the morning so he has no reason to make trouble."

They arrived at the levee at about the time that the captain rang the bell to give the signal that the deck was open for boarding. By the time the steamboat had made the journey up the Mississippi to St. Louis, all the deck passengers were grateful to get off the boat. They were tired, wet, and cold, but as they disembarked from the steamboat, Rebecca said, "I fear we will face greater discomfort than traveling as deck passengers on a steamboat before we reach the Valley."

* * *

"Welcome to St. Louis, welcome to St. Louis!" Horace Eldridge, the general emigration agent for the Church in St. Louis greeted the Saints as they disembarked from the *Natchez*. There on the levee he addressed them. "Each family has been assigned a room in a local boarding establishment near the levee. Tomorrow at nine o'clock in the morning all Church members are to meet at the Concert Hall on Market Street. There you will be assigned to one of two river-boats that will take you to Kanesville within the next few days."

Robert and Rebecca were assigned to travel on the steamboat *Cincinnati*, which they boarded the following day; they arrived in Kanesville on the twentieth of May.

"Oh, Robert, we must find a boardinghouse where I can rest. I am ready to sleep in a real bed for a year," Rebecca said with exhaustion. Her request was soon satisfied, though she was teased by her husband for resting only two hours rather than a year.

That evening the two of them were directed to the tabernacle, where they joined the Saints in a worship service. When it was over, they stood and looked around the great room at the several hundred people, hoping to find someone to give them information as to how they could become part of a wagon company to take them to the Valley.

"Robbie, I think that maybe outside we can find someone to answer our questions. There is too much noise inside to talk," Rebecca suggested.

They started for the door, but in the crush of the crowd they became caught at the doorway. Robert found himself pressed against another man as they tried to pass through at the same time. He looked at the man and started to excuse himself, but stopped midsentence. "Pardon me for bumping into ye like that—" As he looked at the young man next to him, he said first with a question, and then with a shout, "Johnny, Johnny Smith, is that really you? How can ye be here? We thought ye had reached the Valley a long time ago."

As they burst forth out of the doorway, they took hold of each other's shoulders and began to shake one another. Johnny turned and called, "Helen, Helen, it's your brother—right here! Here's Robbie, come and see!"

Helen had finally been able to make her way through the crowd and out of the building as she carried a struggling Willie. When she recognized her brother, she hesitated only a fraction of a second and then ran to him. She handed Willie to Johnny and gave her brother a great embrace. "Oh, Robbie, ye are here. How can that be? Who else did ye bring across the ocean? Is Ma or Jamie with ye?"

Avoiding her question, Robert stepped over to Rebecca and took her hand. As he pulled her to his side, he said, "Helen, this beautiful young lady is my wife, Rebecca."

After several minutes, the excitement lessened and Helen asked hopefully again, "Did the others come?"

Robert sadly shook his head and said quietly, "Ma is dying of the black spit. And Jamie has been made coal master. They could not bring themselves to leave the big cottage. I am so sorry, Helen; I know that's a great disappointment." Helen was silent, looking at her brother as if she could not understand what he was saying. Then a tear made its way down her cheek.

To break the silence of disappointment, Rebecca spoke up. "We need to speak with Elder Smoot about joining his wagon train. They tell us that he will have the Perpetual Emigration Fund people with him."

Johnny answered, "Aye, that is how we will travel to the Valley." With that, he said, "Follow me." He took Helen's hand, and they made their way through the groups of people huddled around each wagon master until they found Elder Smoot. As the last couple speaking with him took their leave, Johnny said to him, "Elder Smoot, ye know me and my wife, but these folks are family and need help from the Fund to get to the Valley as well. Can they become part of your wagon train?"

Elder Smoot said, "Well, they will have to convince me that they are deserving of help from the Fund." Then he looked at Robert and said, "Tell me how you got this far."

Robert explained how he and many of the others had sailed on the *Kennebec* with the help of the Perpetual Emigration Fund and would be dependent upon it to get to the Valley. He ended by saying, "So we are all here in Kanesville and nearly at the end of our funds."

Elder Smoot said, "Since you are family, my wagon company will make room for you. Each wagon is supposed to carry the supplies for ten, so I may have to add another family to your wagon. I recommend that you quickly find work and earn as much as you can to cover unforeseen expenses. Keep in contact with me. In the meantime, here is a printed handbill of the things the Fund will provide for you, and anything not on it, you must furnish. I recommend that you each bring an extra pair of shoes, and each of you men, a gun." With that, he tipped his hat and went on his way.

Robert turned and asked Johnny, "Do ye know where I can get some work?"

"If ye will come with me in the morning when I go up the river to the clay pit, I think I can get ye a position. Follow me and Helen, and we will show ye where we are staying and introduce ye to Mrs. Collins. If she is disposed to do so, she may be willing to feed all of us each morning and night."

"Of course you can take your meals here," the landlady told them.

After hugs and handshakes all around, Helen, Johnny, and Willie stood on the small stoop of Mrs. Collins's house and waved to Robert and his wife.

That evening, before going to bed, Rebecca and Robert sat in the little hotel parlor and read the information on the handbill aloud.

To all traveling with the assistance of the Perpetual Emigration Fund over the age of eight years, each individual is permitted to take one hundred pounds of baggage, including bed, furniture, and clothing; fifty pounds for those four to eight years of age; none to those under four years of age.

A common field tent will be provided to those in each wagon. Each wagon will be furnished with one thousand pounds of flour, fifty pounds of sugar, fifty pounds of bacon, fifty pounds of rice, thirty pounds of beans, twenty pounds of dried apples or peaches, twenty-five pounds of salt, one gallon of vinegar, ten bars of soap. The wagon will have one team of oxen and be furnished with one large barrel for water, which is to be refilled at each river or stream passed. Those assigned to the wagon will also have the use of one or two milk cows, depending on the number of small children in the group. The game caught and killed on the journey will furnish the balance of the food requirements for each wagon.

Those assigned to each wagon may choose to add such additional items as they desire for the journey, which is expected to take three months. It is important for all travelers to note that each able-bodied person is expected to walk during the journey. The wagons are to carry only the sick or the infirm who are unable to walk.

"Oh, Robbie, I am so excited—and a bit scared. This will be such a great journey," Rebecca said as they prepared for bed.

In the morning, the group met at Mrs. Collins's house, and after a simple breakfast, the two men walked to the clay pit and brickworks. Upon their arrival, the owner waved them on to the site and called out, "There's always work here for strong backs."

* * *

When the first of June arrived, Helen and Johnny bid the land-lady farewell and said, "Oh, Mrs. Collins, we will miss ye and your kindness, but we are finally starting the last great part of our journey. We will soon reach the Valley." Putting their bundles over their shoulders, the Smiths gave a short wave of good-bye and hurried to the levee where they met Robert and Rebecca.

Each family included as part of the Smoot Wagon Company met at the levee where they waited for the steamboat *Julia Jane*, talking excitedly among themselves. There were more than three hundred and fifty in the group, most of them from England, Scotland, and Wales.

When the lower deck of the steamboat was full, those boarding last, which included the Smiths and Hogges, were permitted to go up to the second deck. From there they watched the shore slide past. The trip downriver to Atchison, Kansas, took only two days. They arrived the next evening but did not leave the boat until morning. Then they were instructed to wait at the boat until the wagons were brought to the levee. Two hours passed before the first of the ox-drawn wagons arrived.

CHAPTER 49
The Trail West

Elder Smoot began to read the names of the individuals assigned to each of the thirty-five wagons. The five members of the combined Smith and Hogge families were assigned to the thirty-second wagon, along with the family of Joseph Matthews, his wife, Ann, and their ten-year-old son, Tom.

All had grown hot and sticky with the long wait in the warm, humid air when a tall, bearded man everyone called Big Jim led the ox team pulling the thirty-second wagon to the levee. The man held a long rod and the lead rope that was connected to the ring in the nose of the oxen harnessed to the wagon. He called out, "Put your belongings in the wagon box."

As the men loaded the bundles, Willie pointed and said in his childish voice, "Big cows," looking from them to his mother.

Helen asked the man, "What are their names?"

"This one is Bob, and the other one is Sam."

By this time everything had been loaded, and the man with the beard said, "These oxen have been trained some, but all of you are going to need to know how to make them obey. Follow me closely, and on the way to your camp, I'll teach you what you need to know."

Ten-year-old Tom Matthews asked, "Is this all the faster they can go?"

The big man smiled and said, "Yep. This is as fast as they go," and then he laughed and added, "unless they get caught in a stampede, but even then they don't go much faster."

By the time the lesson on how to direct the oxen was completed, the wagon had arrived at the camp. There, Big Jim showed the men how to unhitch the animals from the wagon.

As he took his leave he added, "Remember that it takes a team of oxen longer to stop than it takes them to get the wagon moving, so when you want them to stop, tap their heads and give the command at least fifty feet before you need them to come to a halt—and keep children out of their way, as more than a few have been run over by a wagon when the oxen couldn't stop it quickly enough." With that, he tipped his battered hat to the ladies and left the camp.

After evening prayer, Elder Smoot, who was now called Captain Smoot, stood in the back of a wagon and told the group, "The supplies of flour, sugar, and bacon will be delivered tomorrow or the next day. We are still waiting for some of the cattle to be delivered. Tomorrow we will weigh everyone's belongings to make sure they are within the weight limit."

The following day, the children played, the oxen grazed, and the families became better acquainted with one another. Each of the families carried their belongings to a large, double-hung scale. After their goods were weighed, those with more than the allowed weight had to determine what they would leave behind. Rebecca laughed and said, "Having next to nothing means not leaving anything behind."

That evening, sickness struck the camp. Many of the wagon train members were taken violently ill with stomach cramps, chills, violent vomiting, and purging. Captain Smoot became severely ill, along with at least twenty-five others. Helen pushed the tent flap aside as she entered and said in a hushed and frightened voice, "Some say it's cholera. What if we all die?" She wrapped herself in her quilt and rocked back and forth as she held a sleeping Willie. Johnny put his arm around her. They sat that way most of the night.

By morning, the sound of sobbing could be heard from several of the tents and wagons. Tom Matthews held Willie close as they sat under the wagon watching the adults, telling him over and over, "Everything will be all right. Don't you be scared."

By midmorning, Johnny and Robert hitched the oxen to the wagon and drove the team to the makeshift cemetery where they helped dig the oversized grave where many of their new friends were laid to rest. Seven other graves were either newly dug or partially dug, and weeping families stood around each one. Helen said to Rebecca as they watched the wagon loaded with the dead leave the camp, "I thought the hardest part of our lives was behind us. We lived to get out of the mines and to cross the ocean, but now I wonder how many of us will live to see the Valley."

"Eleven men and women and four little ones were laid to rest in the little cemetery today," Robert said the next afternoon as he wearily sat down on a log near the campfire. The remainder of those who had been ill gradually began to regain their strength over the next three days while they waited in camp for the delivery of the remainder of the cattle and supplies purchased by Captain Smoot.

When the cattle were delivered, Willie wanted to take the lead rope as he called out to his mother, "My cow, my cow." The women of wagon thirty-two were pleased to be given a cow to furnish milk; it also had a six-month-old calf. The breed of the cow was indistinguishable, but it gave milk, and that was what was important. Willie quickly named the cow "Brownie," and the calf he called "Caffie."

When Christopher Langton, a young man in his mid-twenties, came around later that afternoon he introduced himself and said, "Elder Smoot has asked me to assist him in leading this wagon train, and my first assignment is to visit every wagon and teach the folks there how to milk a cow."

Smiling, Helen looked at Rebecca and Ann and said, "I think that this is woman's work." With that, she rolled up the sleeves on her dress.

The day before the wagon train was to start west, a weakened Captain Smoot was helped to the back of a wagon bed where he stood to speak to the group. "These last few days we have buried some of those whose dream it was to go west to the Valley with us. We must give thanks that we were not required to bury more at this time. We must accept that this is a large undertaking and there will be graves along the way, but we know that those we lose go home to a loving God."

Someone handed a chair up to him, and he sat down, exhausted by the effort of standing and talking to the group. "In the morning, we will ring the bell at six o'clock, and at that time all will arise, pack your wagons, complete your breakfast, have prayer, and be ready to fall into line by eight o'clock. The following day, the first wagon will move to the end of the line."

The first day on the trail wore blisters on nearly everyone's feet. The men took turns walking beside the oxen with the rod, but as the wagon wheels tended to be guided by the ruts in the trail, the animals needed little direction. The wagon train stopped for an hour for a midday meal and to rest the oxen. The women handed out biscuits made at breakfast to the hungry children. It required three days to reach the Vermillion River, and by that time many of the children had stopped wearing their shoes. There the children played fully clothed in the water. Helen called, "Tom, will ye please watch Willie so he doesn't drown? It worries me so to have him near the river." Young Tom agreed. The next morning, the wagons forded the river, with the women holding their skirts high with one hand and their shoes above their heads with the other.

They traveled along the Little Blue River toward the Platte, which they reached by the Fourth of July. As they stood and looked at the muddy, thick water, Rebecca said in dismay, "How can we wash our clothes or cook with water that is so muddy we could plant a garden in it?"

No one had an answer. When they camped that evening, Helen remarked wistfully to the others as the women cooked supper at a small campfire, "This is the flattest country God ever made. There's nary a mountain, a tree, or even a pretty valley to be seen. Even the river is flat, brown, and wide. Oh, how I miss the green hills of Scotland. Do ye think there are green hills in the Valley?" Again, no one had an answer.

Willie liked to walk with Tom as he tried to teach the cow and her calf the commands the oxen had been taught. After a while his little legs would tire, and Johnny would carry him on his shoulders until he asked to get down again.

As the men put up the tent one evening, Robert commented, "The nights are warm and pleasant, and if it weren't for the skeeters and buffalo flies, we would nae need to put up the tent."

In late July the wagons reached Lone Tree, which was just beyond the crossing at the Loup River where it met the North Platte. The crossing of the Loup River proved to be strenuous and time-consuming, as patches of quicksand made it necessary to double-, and in one case triple-team the wagons.

As the last wagon was brought across the river, riders going east from the Valley stopped to talk to Elder Smoot. "Pawnee Indians have been scattering and stealing cattle in the area, so your camp will need to double the number of lookouts each evening."

About midnight of the same evening, gunshots and the whooping and hollering of many voices woke the camp. Someone yelled, "Indians!" and the men throughout the wagon company rolled out of their quilts and reached for whatever weapons were available. As the women put their heads out of the tents, they could see by moonlight half-naked figures with flying hair, riding on horseback, whooping and scaring the cattle.

Excited by all the noise, little Willie toddled out of the tent while Helen was watching the Indians. Tom burst out of the tent and began to yell, "They're trying to steal Bob and Sam! They're stealing Brownie and Caffie!" With that, he started to run across the ground toward the frightened cattle that were milling around as the Indians rode their horses through the panicked herd. Willie followed Tom as quickly as his little legs could carry him.

"Willie, come back," Helen screamed. "Johnny, get him! Catch him!" Her voice was filled with panic.

Johnny ran after the child and scooped him up with one arm and then continued to run until he reached Tom. "Tom, you get back to your mother. These Indians would like to steal you just as much as any of the cattle." Johnny's voice was hard with alarm.

Tom stopped running toward the frightened cattle and, looking at Johnny, said, "Yes, sir." He had never heard Johnny use that tone of voice.

As soon as the sun began to rise the morning after the raid, several of the men spent the day searching on foot for any of the animals that had been driven off. They found six oxen in a small streambed two miles from camp. When they brought them back into camp, they were able to determine that there were at least eight additional ox teams and seven cows that were missing.

Two of the other groups of searchers had located two teams of oxen and six cows between them. About midnight, forty-eight hours after the Indian raid, the last team of exhausted searchers arrived in camp with one team of oxen and three cows.

In the morning, after Captain Smoot rang the bell and when everyone had gathered for prayer, he announced, "We are still missing a few teams and several cows, but we must be moving on. The following folks will need to combine their goods with the folks in other wagons." He then read a list of those who had lost oxen and assigned them to other wagons.

For many nights after Johnny had found Willie running after the cow, he would sit upright in a cold sweat, wide awake in the middle of the night. The first time it happened, Helen asked, "What be troubling ye, Johnny?"

He said, "I have the same dream over and over. In it an Indian brave steals Willie. It always scares me just like it really happened."

"It seems to me that about all you can do when that dream comes is offer a prayer of thanks that it did not happen. Now try to go to sleep," Helen said as she lay back down.

CHAPTER 50
Buffalo Stampede

The sound of thunder filled the air, increasing until it shook the ground, the wagons, and the people. The wagons were circling in preparation for the evening camp when the sound started in the east and quickly filled earth and sky. Chris Langdon had not yet dismounted from his horse, so he wheeled the animal around and rode around the outside of the circled wagons yelling, "Buffalo stampede, buffalo stampede! Get into the wagons. Keep your oxen in the yoke. Watch your cattle!"

Helen scooped up Willie and dropped him into the wagon, quickly climbing in herself. "Hold on!" she screamed above the noise of the stampede. "Hold on!"

Ann Matthews climbed in quickly, looking around and calling with worry, "Where's my Tom?" As Rebecca pulled herself up and into the wagon, the herd of buffalo crested the rise in the prairie about five hundred feet to the east of the encampment, coming toward the wagons like a brown flood. The sound of their hooves had become deafening. Johnny and Robert had taken hold of the oxen's yoke and were trying to keep them from panicking. They were still harnessed to the wagon and were growing violently agitated. In their panic, the oxen started to move with the herd of buffalo.

"Hold on, and sit down," Helen shouted as she pulled Willie to her. The wagon moved as the frightened oxen tried to join the stampede. Some of the buffalo broke through and into the circle of wagons, trampling anything in their way. Terrified men, women, and children rushed to climb into their wagons to avoid the hooves and great brown bodies.

The wagon was moving unsteadily over the rough ground as the frightened oxen pulled in panic in the same direction the buffalo herd was moving. The herd streamed past and through the wagon encampment for nearly an hour, breaking wagon tongues and side-swiping wagons, rocking them roughly back and forth. The screams of frightened women and children filled the air.

Bob and Sam finally grew exhausted and, along with the other oxen, slowed and finally stopped to wearily graze. To avoid being trampled by the buffalo, Johnny and Robert had let go of the oxen and grabbed onto the wagon seat where they had held on for dear life throughout the jolting ride. Finally, the buffalo grew calmer and were scattered for several miles over the prairie, grazing as if nothing had happened.

Everyone climbed down from the wagon, and as they led the oxen back to the campsite, they found others whose wagon wheels had been damaged when they had been pulled into prairie-dog holes. Before they reached the campsite, they could see Tom Matthews and his father walking briskly toward them. When Tom recognized the wagon, he started to run toward his mother as fast as his ten-year-old legs could carry him.

The rest of that day and much of the night was spent mending wagons. The sound of saws and hammers was heard late into the night. Willie cried himself to sleep because he could not find Brownie.

The next day Johnny borrowed a horse, and he rode out with Ralph Rowley, Bill Reeves, and Dan Thomas, who were also on borrowed horses, to look for lost cattle. After nearly two hours, they finally heard a cow bellowing. They finally came upon Brownie, who had one leg caught in a fallen log near a small creek. "My cow, my cow!" Willie called out when he saw them returning to camp.

* * *

The first week of August found the Smoot wagon company beyond Scott's Bluff but several miles short of Fort Laramie. The buffalo herd that had stampeded the cattle had continued to graze around the wagon company for several days as they had moved westward. "How my mouth waters for a big buffalo steak," Joseph Matthews said, "and we would have one if President Young had not promised the Indian tribes that we wouldn't kill the buffalo." The next day some of the men came upon a herd of deer, and then there was fresh meat in the camp.

The wind blew relentlessly, and the flies and insects followed the wagon company as if they knew the way to the Valley. The soles of the children's feet were as hard as tanned leather. Everyone suffered with swollen and chapped lips. When Rebecca saw herself in the reflection of a quiet stream she said in horror, "Oh, I look a hundred years old," and she sat down and cried.

"Will the water ever get cleaner?" Helen complained as the women were straining it through rags to remove most of the mosquito larvae and other floaters.

That afternoon as the women talked and walked beside the wagon, young Tom came to Helen and said, "I can't find Willie anywhere. I've been trying to watch him like you said, but I can't find him."

Helen called out, "Willie, Willie, where are you?" Her voice was firm.

A little voice answered, "I be right here, Ma."

No one could see him, so she called again, "Willie, where are you!" This time she spoke with urgency.

"Right here, Ma, by Sam and Bob."

The women ran to the ox team, and there was Willie, standing on the wagon tongue with a hand high on the back of each of the oxen as the wagon continued at a steady walking pace on the rutted trail.

Helen called to her husband, who was walking ahead of the oxen talking with Brother Matthews. "Johnny, will ye get your lad off the wagon tongue before he falls off and gets run over by the wagon?" Her voice was full of alarm.

As Johnny turned, he could see Willie grinning at them over the back of Sam. His father stepped between the two oxen and lifted his son off the wagon tongue. When he carried him back to his mother, he said, "Ye must never do that again, Willie. Little Jimmy Brown was riding on the wagon tongue, and when he fell off, the wagon wheel went over him and killed him. Ye don't want that to happen, do ye?" Willie shook his head uncertainly. His father continued as he handed him to his mother, "Ye don't want to make your ma cry, do ye?"

"Nae, Pa."

"So ye promise ye will never do that again?"

Willie did not understand the death of Jimmy Brown, but he knew he did not want to make his mother cry. "Aye, Pa, no more rides so Ma won't cry."

CHAPTER 51
New Midwives

Exhaustion had begun to wear the travelers thin—their clothing, their flesh, their cattle, and their strength. Even hope had worn thin. The days passed with the oxen pulling the wagons up the almost imperceptible but steady incline toward the mountains that had been visible in the distance for many days. They stood against the sky in varying shades of blue, with white caps of snow on the highest peaks.

After the wagon company left Fort Laramie, the night air grew cold. Families huddled together at night in the worn tents. As they reached the last crossing of the Platte River, Helen stood still as she looked at the water. When her brother approached her she said, "How will we cross? We have no money to pay the ferrymen, and the river bottom is full of quicksand."

Her fears were quieted when Rebecca moved from wagon to wagon telling everyone she could find, "Captain Smoot says the men at the ferry will take us across at no cost. Do ye hear me? Captain Smoot says we can cross on the ferry at no cost."

When the wagon company reached Red Butte for the evening encampment, Chris Langdon rode from wagon to wagon asking, "Can anyone here help deliver Sister Murdock's baby? We buried our midwife near Scott's Bluff."

When he reached wagon thirty-two, he asked again, "Can you help Sister Murdock? Her baby is coming."

The women looked at each other, and Rebecca's eyes grew large as she shook her head. "Nae, I can nae face the thought of losing someone the way we lost Janet."

Helen put her arm around Rebecca and said, "You stay here. It will be all right." Then she motioned for Ann Mathews to come with her to help. "We have had little experience in delivering bairns, but we are mothers. We are willing to help," Helen said, speaking for herself and Ann.

Chris pointed out the Murdock wagon, and, picking up her dishtowels, which had been drying on the back of the wagon in the sun all afternoon, Helen led the way. Ann, hurrying to catch up, said to Helen as they rushed toward the wagon, "I hope you know more than me."

"I think the best thing will be to let nature do what needs to be done," Helen responded.

Nature had almost completed what needed to be done by the time the women reached the wagon. John Murdock was greatly relieved to be shooed away with instructions to build a fire and warm some water. While Ann held the baby and wrapped it in dish towels to keep it warm, Helen obtained a short piece of rawhide and tied off the cord. When the water was warm, the baby's father carried the pot of it into the wagon where the women gently washed the newborn girl.

Helen washed the face of the weary mother and offered her a drink of water.

Ann wrapped the baby in a quilt and put her in her mother's arms. "The Lord sent this little one to fill the empty place in your heart left by the loss of the little girl that you buried on the trail." She added, "Now you must rest. Send your husband to get us if you need us in the night."

Within a day, the word had spread throughout the camp that there were two new midwives. Helen laughed and said, "One birthing does not a midwife make."

But four days later, as they camped at the Sweetwater River, David Jones came to the women as they prepared supper and said, "My wife, Ellie, is in labor and sent me to bring you to help her."

The two women hurried to the Jones wagon and could do little more than tell Ellie to push. The baby boy cried strongly, and the women laughed with pleasure as they washed him and handed him to his mother.

As they walked back to finish cooking supper two hours later, Helen said, "One lad and one lassie; do ye think that makes us experts now?" They both laughed heartily.

* * *

At Independence Rock, the camp held a celebration. One brother got out a beloved violin, and though it had only three strings, he could play up a melody that made even the weariest foot tap. Another took out a banjo that had not been played since the owner had buried his wife near Lone Tree. For the night, many of the travelers forgot their grief and danced until nearly sunrise. Even Robert and Johnny managed to learn the Virginia reel, though Joseph Matthews was content to watch.

The crossings of the Sweetwater River came so often over the next two weeks that many in the company began to take cold. Though the weather during the day was pleasant when clothing was dry, in wet clothing, none of the weary travelers were warm enough. The men often had to help the wagons across the river to keep them upright. By the fourth crossing, Robert was coughing and feverish in his cold and wet clothing.

Near Rocky Ridge, between the fifth and sixth crossings of the Sweetwater, Chris Langdon came to the tent where the women were settled for the night. "Sisters, can you come and help with another birth? Sister Calvin is in labor, and I fear for her. She has not been well since her husband died of cholera."

The two women did not take time to change from their night dresses, but each simply threw a shawl over her shoulders and hurried to the wagon. Sister Calvin was white-faced, and her hands were cold and wet with perspiration. As they lifted the wagon cover and climbed in, she whispered, "Please, save my baby." After a moment she spoke again, weakly, "Save my baby—and if it's a boy, name him Robert Campbell Calvin after his father." It literally took the last ounce of her strength to speak.

Chris Langdon had built a fire and had water heating in a large pot. The baby was born blue and not breathing, so without waiting for Chris to lift the pot into the wagon, Helen climbed out, carrying the baby in one arm. She put her hand in the water, and feeling the warmth, she unwrapped the baby and lowered him up to his chin into the water. After about a minute, she lifted him out and allowed the cold breeze to dry him. Then she put him back into the water for another minute. Then she again lifted him out into the cold night air. She repeated this two more times, and finally, the last time she lifted him out, he moved and gave a weak whimper. She wrapped him in a quilt and dried his head, saying, "Robert Campbell Calvin, now what will we do to keep ye alive?"

Ann had stayed with Sister Calvin until she could see that there was nothing she could do. The mother's body was growing cold quickly.

After Ann climbed out of the wagon, she and Helen talked for a few minutes. Helen stood holding the infant close to her heart, enveloped by the memories of the baby buried on the hillside in East Lothian and the other that lay in the churchyard in Edinburgh, but after a few minutes, she shook her head and said with urgency, "The bairn must have a wet nurse."

Ann said thoughtfully, "There are two women who could serve as a wet nurse, as they both have new babies."

"Aye, but only one has buried two children on this journey. Let's go to Sister Murdock and see if she will take him."

The two, accompanied by Chris Langdon, made their way to the Murdock tent where he called out, "Brother and Sister Murdock, we need to speak with you."

Brother Murdock poked his head out of the tent flap. "What's the trouble, Brother Langdon?"

"We have a motherless baby boy here who needs a wet nurse. Do you think your wife could take him?"

"Take another infant, Brother Langdon? I don't see how . . ." Before he could end his sentence, his wife had thrown back the tent flap and said with arms extended, "Give him to me. I can raise him like a twin."

"But my dear, how can you nurse two babies?" her husband asked.

"With love, husband, with love. Just as little Mary has filled the place left by the death of our Charlotte, this tiny boy will fill the empty place left by the death of our Jimmy."

With that, Robert Campbell Calvin had a new home and a new mother, at least until other relatives could be found in the Valley. In the morning, as they stood at Sister Calvin's grave, Helen could have sworn that there was a smile playing around her lips as the blanket was folded over her face and she was laid in the ground.

CHAPTER 52
Exhaustion and Injury

The next day was taken up with the task of getting the wagons up the five-mile trail to Rocky Ridge that was used to bypass an impassable section of the Sweetwater River. To get their wagon up the steep and rocky trail, Johnny and Robert had lifted the remaining supplies out of the wagon to lighten the load for the oxen. Most of the teams had begun to show the wear of the trail and were unable to pull their wagons up the incline without being double-teamed. The able-bodied men pressed their shoulders against the back of each of the wagons and pushed as the oxen pulled.

A task that with strong oxen and men could have been accomplished in two or three hours took nearly twelve. To make matters more exhausting, as the last ten wagons were still waiting to begin the climb, a quick and cold rainstorm struck. The hail and large raindrops were driven by a cold wind, which lashed at the exhausted travelers, people and beasts alike. Though it was only late August, the temperature dropped until everyone shook with the bitter chill in the air.

Helen stood apart from the group and prayed aloud with a voice filled with desperation, "Dear God, help us! We are so tired and cold. Please help us!" Her prayer was more than a plea; it was nearly a demand. The storm passed quickly but left behind cold, wet humans and animals.

As the last wagon was being pulled laboriously up the incline, the wagon tongue snapped, and the wagon slid to the right across a wet, sloping rock surface where Robert had been pushing near the rear wheel. It knocked him over, and only his leg stopped the wagon from sliding farther back down the hill. His leg was pinned under the iron tire band on the wheel as he cried out in pain.

While six men held the wagon in place and lifted it, Johnny and Joseph pulled Robert out from the under the wheel. Rebecca could see the leg swelling and the blood swiftly seeping through his worn pant leg when he was carried to her. She tore a strip of cloth off her worn apron and tied the cloth firmly around his leg, pulling it as tightly as she could to stop the bleeding and swelling. "I don't know what else to do for ye, husband," she said, her face full of alarm. "Will ye be able to walk?"

"'Tis nothing," he said, though the agony on his face was evident. "Many's the time I been hurt worse than this in the pits." But he was gray with shock and pain.

The camp at Rock Creek was sixteen more miles, too far for the exhausted wagon company, so the men struggled to put up the tents, and the families huddled together through the cold night.

The next day, the group labored to reach Rock Creek for the night encampment. "You will ride in the wagon," Rebecca insisted with a resolve in her voice that her husband would not have opposed, even if he had felt up to it. As the women fixed supper that evening, Helen said, "I hope that these past two days are the last of such hard going, as I don't see how we could face that kind of trail again."

As they sat down to eat their cornbread and beans, Brother Matthews said quietly, "Sister Smith, you are in for a disappointment, as I hear that the last hundred miles from Fort Bridger into the Valley will be difficult, in some places as trying as what we traveled the last two days." In exhaustion and disappointment, Helen sat quietly throughout the rest of the meal, not speaking further, hardly touching her food. Tears brought on by exhaustion and worry for her brother trailed down her cheeks. Ann sat down next to her and put a comforting arm around her shoulders. That night Rebecca slept in the wagon next to Robert, trying to keep him warm enough to stop his shaking. In the morning, Robert continued to ride in the wagon.

* * *

Several days later the wagon company reached the Bear River. Captain Smoot had told them that this was the last major river crossing before they reached the Valley, after which he would leave by horseback to tell the Church leaders there of the progress of the company. That night many of the company danced and sang again. Robert sat in the wagon and shivered with the cold the others did not feel. Rebecca wrapped a quilt around his shoulders. She couldn't help but think that he suddenly looked like an old man. She turned her face away at the thought to hide her tears.

When the wagon company entered Echo Canyon, the tall, red rock walls towered above the stream that made its way through the bottom of the canyon. The children discovered that their laughter and shouts would echo through the canyon, so they took up a shouting contest to see who could make the most noise. Finally, parents with ears overwhelmed by the noise insisted that they become quiet. "You will stop the noise making," Joseph Matthews firmly told his son and his friends. The wagons made slow but steady progress, giving the children time to play in the stream amid the willows.

The next day, Captain Smoot rejoined the company just as they exited Echo Canyon and began the trek up Big Mountain. The trail up the long incline was exhausting for the tired oxen and pioneers alike. The peaks of the snow-covered Wasatch Mountains towered high above them. That great hump, the highest point on the entire trail, required three days to conquer. Chris Langdon rode from wagon to wagon, telling everyone to take heart, as they were within two or three days of entering the Valley. "We will descend into and through Emigration Canyon, and you will see the Valley very soon." His words were followed by cheers of gratitude and, for some, tears of exhaustion.

As he started to move on to the next wagon, Rebecca stepped up and took hold of the horse's bridle. "Please, Robert must have a blessing. He is so sick I fear for him." Langdon dismounted and climbed into the wagon. When he saw Robert's white face and clammy skin, he knelt down by him and asked, "How long has he been this way?"

"Since before we crossed the Bear River."

Langdon and Johnny laid their hands on Robert's head, and Chris stated firmly in his prayer, "You have labored long and hard to bring your family to the Valley. The Lord wants you to live so you and your posterity may experience the blessings that await you. I bless you to sleep that you might be healed." Robert drifted into a heavy sleep for the first time since his leg had been injured.

The next three days were filled with slow progress through the rugged canyon, but Robert slept a feverish sleep filled with dreams and murmurings that frightened the others. When he would wake enough to groggily look around the wagon, Rebecca would insist that he drink some cold water. Helen asked Rebecca each evening, "How does he feel? Is he still so feverish?"

Rebecca's answer was always the same. "He sleeps all the time, except when he is out of his head. Mostly he doesn't even know I'm here." Each night she held his hand as she lay next to him in the wagon and begged, "Robbie, can you hear me? Please get better. Please get better. I'm with child, and I don't know how I would live without you." Then as she wept she would plead with God to spare him. Helen tearfully pleaded for her brother in her prayers as well.

The tired oxen had to be rested several times as they made their way through Emigration Canyon. In many areas, the wagons had to use the riverbed as a road. Well after dark on the third day they had spent in the canyon, the exhausted members of the wagon company made camp on a more level area at the western mouth of the canyon. In the far distance a few faint glimmering lights could be seen—or perhaps they were just the glimmering reflections of the hopes and wishes of the weary travelers.

In the morning, just as the sky had begun to lighten, Johnny left the tent and quickly returned, shaking Helen awake. "Come, see the Valley," he whispered excitedly. "We have reached Robbie's promised land."

Rebecca had been sleeping next to Robert, listening for his breathing. When Johnny stuck his head in the wagon and urged her to get up and see the Valley, she rose halfheartedly, and though she was still in her nightdress, she climbed down from the wagon at his urging. As the eastern sky above the mountaintops grew brighter, the three of them stood looking westward. They could see many small, gray, adobe cabins in the distance enclosed in the adobe wall of a fort, and a few others laid out in a north-south, east-west grid outside the walls of the fort. Even in the early morning, the community was awakening. The smoke was rising from the chimneys of small cabins in the outlying areas.

"Look, look at the light on the water of the great lake to the west," Johnny almost whispered in awe. Then he said excitedly, "Let's tell everyone." In his bare feet, he moved from tent to tent and wagon to wagon, calling out, "Come, see the Valley! Wake up, we're finally here!"

Worry over her husband's illness had left Rebecca drained, unable to share in the excitement. She turned to return to the wagon where her husband lay, but as she did so, she bumped into a tall man who stood behind her. She looked up to see her husband's smiling face. "Robbie, you are awake!" Her voice was filled with relief.

"Aye, Rebecca, I am awake and feeling better—or at least better than I have been for awhile." Rebecca leaned against him and sobbed, repeating the words, "Praise be to God, praise be to God!" Helen stepped up and put an arm around each one of them.

Within a few minutes everyone in the entire company was awake, and those strong and well enough stood near their tents, looking westward, their exhaustion nearly forgotten.

CHAPTER 53
The Valley

As the weary travelers stood looking to the west, they could see a group of men on horseback and several in carriages winding their way up the incline coming toward them. After watching the approaching group for about half an hour, they could hear strains of music, and someone cried out, "There's a band in the front carriage. They've come to greet us with a band!"

By the time the carriages and riders had reached the encampment, everyone had dressed, and the tents had been hurriedly taken down and put into the wagons. When the largest carriage, which led the procession arrived, Captain Smoot stepped forward and assisted one of the men in the wagon to descend. He wore a black waistcoat with tails, and a top hat. He was a broad-shouldered man with a head of shoulder-length dark hair. The word went around like a wave in a tidal pool, "That's President Young. That's Brother Brigham! Brother Brigham has come to welcome us!"

The band, which filled the other seats in the carriage, began to play again with vigor. Despite their weariness, some of the wagon company began to dance to the music. Then, as they looked for places to sit to catch their breath, the band took up the familiar and melancholy tune, "Come, Come, Ye Sants." Gradually, everyone began to sing the beloved hymn.

Come, come, ye Saints, no toil nor labor fear;
But with joy wend your way.
Though hard to you this journey may appear,
Grace shall be as your day.
'Tis better far for us to strive
Our useless cares from us to drive;
Do this, and joy your hearts will swell—
All is well! All is well!

Why should we mourn or think our lot is hard?
'Tis not so; all is right.
Why should we think to earn a great reward
If we now shun the fight?
Gird up your loins; fresh courage take.
Our God will never us forsake;
And soon we'll have this tale to tell—
All is well! All is well!

We'll find the place which God for us prepared,
Far away in the West,
Where none shall come to hurt or make afraid;
There the Saints will be blessed.
We'll make the air with music ring,
Shout praises to our God and King;
Above the rest these words we'll tell—
All is well! All is well!

As they began the fourth verse, their voices grew quieter.

And should we die before our journey's through,
Happy day! All is well!
We then are free from toil and sorrow, too;
With the just we shall dwell!

By that time, Rebecca was weeping uncontrollably, and Robert asked, "What's got ye so upset? Nae, don't cry. Rebecca, we should be happy. The journey's over. We're home!"

"Dear husband, I was sure I would enter the Valley a widow, and our child would be fatherless. My faith was gone." Looking up at him she smiled through her tears. "But my husband is well and strong, and we will enter the Valley together. I cannot stop my tears of joy." At the news of the coming birth, Robert held her close and smiled but said nothing. That secret could wait awhile before it was shared.

Many of the men and women had begun to weep as they sang, suffused in the memories of those who lay in the graves along the trail. But as the final lines were sung, the voices grew strong and full, making the canyon behind them and the desert spread at their feet ring with joy.

But if our lives are spared again
To see the Saints their rest obtain,
Oh, how we'll make this chorus swell—
All is well! All is well!

For a few moments, all stood silently as the notes echoed and died away. Then Captain Smoot climbed into the back of his wagon where he could be seen by all and announced to the wagon company that they had been blessed with the music of Pitt's Band as a greeting, and more importantly, the First Presidency, several members of the Quorum of the Twelve Apostles, and many community leaders had come to greet them.

"These good people have even brought us breakfast." With that, many of those in the carriages began to distribute melons and baked goods brought by those in the greeting committee.

The wagons were lined up for the trek into the Valley accompanied by the music of Pitt's Band, with Brigham Young's carriage leading the way. When Rebecca urged her husband to ride in the wagon, he said firmly, "I will walk, my dear Rebecca. I will walk into the Valley with my wife." He took Rebecca's hand. His sister took his other hand, and he laughed and said, "I think I am the only man present with two women to look after me."

With that, Johnny joined them and said with a smile, "Ye will only have part of Helen's concern. The rest is mine." With Willie on his shoulders, he put his arm around Helen, and though Robert's limp was noticeable, they walked together toward a new future.

The children in the wagon company had caught the excitement of the occasion and danced and romped beside the wagons as they made their way westward on Emigration Road. As the wagon company moved west toward the Temple Block along South Temple Street, a cannon sounded over the city with nine rounds of artillery to welcome the weary travelers.

Helen jumped involuntarily at the sound of the cannon.

Robert saw her start at the sound and laughed. "My dear sister, I believe that is part of our welcome." Reading her thoughts, he added, "And here in the Valley, we will never have to fear the firedamp again."

As the wagon company moved slowly through the streets, people came out of the shops and homes and applauded and shouted their greetings. Some ran into the road to shake the hands of the men of the wagon company.

Slowly, the tired oxen pulled the wagons past the Temple Block. There everyone could see an unfinished, red sandstone wall around the block and inside it, a variety of shops, including a foundry, a great waterwheel on a small creek, and a carpentry shop. The word traveled through the group that there, inside the wall, the temple would be built.

They continued to Second West Temple Street and turned north. One long block later, just beyond First North Temple Street, they were directed to pull their wagons onto Union Square, where it was apparent that many wagon companies had camped before them.

After every wagon had pulled onto the square, the members of the wagon company were called together so President Brigham Young could address them. As he stood in his carriage, high enough above the crowd to be heard, he began, "First I will say, may the Lord God of Israel bless you, and comfort your hearts." The entire company responded with a fervent "Amen."

He continued in a voice that could be heard throughout the camp, "I will say to this company, they have had the honor of being escorted into the city by some of the most distinguished individuals of our society, and a band of music, accompanied with a salutation from the cannon. Other companies have not had this mark of respect shown to them; they belong to the rich, and are able to help themselves."

At that Helen whispered to Johnny, "This is the first time I have ever been told that we are worthy of special privileges because we are poor. 'Tis a strange thing to think on."

President Young continued, "We have prayed for you continually; thousands of prayers have been offered up for you, day by day, to Him who has commanded us to gather Israel, save the children of men by the preaching of the gospel, and prepare them for the coming of the Messiah. You have had a long, hard, and fatiguing journey across the great waters and the scorched plains; but, by the distinguished favors of heaven, you are here in safety." As President Young spoke, his words were consumed by the members of the wagon company as if they were food and water for the soul.

When he was finished speaking, Brigham Young stepped down from the wagon and moved through the crowd. He shook hands with the men in the group, tipped his hat to the women, and then made his way back to his carriage. There he waved farewell with his top hat as his driver turned the carriage and the band began to play a rousing tune.

After President Young had left, Captain Smoot climbed into the back of his wagon and called the members of his company together again. "Today is September third, and we have arrived in

Zion with the greeting and welcome of our Church leaders." As a great cheer arose and then quieted, he continued, "It is appropriate that we offer a prayer of thanks for our safe arrival." He removed his hat as did all the other men, and as everyone bowed their heads, he prayed, "Great God of heaven, Thou hast brought us here, through sickness and hardship, through heat and cold, over mountains and through quicksand, and we offer our thanks to Thee for our safe arrival. Now we can worship in peace and in accordance with our conscience without fear of persecution. Please give us the strength to build Zion strong and true and to Thy glory."

At the conclusion of the prayer, each of the two young Scotsmen put his arm around his wife. As they stood together looking at the great mountain peaks to the east of the Valley, Robert said quietly but firmly, "Now we will make a home of our own in our promised land, and here we will help build a temple to our God in the sunlight." He paused and added with gratitude, "And we will never be forced into the darkness of the pits again."

Epilogue

The years ahead would never be easy for the families who struggled to leave old countries, old customs, and old religions to gather to their Zion in the Great Salt Lake Valley. Before permanent dwellings were finished, many would be sent by Brigham Young to colonize one of more than four hundred settlements established by the "Mormons" throughout the western United States, Northern Mexico, and Southern Canada. These religious pioneers would dam the rivers, dig the irrigation ditches, farm the virgin soil, plant the trees, and help tame a massive part of the continent. No matter where they settled, they would labor to wrest a living from a harsh and dry land, and would see times so hard within the future years that for weeks at a time some of them would be forced to subsist on sego lily bulbs, pigweed, thistles, and pine nuts.

In just five short years, the American government would send one-third of its standing army to put down a nonexistent "Mormon rebellion," stopping the work on the Salt Lake Temple. In 1858, after work on the temple was begun again, Johnny would use the skills acquired in the pits of Scotland to become a stonecutter, rough-cutting the great granite blocks in the quarry at the mouth of Little Cottonwood Canyon. The big hammers, picks, drills, and black powder that were used to free the blocks of stone from the mountainside were familiar tools in his hands, but the sun and fresh air—and more importantly, the purpose for which he worked, would make this endeavor entirely different than the work of earlier years. Throughout all the years of his life, he would be proud of his efforts to build the Salt Lake Temple

Because of his bad leg, Robert would become a teamster, driving one of the fifty teams and wagons that hauled the great chunks of granite the twenty miles from the quarry to the Temple Block. The great stones, each weighing from one to nearly three tons, would take as long as four days to bring from the quarry to the Temple Block, each one pulled by two teams of oxen. The heaviest stones were hung under the wagon beds, and the task for the oxen was so great that sometimes spectators would stand in reverent awe as the teams and wagons made their slow procession toward the Temple Block. There, after they were shaped by the experienced stonemasons from Britain, the great pieces of granite were sometimes stacked like rows of dominoes toppled by a giant, awaiting their place in the great House of the Lord.

For many years, the men working on the temple and other public works would be paid out of the tithing of the Saints, some-times in scrip that could be used at the tithing storehouse or at some of the merchants on Main Street. Other times they were paid in produce and stock. On one occasion, Johnny was paid with a pig, which he sold for thirty-one dollars. Occasionally they would be paid in cash, but only when times were good.

The Salt Lake Temple would stand unfinished while the men of the Valley worked for the transcontinental railroads. Brother Brigham would sign a contract promising to provide five thousand men to work for the Union Pacific Railroad to bring the Saints a desperately needed cash infusion. Again, Robert and Johnny would use their black powder skills as they worked to smooth the rail bed and remove the rock overhangs in the mountain passes. And among hundreds of others, they would cheer at the Union of the Rails, as the Golden Spike was driven to unite the nation at Promontory Point, Utah Territory, in 1869.

As the years passed, both couples would raise large families, and in each one, the oldest daughter born in the Valley would be named Isabel.

To the great joy and satisfaction of both young couples, Richard Smith's heart was softened, and in response to a letter of encouragement from Johnny and Helen, he brought his family to the Valley four years later with the help of the PEF. After Isabel's death, Helen's brother James eventually left the coal master's large cottage, and he and his family, along with his younger brother David, eventually settled in Cache Valley, Utah Territory. The Smith and Hogge men became stonecutters in Logan Canyon, where they harvested the great blocks of stone that formed the Logan Temple.

The gentle little landlady, Mrs. McEwen, eventually joined her husband and son in the quiet cemetery in Edinburgh, but not until her boardinghouse had served as a way station for many more families on their way to the "promised land."

In the years since this mighty immigration took place, many have wondered just why these immigrants continued a long journey that could have ended hundreds, if not thousands, of miles sooner. The vast majority of those seeking a new life in America stopped and settled as quickly as possible after their long and rigorous voyage across the Atlantic Ocean. Many historians have expressed wonder that these religious immigrants felt the need to endanger their own lives and those of their loved ones to struggle farther across a vast continent in the face of tremendous hardships to complete their journey to the Great Salt Lake Valley in the Rocky Mountains. Perhaps the best, and maybe the only, explanation can be found in the fact that faith is the greatest mover of mountains, or ships on the sea—or wagon companies on the plains.

Selected Bibliography

Arnot, R. Page. *A History of the Scottish Miners: From the Earliest Times*. London: George Allen & Unwin Ltd., 1955.

Barrowman, James. "Slavery in the Coal Mines of Scotland." *Journal of the Monmouthshire Colliery Officials Association*, Vol. 1, 1897, 195–198.

Carter, Kate B. ed. *Our Pioneer Heritage*, 20 vol. Salt Lake City: International Society, Daughters of Utah Pioneers, 1958–1977.

Hartley, William G. *"Don't Go Aboard the Saluda!": William Dunbar, LDS Emigrants, and Disaster on the Missouri*. Riverton, Utah: Millennial Press, 2002.

Hayt, J. A. "Industrial Accidents," Section 12.4. *Scotland in the 19th Century*. Published in the Glasgow Digital Library. Retrieved 2006–05–25.

Jenson, Andrew. "Mode of Conducting the Migration." *The Contributor*, Vol. 13, 1892, 181–185.

Larson, Gustive O. "The Emigrating Fund in Europe." *Prelude to the Kingdom*. 155–167.

Old Mersey Times. "Leaving of Liverpool, 1848." Southport Visiter (sic). Liverpool: 1850. Reprinted 2002. Retrieved 2006–06–27.

Raynor, W. A. *The Everlasting Spires.* Salt Lake City, Utah: Deseret Book Company, 1965.

Talmage, James E. *The House of the Lord.* Salt Lake City, Utah: Deseret Book Company, rev. ed. 1976.

The Church of Jesus Christ of Latter-day Saints. Church History. "Church History in Scotland." Retrieved 2006–05–27.

_____, comp. *Coal Mining in Scotland 1840–1920.* Published by Glasgow City Libraries and Archives. Retrieved 2006–06–24.